"You know, the world doesn't seem so bad to me." He looked up at me. Each feature on his face seemed to react separately. First his eyes sparkled; then his head rose; then a smile crept across his face.

"Okay, you. I spilled my guts. What about you?"

"What about me? I'm not in a relationship."

"Why not?"

"'Cause I'm not a relationship type of gal." It sounded nice. Better than, "I can't seem to get anyone I like to like me back."

"Again, why not?"

"Not good at them. Look, Todd, if I have to read books on dating, then I'm probably no good in a relationship." Great, I thought. My secret's out. The mother of all don'ts. The don't that's such a don't you don't need to say it. DON'T ADMIT YOU READ BOOKS ON DATING.

Todd slowly sat up in interest. "You read books on dating?"

DATING 101

JEAN MARIE PIERSON

No Good Girls

LOVE SPELL NEW YORK CITY

LOVE SPELL®

March 2008

Published by

Dorchester Publishing Co., Inc.
200 Madison Avenue
New York, NY 10016

ISBN 10: 0-505-52756-1
ISBN 13: 978-0-505-52756-1

Printed in the United States of America.

10 9 8 7 6 5 4 3 2 1

Visit us on the web at www.dorchesterpub.com.

No
Good
Girls

Blessed are those who have not seen
yet believe.

John 20:29

What the hell did I know?

First rule of writing is to write about what you know. Looking at a blank piece of paper, I thought, well what's that? What could I claim to know enough about that would fill the 119 pages that constitute a screenplay? I reminded myself that I've done this before. My first, unsold screenplay was about Christmas. Brilliant. I knew my holidays. Even a Buddhist monk can speak with some authority on the meaning of Christmas. So how should I begin this one? Let's start out with things I actually know.

1) I know how to write a screenplay about Christmas.

2) I know how to fix an updraft carburetor.

3) I know how to whistle.

4) I know the only thing more boring than a book on birds is an author reading aloud from a book on birds.

5) I know I hate my job.

6) I know I hate my job because it doesn't allow me to write screenplays about Christmas.

7) I know I need my job.

8) I know that books on how to get a man only work on men who think like women who write books on how to get a man.

9) I know *he's* out there in Manhattan.

10) I know the only books that will help me find him are *The Art of War* and an atlas.

11) I know that my New York Minute will hit any time now.

Add a little geology and a splash of Penn State football trivia from the 1990s and that might be a good sampling of the things I could write about. I wouldn't say I'm exactly an expert at any of the above. Possessing a good working knowledge would be more like it. But I do have great friends. That's where I'm a pro. A pro or just extremely lucky.

Okay then, that's a good place to start.

NO GOOD GIRLS

screenplay by Geraldine Agnes O'Brien   Draft #1

INT. DINER   NIGHT

Three women in their mid-twenties, GERI, MARIA and
EMMY, sit at a table in a New York City diner. GERI writes
feverishly in a notebook as Maria tells an animated story
with her mouth full.

> MARIA
>
> So Pat and I were just standing over these scumbags
> with our guns out and our adrenaline friggin' pump-
> ing. I mean, this is the day that a cop lives for. That
> you hear stories at the station about. It was crazy! Get
> this, they were actually cryin' for their mommies!

> GERI
>
> They were eleven.

> MARIA
>
> Doesn't matter. Anyway, their shit was everywhere.
> They knew they were screwed. So I knelt down and
> told those little perps . . .

> GERI
>
> (mumbling to herself) I don't make the laws . . .

MARIA

I don't make the laws. I just enforce the ones the mayor tells me to.

EMMY

That's so amazing, Maria.

MARIA

Yeah, well those little bastards learned the hard way that littering is no goddamn joke. And Geri, don't take this down.

Geri, the writer, looks up from her pad.

(cont.) MARIA

This is private stuff here. I don't want you putting me in some lame-o art flick.

GERI

If you're in it, then it's probably not art.

EMMY

What's your new screenplay about, Geri?

GERI

It's about us. Only . . . cooler.

Emmy and Maria chew their food and look at Geri in silence.

(cont.) GERI

What?

MARIA

Out of all the ideas in that huge head of yours, we were the best you could come up with?

GERI

May I remind you we are hip, trendy, city girls doing hip, trendy city things.

MARIA

We're not hip.

EMMY

The trendiest thing I did last week was eat Thai.

GERI

And in my screenplay Thai is a guy.

MARIA

Great! Just what the world needs. Another dopey chick flick. Do me a favor, will ya? No scenes where we're singing. I hate that. Every friggin' chick movie has someone singing. That's stupid.

GERI

Noted.

MARIA

If I'm in it, I want to kick some ass. Like Buffy.

EMMY

And if I'm going to be in it, then I want a love story. One where a guy who looks like Brad Pitt falls desperately in love with me and I just pretend he doesn't exist.

MARIA

Who are you kidding, Emmy? You do backflips for guys.

EMMY

Well, if I do, then just shoot me.

GERI

No, you guys got it all wrong. There's not going to be any fight scenes or models in this. I'm thinking gritty reality. It's going to be a contemporary essay on how women can be misled by the romantic illusion of . . .

EMMY

Waxing?

MARIA

Douching?

GERI

The New York Minute. How girls like us expect New York City to change their lives overnight. And in this we are witty. So, come on, Maria. Say something witty about, I don't know . . . vegetarianism.

MARIA

Eat me, not a cow.

GERI

Okay, most people don't think "Eat me" is very witty. Now let's just pretend Kurt Vonnegut is writing in the next booth . . .

MARIA

I'd say, "Kurt, eat me, not a cow," and if Mr. Volkswagen wants to use it in his next movie, fine. If not, fuck him.

EMMY

What's going on with your Christmas script?

GERI

It's on Universal's slush pile.

MARIA

So if they buy it, your carolers will most likely be set
on fire on Vin Diesel's doorstep.

EMMY

No way. Geri's no sell-out.

GERI

Emmy, at the rate I'm going, I'd make those kids into
s'mores if it would sell.

MARIA

There's your gritty reality.

A WAITER walks up to the table.

GERI

Help me, sir. Say something witty.

The WAITER pauses in thought.

WAITER

Eat me.

1

The Price of Wishes

The price of wishes had officially gone up. As I walked out of the Soupberg Diner into the open air of Manhattan's Upper East Side, with the first pages of my new screenplay sizzling in my messenger bag, I found myself debating. Not whether Angelina Jolie would be too pretty to play me in this screenplay, but whether the waiter who just asked me to eat him actually peed on my bacon cheeseburger. So if ever there were a time to make a wish, it was now.

A few short steps away on the corner of Seventy-second and Second Avenue sat Max, our neighborhood homeless man; or as he liked to call himself, freelance minimalist-lifestyle expert. He was staked out in his usual place, wearing his usual garb and holding up his usual hook: a tattered Jack Daniel's box with the words "MAKE A WISH— 50¢" written in dried ketchup. The sign was taped to a nine iron as a way to draw attention to his secret powers of wish granting while also being a handy way to keep himself from falling off his industrial-size spackle pail. I couldn't understand how Maria and Emmy never noticed him outside of the Soupberg Diner. After all, how often do you run into a homeless man who looks like Santa Claus wearing a garbage bag? This night the *50¢* part of his sign had been crossed out and replaced by *$1*. Curious to see the reason behind the fare increase, I gave him his expected bowl of corn chowder and some peanut-butter crackers.

"MTA fare hike. Two bucks a ride now," he said, reaching for the soup.

"Does that mean my wish will come true twice as fast?" I asked.

"Does the subway come twice as often as it did before?"

He made a good point. I reached into my pocket and produced a shining new Sacajawea gold dollar coin. As soon as I put it in the bowl, he grimaced.

"I hate those."

"It's legal tender, Max. It counts." But secretly, I agreed with him. Even though I liked the fact that a Native American woman was finally getting the recognition she deserved, a thousand plus years after the fact, I hated when I got eighteen of them as change for a twenty from the MetroCard vending machines. It made my wallet feel like a brick and made me constantly overpay for a pack of gum.

"But the triple cherry slot machines don't take gold dollar coins."

"She's Native American. They have to take it."

"Got any singles?"

"I gave them to an insulting waiter."

"How about those state quarters? I need Mississippi . . ."

"Max, you're wearing a Hefty bag! You're homeless, remember?"

Just as that kind remark hung in the air, a woman walking her French bulldog overheard my comment and called me a bitch under her breath. And she would have been right, too, had I not sworn I'd seen Max stroll out of the Polo store on Seventy-second Street, wearing a tuxedo and swinging a large shopping bag. The doorman of the store even called him a cab and waved him off like Donald Trump at Christmas. But the guilt soon stung me. This could be my daily dose of being wrong. For karma's sake, I dropped another dollar coin into the bowl.

"Here ya go, Maxy. Sorry about that."

Max just shook his dusty head and laughed at me. He dunked a peanut butter cracker into his soup and took a bite. His beard caught all the crumbs that flew out when he talked.

"Geri, you're a good kid. A bit of a potty mouth but a good kid nonetheless." He reached over and picked up the small black cauldron at his feet.

"Here," he said, handing it to me. "Give it a good hard shake."

There it was. The infamous bowl of wishes. In the middle of this little black cauldron sat a worn, chipped brass bell balancing on a mound of loose change. My two gold dollar coins topped the heap.

"Come on. You know the drill."

And I did. But the last six times I rang that bell, the only wish that seemed to come true was that I would find love in the least likely place. That turned out to be walking in on a forty-year-old woman giving a blow job to a twenty-something waiter in a bathroom stall at Brother Jimmy's Bar and Grill. It seemed that if the bowl was to work, it not only needed a dollar but specifics and faith. None of which I possessed much of after the age of eight. If there was one thing that my life seemed to be hell-bent on teaching me, it was that any jingle that was jangled from Geraldine Agnes O'Brien fell on deaf ears.

"You make a wish for me," I told Max.

He gently placed his dinner on the sidewalk. "Suit yourself, oh ye of little faith."

Max rubbed his hands together as he peered into my face. He tried to excavate from my puzzled expression what sort of wish I would want granted. After an uncomfortably long moment of direct eye contact, he put his hands on his knees and stared up into Manhattan's evening sky. I looked up as well, wondering what Max could actually be staring at. His eyes rolled around the few stars that could peek through the constant pink glow of the city's atmosphere. In Manhattan, it's almost impossible to find the moon in the early evening. The lights of the city seem to outshine outer space. As if New York has no use or need for a moon in the first place. Max's body rocked back and forth as a slow hum vibrated through his throat. After a minute of watching Max fall into some kind of soup-induced trance, I felt completely insane. Forget this, I thought. I could be here all night.

Bending close to his ear, I whispered, " 'Night, Max. Stay safe and keep warm." And with that, I walked up Second Avenue toward home. Max made no motion toward ringing that bell.

Tuesday night on the Upper East Side is like Friday night in Pittsburgh. All of the rich and rich-in-waiting seemed to be outside, taking advantage of the warm late spring night. Handsome couples sat at sidewalk cafes enjoying the fresh air and a cigarette as they dug into monstrous salads covered with oil and cheese. Women in velour sweatpants fussed over the mini-turds that their mini-dogs left behind. Older couples walked hand in hand down the sidewalk discussing the lecture at the 92nd Street Y on rustic whole-food cooking while enjoying their fat-free, low-calorie, brownie-batter yogurt cones. As I walked past these outdoor diners, smokers and yogurt connoisseurs, I caught a glimpse of Emmy and myself five years ago. Two fresh-out-of-college girls were holding another girl's hair back as she threw up on the sidewalk in front of our neighborhood bar, Doc Watson's. I sidestepped the vomit and the heartfelt, "I so fucking love you guys," and asked myself the same painful question that I'd asked myself every day since

I moved to this fateful town. When did New York cool turn so . . . state college? Why was I not in the hard-core artist section of the Lower East Side having sex with Ethan Hawke look-alikes? Why was I not lugging cables around for a film shoot or beating tourists away from the craft services table? How did I, the cool, edgy writer, land in the brunch capital of the world? Where everything was so "okay" that I took every opportunity I could to endanger myself just to feel the thrill of being alive? Was I abnormally brave or crazy from boredom? I figured it had to be one or the other. After all, I was the only one on the block who didn't hit the deck when the bang barreled down Seventy-eighth Street.

Instead, I did what anyone who has lived in Manhattan more than five years did. I stopped, waited two seconds and did the math. 1 bang + 0 scream = 1 car backfiring. 1 bang + 1 pause + 1 bang = 2 sets of tires running over a steel grate. 1 scream + 1 pop + 1 pop + 1 pop + soft patter of feet = 911. But this bang I knew all too well. It came from my neighbor's 1984 Nissan Maxima. A distress signal sent out by the car to its owner that it wanted to die.

Todd's car was the easiest one to spot on Seventy-eighth Street. Out of all the SUVs, kidnapper vans and black Town Cars that normally lined both sides of the block, his usually sat catty-corner under the streetlight with a soft stream of smoke leaking from under the hood. This night was no different. With the hood up and half a tool box splayed out on the sidewalk, Todd grunted as he banged a screwdriver on his battery.

"How's it going, Todley?" I asked as I peeked over his shoulder at the engine. His wide shoulders and tall frame doubled over the engine did not allow for a clear view of anything. Todd turned his head and peeked back at me, giving me a tired but sweet smile.

"Hey there, Geri girl. You look amazing."

"I bet I do." I chuckled as I plopped my messenger bag down. "What's it this time?"

He tucked in his chin and pouted like a girl. For a handsome, square-jawed man, he looked ridiculous. Adorable but ridiculous. "It won't start, Geri. Why?"

" 'Cause it's old and made in Japan."

"But why?"

Rolling up my sleeves, I nudged him out of the way and took a quick look at the engine. "Well, with this car it could be a number of things. A discharged battery, a busted catalytic converter, warped engine heads, a bad ignition switch or neutral interlock. Or . . ." I stuck my nose close to the engine and sniffed. "Or it's just a pile of crap. What does it do when you put the key in and turn it?"

"Well, it started initially . . ."

"So we all just heard."

"But then it died. Now it just clicks."

"It's probably the battery." I walked over to the toolbox and pulled out a pair of his oversized work gloves. But as I shook my head in disbelief that a chiropractor would drive such a death trap, he threw me one of his smiles that made his cheeks dimple so deep you could stick your finger in it. One of those smiles that always made my brain say for a split second, *if only.* If only Todd Boyd wasn't my downstairs neighbor of five years. If only he didn't have a long-term girlfriend who looked like she modeled sweater sets for JC Penney. If only he drove American. But as always, the second passed. And I let it go. "By the way, did you ever wind up getting that wrench kit?"

Todd bent over and removed the first tray of his toolbox, revealing a row of shiny new Crescent wrenches. He held one of the gleaming silver tools up to the streetlight for me to examine.

"I did good, right?"

Upon closer inspection, I could feel my heart drop. Wrinkling my nose, I said, "You bought SAE wrenches."

"Like I said, I did good, right?"

"Todd, SAE are used for American cars. Your car, my dear, uses the metric system." By the look on his face it appeared that I had just let the air out of his tires. Not wanting to disappoint the only man other than my father who'd ever bought a tool set on my recommendation, I reached over and rubbed the side of his arm for encouragement. When my hand slid over his triceps, he instantly flexed. "Don't worry," I said, barely suppressing a smile. "You can make do with these. Just remember, with a bit of metal wire a half-inch wrench will do in a pinch for a 12 millimeter."

The smile returned to his face. "Hey, some girls like flowers. Some like tools."

"And I've liked my fair share of tools. We all can't be as lucky as Cassie."

This breakdown marked the third time in a month that I'd spent quality time with Todd under his hood. Which was not a very bad place to be. His brown bomb not only kept my knowledge of foreign engines fresh but enabled me to hang out with the only neighbor I really knew in the building. He sat on his bumper and rifled aimlessly through the toolbox as I scrubbed the rust off his terminal caps.

"So other than car troubles, how's everything going?" I asked as I tried to loosen one of the caps. He paused for a moment and fumbled with a clamp. Noticing the silence, I glanced back at Todd. His face had lost its smile. All was not good in Apartment #18.

"Know anyone who needs a roommate? I'm looking," he said as he clicked the clamps to his belt buckle. I shifted my attention back to the battery.

"I don't know anyone who would want to live with a couple," I said. "Could you pass me a rag?"

He leaned in next to me to examine my handiwork. The clean smell of a newly washed shirt and Speedstick replaced the odor of burnt oil. "It's just me," he said as he handed me the rag. I stopped working.

"And Cassie?" I asked.

He shook his head. "Over. It was a long time coming."

"I'm sorry to hear that." And I was. The last time I fixed his fuel injector, he was thinking about buying a ring. Between the fuel injector and the battery, their relationship seemed to have hit the skids. I didn't know much about Cassie except that she worked as a hairdresser in Midtown and had an addiction to Altoids. In five years I'd only passed her a handful of times in the hall. She never spoke to me. Even when I held the front door for her, the most I would get would be a nod of recognition and a strong whiff of peppermint. But on appearance alone, Cassie and Todd seemed like a genetic match. Both were extremely fit, with black hair so thick you couldn't even see a part. Their eyes were the kind of gray-blue eyes I've only seen in cats, and their skin was the color and texture of my grandma's china. It would be safe to assume that if one of them needed a kidney, they wouldn't need to go far to find one.

But though Cassie would walk over me in a fire, my relationship with Todd couldn't have been more different. Ever since the day I slim-jimmed his car door open, Todd and I could never pass each other without stopping to have a twenty-minute conversation. Between questions on how my dad taught me about big block engines to how many query letters I'd sent out that week on my screenplay, Todd seemed to genuinely care about the comings and goings of my life. He also seemed to be open about his. To a point. He never hesitated to tell me about the characters he'd seen at the chiropractic office he shared with his father in Queens or stories about his days on the swim team at UMASS. But when I asked him about the woman he lived with, the only thing he would say was that they'd dated in high school and that Cassie's dream was to get out of doing hair and move into facials. Nothing more.

As I scrubbed the wire brush around the battery, I tried to figure out why a man who never threw anything out, no matter how old or broken it seemed to be, would break up with his girlfriend of eight years. And what girl in her right mind would leave a guy who could give her free adjustments and bought ratchet wrenches?

When I turned my head to answer, I found his face uncomfortably close to mine. So close that I could feel his breath on my cheek. So close that I only needed to whisper to be heard. "I'll keep my ears open. If I hear something, I'll let you know."

Then I did hear something. The bell. Max's bell. The bell I'd rung unsuccessfully for true love, a million-dollar deal for my screenplay and a cool new job seemed to be going off right next to my left ear. That sound made me jerk up so fast that I smashed my head on the inside of the hood.

"What happened?" he asked as he reached for my pulsing skull.

"Did you hear that?"

"What?"

"That bell."

"You mean the one ringing in your head right now?" he said, half concerned and half chuckling. In a daze,

I looked up and down the street for Max and his movable feast of garbage. Nothing.

Rubbing my head, I turned to Todd. "Try it now."

Todd hopped behind the wheel and turned the key. The heap turned over beautifully. Dad would be proud, I thought. He would have grabbed me in a big bear hug, kissed the top of my head, then pushed me into the house to get the grease out of my clothes before it set. Todd's reaction was similar. He jumped out of the car and threw his hands in the air as if I'd just scored a touchdown.

"Geri, you're a goddess!" he cried before running over to me. He wrapped his thick arms around my five-foot frame and spun me in the air for joy. This, I find, is the normal reaction of people who get their car fixed for free.

"I owe you a drink."

"It's okay, Todd. Really, you don't need to . . ."

"I insist. For all the times you've got me out of a jam, it's the least I can do." He placed me safely down on earth. My knees buckled once my feet touched the ground. A feeling I blamed on the bump on my head instead of the knot I felt tightening in my stomach. Todd ran back over to the car, threw all the tools into the box and slammed down the hood. "Look, I have to go on a call now, but how about we go to Doc's? Thursday work for you?"

"Thursday's fine."

"Great. I'll meet you there at eight," he said as he hopped in the car. Still wearing his work gloves covered in battery crud, I routed through my hair to find the ravine the hood had left in my skull. He rolled down the window and stuck his head out. "And put some ice on that bump. I don't want you to get amnesia and forget about our fate."

"Our what?"

"Date, Geri. Our date." He laughed as he drove the brown

bomb away. His car stopped at the red light on the corner of Seventy-eighth Street, then disappeared into the traffic streaming up First Avenue.

Date, I thought to myself. *I have a date.* Not a real date, but a night out with someone who didn't have ovaries. Someone cute who I could pretend asked me out after noticing me across a crowded bar instead of someone who wanted to thank me for fixing his car. I wondered how much of a date it would really be. Then my fingers found the lump on my head and the shooting pain that accompanied it. *Great.*

A taxi blew its horn behind me, giving me a gentle nudge to get the hell out of the middle of the road. I grabbed my messenger bag filled with query letters and self-addressed stamped envelopes and continued on to the six-story red brick walk-up that Emmy, Todd, Cassie and I called home.

At night, our building seemed identical to the other fifteen cookie-cutter walk-ups that sidled up next to each other on our street. But during the day you could see the one detail that made our building different. The fire escape. The ironwork that ran up the front of Number 318 looked as if it belonged to a hotel in the French Quarter of New Orleans rather than on the Upper East Side of Manhattan. Hundreds of swirls made by curled iron bars covered in chipped brown lead paint laughed in the face of the safety codes that all the other building's perpendicular railings were forced to adhere to. And although those occupants stood a chance of making it out alive during a fire, I loved the shadows the bars made at night around my bedroom.

Reaching in my bag for the keys to the front door, I heard it again: Max's bell. Determined to find him, I darted back onto the street, but the only person I could see was a lone Chinese delivery boy peddling the wrong way up Seventy-eighth Street. His thumb gingerly plucked the bell fastened to his handlebars.

Max's bell. Now that would be crazy, I thought as I shook my pounding skull. *This is just me being crazy.*

2

If Crazy Falls in a Forest

"No, *this* is you being crazy," he said. He always got nervous when I stood on the railings of the fire escape. Straining to reach the watering can over my head to feed the philodendron, I tried to explain to him, yet again, that it was not just easier for me to do it this way, but safer for everyone else as well. Emmy's hanging plants grew so large and so heavy in the spring that trying to bring them down off the railings to water them would require a fork-lift. After all, no one wants to worry about killing a pedestrian with a planter at seven in the morning. If *I* fell, the person walking underneath would at least stand a better shot at moving out of the way. A screaming female grabs your attention quicker than a fifty-pound planter's silent fury. And safety aside, the unobstructed view of the sky that appeared between the high-rises took my breath away. Still, J. T. didn't buy it.

"I'm not crazy," I explained. "I'm saving time and maybe a life."

"So what are you saving when you do your pull-ups on the fire escape? A gym membership?" he asked. I could feel his eyes digging into me. "I can't save you, you know."

"I don't want to be saved," I said as I stuck my finger into the moist soil. "I just don't want to kill Emmy's plants again."

"Okay then. But if you fall and splatter that pretty little face of yours all over the pavement, you'd better not come crying to me," he scolded. I turned around to get a better look at him. His white pressed suit gleamed against the brick. With his long legs crossed at the ankles, his arms folded and sporting a wry smile, he shook his head and tut-tutted me like a two-year-old. "I adore you, Geri, but have no intention of cleaning up after you."

Looking past my bare feet gripping the fire-escape railing, I saw the morning urbanites hustle along the sidewalk below. They scurried to work with their mochaccinos firmly in hand and their bleeping Nextels latched onto their belts. Not a one looked up to catch my high-wire act four stories above. As I dropped my watering can on the fire escape, I wondered, if a tree only makes a sound in the forest when someone is around to hear it, are people only crazy if someone catches them doing something nuts? Watching the sheer intensity of people bound to work on time, I figured I wasn't crazy. I was just invisible.

"Think I can do it?" I asked him. J. T. let out a sigh and began to examine his cuticles.

"Are we doing this again?"

Inching my feet a hip width apart, I bent my knees slightly to improve my stance.

"Every second I can balance on this railing will be another million a producer is going to pay for my screenplay." My hands slowly pulled away from the pot that hovered in front me. "I made it to ten last time. What do you think about fifteen?"

J. T. bit a hangnail. "You'll get to seven."

By the time I hit four, I felt my feet begin to slip. My arms thrashed in the air until I grabbed hold of one of the planters. With a swift yank, I lost my balance, fell off the railing and landed with a bang back onto the fire escape.

The philodendron followed, coating my cheap Burlington Coat Factory beige suit with a layer of potting soil. He squatted down next to me and put his face near mine.

"Keep going this way and we will never get a chance to meet. And how angry will I be at you then, kitten?" he said as he brushed a few particles of mulch off his trousers. The morning light caught the gold in his blond curls, making his head sparkle the same way the sunlight does when it bounces off the bay. J. T. swept a few stray strands of hair away from my eyes.

"Now you know that only *I* can make it to fifteen." He demonstrated this by hopping gracefully up onto the railing and doing a little soft shoe dance. "You, my dear, will just have to wait."

And with that, he gave me a wink, jumped off the fire escape and disappeared into the ether below. I rolled over and looked through the iron bars, hoping he would materialize on the sidewalk. But I saw nothing other than our elderly landlord sweeping the front stoop. Then I heard Emmy call from inside the apartment.

"Geri, are you okay? I heard a thump."

"I'm fine, Emmy," I said without so much as moving a muscle. But was I fine? Probably not. At least I knew what I wasn't. I wasn't crazy. I was sane. Incredibly sane. Because I was lucky enough to have what no other twenty-seven-year-old woman on the Upper East Side had. I had an imaginary friend. And his name was J. T.

"Geri! You all right?"

I crawled back through the window into the spacious, 400-square-foot apartment I shared with my best friend, Emmy. The first thing I learned when Emmy and I moved into Manhattan was that space was relative. Whatever I thought the average American considered reasonable in apartment sizes and office-appropriate skirt lengths would have to be completely reassessed. Our apartment was a classic pre-War walk-up, although I was never quite sure if pre-War meant World War I, Civil or French and Indian. We rented a "technical" two-bedroom apartment. Aside from the kitchenette and bathroom, there were two rooms that could fit a twin bed and a sac of laundry. Nothing more. It was the kind of apartment that usually prompted anyone from Manhattan to say how lucky we were to have our own bedrooms. Anyone who didn't would just look around nervously and say how Manhattan's a great place to visit but they would never want to live here.

"What happened? I heard a bang," Emmy said as I made my way into the kitchen and over to the refrigerator. Emmy ran between the rooms, filling her schoolbag with students' homework papers, lesson plans and other sundry school stuff. She looked chipper and alert. Had I not known her since kindergarten, I would think she ate her toast with a thin spread of Ecstasy. She stopped abruptly in the kitchen and looked me over. Dabbing on a layer of strawberry lip balm with her pinkie, she asked, "What happened to your suit?"

"The plant fell. Em, how long have you been up?"

"Since four thirty. Had to grade papers. Early bird does catch the worm, you know."

"So does the last person to finish a bottle of tequila, but you don't see me aiming for that honor."

She giggled as she tied her long blond hair into a teacherly, sexless bun. She winced as she tucked in the loose strands.

"Geri, no wonder you don't like your publishing job. You're tired. You'd feel better getting a jump-start on your day. Maybe doing some yoga in the morning would help."

I poured myself a bowl of Cap'n Crunch. "Emmy, if I got

that much of a jump-start, I guarantee by lunch you would find me taking a nap in the coat closet."

She cocked her head in disbelief. "Oh, please. You would never do that."

Little did she know I've caught forty winks in the company coat closet. And the small boardroom by the freight elevator. And on my boss's office couch during sales conference.

"Well, for any teacher worth their salt, the day is half over," she said as she gathered her textbook and a few stray pages of homework. Emmy cared about kids and their little brains so much, it made my heart bleed. When she wasn't teaching advanced calculus and trigonometry at The Day School on the Upper West Side, she volunteered at Lenox Hill Hospital, holding infants with HIV. Back in high school, our guidance counselor diagnosed Maria and me as "clinically brain dead" in math. If it wasn't for Emmy letting us cheat off her in Sequential 2 class we'd most probably still be sitting in the second row of Ms. Morro's classroom trying to figure out what integers were.

"Oh and Geri, can you please take those down?" She pointed to the rejection letters tacked up on the refrigerator door. "You know how I feel about them."

I'd gotten into the habit of saving my rejection letters. I read in some article in *Vanity Fair* that it built character. At the rate they were flying in, I was building a character the size of the Statue of Liberty. But Emmy believed our food shouldn't be near all that bad karma.

"But Emmy, I'm almost at fifty."

She yanked one off and passed it to me in disgust. It was my favorite. Written by an assistant at William Morris, it read, "We don't believe Geraldine's writing is strong enough for us to warrant reading her whole screept." *Screept?*

"Now, Geri . . ."

"Lots of writers keep their rejection letters. It gives them drive."

"I think it's masochistic. And it's probably what's making our milk go bad earlier than the expiration date."

Not willing to argue with the power of bad karma, I conceded. "I'll take them down if it bothers you."

Emmy stopped packing and stood with her hand on her hip, pointing that teacherly finger at me.

"It should bother you. All these letters are from people who are going to eat their words when you become famous. And it will happen because you are a great writer, Geraldine Agnes O'Brien. You always were. But until that day comes, I don't think it's good for your chi and our perishables to be looking at all that rejection every day. Trust me. You'll feel like a million bucks after you do it."

"Okay, Mother Kozak. Is that all?"

"As a matter of fact, no. That's not all." Just then Emmy smacked a box of Borax in front of me. A puff of white dust escaped from its lid. She stood over me waiting for some sort of answer.

"Care to explain this?"

"Borax? Well, it's a detergent in powder form. You sprinkle some on a sponge or directly on a surface you feel isn't as clean . . ."

"You saw Todd last night, didn't you?" Looking into her squint, I knew I was busted. Borax only existed in the apartment because Dad taught me long ago that Borax and lavender were the only cure-alls for getting grease off your hands. And each time I left the Borax box out, it meant Todd's car had exploded. And each time Todd's car exploded, Emmy felt that it was karma or God or the engineers at Nissan trying to tell us that Todd and I were soul mates.

"His battery cables rusted. No big deal," I said, munching

on my cereal. Instead of looking at her, I pretended to read the nutritional information on the side of the box.

"Isn't that like the fourth time in two months?"

"What can I say? He drives a shitmobile."

"I think it's an excuse to see you."

"Really? He takes his life and the lives of his passengers in his hands solely for the purpose of spending time with me? A woman who lives one floor above him? I don't think so, Emmy." Explaining was no use. The smile wouldn't melt off her face. I could feel my eyes rolling up to the ceiling. "Besides, I wouldn't date him. He's rebounding. He broke up with Cass . . ." but before I even got the word *Cassie* out, she broke into a squeal.

"It's a sign! It's a sign! Go for it, Geri! You guys have chemistry."

"No. He drives a deathtrap and I have an odd ability to fix fanbelts. That's all."

I suddenly lost my appetite and emptied the bowl into the sink. Emmy ran into her room and rifled through a small stack of books. She pranced back into the kitchen and proudly held up a volume titled, *The Love You Always Lose: How to Get Him and Keep Him in the First Three Dates* by Kelly Cox.

"For when he asks you out. I found it extremely informative," she said as she handed it to me.

"You've got to be kidding," I said as I idly flipped through the pages. " 'Chapter Three—Don't curse or swear.' " I slammed the book shut. "Fuck me, I'm out already."

"Don't be so quick to judge. Reading it couldn't hurt." She noticed the time on our rooster wall clock. "Oh, shoot, I'm late." Emmy picked up her duffel bag and headed toward the door. "I told my students I would pick up bagels from Zabar's for their study break. I'll see you later for lunch."

"Remember, Emmy," I called out after her. I opened the

book and read aloud. " 'Don't say I love you first. It gives away your power in the relationship and makes you seem desperate and needy.' "

She just laughed. "Love you, crazy girl."

"See, now I think you're needy. I don't think I can handle this relationship. You'd better move out."

Emmy just smiled as she unlocked the padlock, the deadbolt and the chain. Before leaving she looked up at the large crack running through our plaster ceiling.

"You know something, Geri?"

"We need to spackle?"

"No. I think this is going to be a great day." And as she walked out of the room, her Happy perfume still lingered in the air. It amazed me how someone who hadn't had a boyfriend in close to three years could remain so optimistic about dating. Even with no prospects in sight.

As I packed my messenger bag for work, I figured that it would be better not to tell her that Todd and I were meeting for drinks. She would probably force me to get a makeover or buy a new outfit. And as I took a look in the mirror and examined my black wavy curls that I always cut myself, my square jaw and my winter-white skin that never tanned, I laughed. Chemistry. Right.

I took another look around the apartment to make sure all the lights were off and that the iron, which still sat in its original box, remained unplugged. I went through this routine eight times before I left. But before I walked out the door I turned around and grabbed the dating book off the coffee table. Stuffing it into my bag, I thought, she could be right. Even though it isn't a date, it still couldn't hurt.

3

Extreme Routine

My guidance counselor in junior high school said that nothing could get us down or make us cave into peer pressure to do something stupid like smoke pot, set off m-80s in our band teacher's garage or jump off the Goose Creek Bridge at low tide, if we were constantly centered and in a happy place. But it's hard to find your happy place when you can feel your chief financial officer's nutsack on your hip in the company elevator. Normally in the mornings, I waited for an elevator that didn't exceed the estimated weight limit clearly noted on the inside door. But when I heard the people piling on debating whether the meeting was on the twelfth or the fifteenth floor, I figured that I'd better squeeze in. This meant cramming onto the elevator with about twelve men in suits holding their morning coffee next to their Adam's apple and ten women carrying multiple canvas handbags, one of which always sported the Junior Varsity Publishing company logo of a tiger holding two pom-poms. Once the doors closed, all conversation ceased and all eyes focused on the numbers lighting up. I used to wonder why people who knew each other refused to talk or even look at each other on an elevator. Hedda, my boss, explained this phenomenon by saying it was harder to yell at someone at a ten thirty meeting if you asked them where they got their shoes at eight.

As we got closer to my floor, I couldn't shake the feeling that I was forgetting something. This feeling did not occur all that often, since my life at Junior Varsity Publishing was of such extreme routine that the Swiss could use me to calibrate watches. The only thing that rolled up on my mental Rolodex was to ask my friend and coworker Sally about her date with Paul.

Sally Schoenfeld was really the only true city girl Maria, Emmy or I knew. Born and bred in Queens, Sally knew how to nab the best pantsuits, men and Greek food in the five boroughs. And although she promised her parents she would marry a Jewish doctor, Sally dated the most glaringly non-Jewish men around. This time, her parents had set her up with Paul Cohen, a urologist from Riverdale. So other than asking her if Paul had broken the cycle of gentiles, I drew a blank.

Once the doors opened on the twelfth floor, I pried my way past the crowd out into the open air of the Junior Varsity lobby. As I looked around, there didn't seem to be any unusual bustle for a Monday. Everything looked exactly the same as the work day before and the work day before that. All the days of the last five years bled together as follows:

First came Berta, the twelfth-floor receptionist.

"Hello, Berta," I'd say. Berta, our eighty-year-old Hungarian receptionist, would be reading a romance novel, the cover of which normally sported a fit, mildly sweaty, self-tanned Caucasian male wearing Navaho tribal headgear, a loin cloth and some mukluks. She wouldn't even look up when she asked me in her thick Hungarian accent the same question that made me feel like a colossal failure each and every morning.

"So? How's the writing going?"

"Fine. Thanks." And technically it was. My first screenplay was finished and my suicide note was coming along smashingly.

Then, Howard, the twelfth-floor mailroom man, would come through the double doors with his cart. A slick fifty-year-old man, Howard applied Drakkar Noir with a washcloth. The same cologne an old boyfriend of mine wore at college.

"Hey, Geri! Always on time. Like the sun!"

" 'Morning Howard," I'd say as I passed him. He would hold the door open for me with his free hand, and for the two seconds it would take for me to walk past him, I would get the urge to have sex and write a term paper.

After I rounded the corner past the crispy brown tips of our welcoming office palm and an old poster of Kibbles the Karate Kat (which they later changed to Kibbles the Karate Cat after they realized that the initials KKK didn't look quite right stretched across the front of a feline superhero's chest and looked even worse when left as a calling card on the crime scene), Daisy Dickinson would hustle past me on the way to the bathroom carrying a small bag filled with her own private stash of toilet paper. At exactly 8:55 her second Mocha Grande caused the first one to work its way through her lower intestine, causing a swift flight to the ladies room.

" 'Morning, Daisy."

"Hiya, Geri!" she'd say, her eyes gleaming bright from caffeine. Daisy's freckled skin, Raggedy Ann red hair and Southern accent gave her an air of down-home country goodness. You didn't have to be around her long to know this was only a defense mechanism Mother Nature had given her so that people didn't succumb to the urge to throttle her after she opened her mouth. Everything she said was an insult in the form of a politely worded question. If she wasn't the president's executive assistant, she would have been buried under the file cabinets years ago. "Your Duane Reade run out of Tide, too?"

"What?"

"Oh, nothing. Was the Six train platform too crowded for you again?"

My watch read 8:56. As usual, right on time. I ignored Daisy and went straight to my desk. When I plopped my messenger bag onto the faux-wood surface, the paper that overflowed from Sally's tumbled down onto mine. Our desks faced each other, making us look like we were in some form of primitive typing duel. But even though we were both assistants to the vice president of marketing, our respective work spaces were diametrically opposite. My space looked barren. My bulletin board displayed a picture of Elvis, my Dad's 1960s lime green Muntz Jet and a checklist of agents, producers and production companies that I had yet to send my screenplay to. On my desk sat nothing more than a stapler that could only fasten three pieces of paper together before the staple warped, a mug filled with pens that didn't write and a blotter calendar inked up only with the first and last days of my menstrual period. The only thing that really worked on my desk was the Bill Clinton bobblehead doll that Sally gave me on my third year anniversary with the company. I'm not a huge Clinton fan, but Sally got tired of people asking her if I was a temp.

Sally's desk, on the other hand, looked like an outlet center for Kinko's. Packing labels, spreadsheets, colorful J. V. children's books, publishing schedules from before we graduated college, were all proudly displayed and in clear view of any company executive who might happen to walk by. Her work space screamed "go-getter," while mine screamed "gone fishing."

I searched Sally's day planner and bulletin board for any signs of office activity. Apart from an informative company meeting on our new sexual harassment policy and a few office holiday grab bag ideas, I found nothing. Since the coast seemed to be clear, I figured I would get to work on writing more query letters for my screenplay, *What Child Is This?*, a young adult Christmas comedy about kids, caroling and leukemia. No time like the present to throw them in the mail to start the rejection process.

Just as I sat down to type, Sally appeared in a fitted black business suit, carrying a stack of handouts.

"Sally! How'd it go with Paul?" I asked as I watched her dig a staple out of a pile of papers with one of her long, French-manicured fingernails.

"You mean Carlos."

"What happened to Paul?"

"What usually happens when Mom yells over the kugel, 'Did you know our Sally graduated top of her class at Fordham and still kept her virginity? Isn't that fantastic? Do you like tongue?'"

"Yikes. But Carlos doesn't have a real Hebrew ring to it."

"I'll tell them it's Ephraim in Yiddish."

Sally being a virgin is like a tomato being a fruit. Technically, it is. The rest of the world, however, doesn't see it that way. Sally prided herself on never having "known a man" but after she explained to the three of us in great detail how to make a man climax by using only the first two digits of your pinkie and an open mind, we suspected she'd known a few vegetables.

Sally stopped her frantic digging once she caught a glimpse of my outfit. She straightened up and examined me through her Dolce & Gabbana black-rimmed glasses. Her ebony hair was tucked neatly behind her diamond-studded ears.

"What's that?" she asked. She waved her finger wildly at me as if she was trying to cast a spell that would pouf me into a pumpkin.

"What's what?"

"That black shit."

I stuck out my jaw and did my best impression of Ally Sheedy from *The Breakfast Club.* "I like that black shit."

"Geri, it's soil."

"Oh, this?" I said, noticing a leaf hanging half out of my pocket and the dirt skidmarks smeared over the left side of my blazer. "I fell."

"Where? Out of a tree in Central Park? Look, you'd better clean up before the meeting. What did you come up with for your proposal?"

Then it hit me. "That's not until the eighth," I said as my eyes drifted over to the cursor pulsing on the *8* of my May 8 query letter. My skin grew clammy as I began to break into a hot flop sweat in my thirty-dollar, 100 percent polyester suit. Even though I didn't like my job as a marketing assistant at Junior Varsity Publishing, I couldn't get fired. I'd gotten fired once in my life. I'd never make it if I got fired again.

She took off her glasses and rubbed the bridge of her nose. "Please say you thought of an idea for Hedda's kids' historical series."

"Sure."

"What is it?"

I gulped. "A surprise?"

"Oh, God, not again," she said as she gathered her reams of handouts. "I'll meet you in the boardroom, Geri."

Crap, I thought. My boss expected Sally and me to come to this meeting with ideas. To prove ourselves to the other managers. We were her protégées. Her new young energy. Her think tank. But my tank was empty. My mind drew a blank. I knew the answer would come. I just needed some inspiration. And with that, I crawled under my desk, pulled out the plug of my computer and licked the power strip.

That's when the lights went out.

It wasn't until I looked at myself in the bathroom mirror that I realized why everyone in the conference room was staring at me during my presentation as if I had just come out of a coma and asked if Reagan got elected again. It wound up that electrocuting myself not only jogged my brain enough to give me a marketing idea for a new line of kids' books but also caused my left pupil to dilate completely. I thought that maybe if I looked directly into the florescent light, my pupil would go back to normal. Instead I just got a migraine. I wasn't too worried about everyone else's reaction. Just Sally's. All she could do was pace anxiously behind me as I held my face up to the light.

"The Donner Party?"

"Hey, it was the best I could come up with."

"No, Geri. Your best was the Joan of Arc doll that changed colors in hot water. This . . . this was crap!" she said as she inadvertently pointed to an open toilet stall. Just at that moment Daisy Dickinson walked past. After witnessing me pitch my big idea to the managers, she probably thought I was too dumb to know what shit was.

"Okay, so it wasn't great. But don't take this the wrong way, Sal, your idea wasn't that much better."

Sally folded her arms in a huff. "I think the story of the suffragettes would make a great series."

"No offense, Sally, but if I can't even muster the energy to read about how I got the right to vote, how am I going to sell that to a second grader? Can you honestly see a kid

saying, 'Daddy, can you read us the one about Lucretia
Mott again?' "

"Well, you certainly didn't bring the women's movement
forward today with half of Nebraska smeared on the front
of your suit and your psycho eye glaring out at everyone.
You freaked out most of the people in there." Sally began
to chew on her cuticles. In the land of Sally this meant her
anxiety was at level orange alert.

"It wasn't as bad as you think. Look, we're up against the
New Deal and the history of wheat. Both are snore city."

Sally stood behind me and faced me in the mirror. Her
eyes were filled more with concern than fear. "It's not that
our ideas sucked, Geri. The fact is that you don't care. Your
suit screams it. And some of us do care. Some of us care a
lot." She looked down sadly at her chewed-up cuticles and
busted fingernail. She was right. Some people, like Hedda
and Sally, cared. And on some level, I must have cared too.
Only nothing in my head, heart or soul would let me act
like it.

"I'm sorry, Sally. I should have thought ahead."

"Geri, I like this job. I worked really hard to get out of reception into this position. And until I have real nails, I
need this job."

"I'll ask Hedda if . . ." but then I stopped. I could smell
her. You always smelled her before you saw her. Hedda
Jove, Vice President of Marketing and grande dame of
Junior Varsity Publishing. The only thing she loved more
than a four-hour lunch or a quickie Vegas wedding was her
signature scent, L'air du Temps. Sally and I silently counted
down the seconds until she barged into the ladies room.

"Geri! There you are! What a presentation!" she cried as
she clasped her hands together in joy. Her nineteen-karat
sapphire lodged comfortably on her knuckle.

"Thank you, Miss Jove, but I can explain. Sally's idea, as

I'm sure you'd agree, was so much better than mine that I felt I couldn't compete so . . ."

"Geri, stop. Call me Hedda," she said.

"Okay. You see, Hedda, I know you're probably not happy about the idea of exposing kids to cannibalism, but . . ."

"Not happy? The board was thrilled! They're already talking about releasing the series during good nutrition week." I stared at Hedda with my one good eye and waited for the punch line. Sally looked at me as if she'd just smelled a turd.

Hedda was who I imagined Sally would be in twenty-five years if she had money, extensive microdermabrasion and a couple of ex-husbands to keep her last name in rotation. After asking Sally twenty times where she got her nails done, Hedda had pulled her out of reception and in to work with me. But although Sally and Hedda shared a common love of acrylic tips and Louis Vuitton Speedies (which I found out were not ham sandwiches), Hedda seemed to think that I possessed the stuff Corporate America was made of. But like my Grandmother, who would look up at my acne-pocked fourteen-year-old face through her cataracts and said, "Pimples? Your skin's like silk," Hedda believed what she wanted, despite the facts that stared her in the face.

In the middle of the gray and red company bathroom, Sally and I stared at Hedda as if she had just lost her mind. Hedda gushed on. "It's traditional values! Wal-Mart will love it! And isn't that what America is trying to get back to? Family vacations, camping trips, eating together . . ."

"You mean eating each other," Sally corrected.

"Same thing." Hedda's eyes drifted off into a dreamlike state of inspiration. "We can market it through Halloween. I can see them lining the shelves of Barnes & Noble now.

Great and Gross American Disasters. It will teach kids how hard it was back in the days of expansion. And really, what kid would sit in front of a video game when he can read this?" She broke from her trance and looked into the mirror to fix the mound of brilliant blond hair that spun up like a hive on top of her head. "And to boot, these stories fall into the Titanic-style disaster, which is just so wonderful."

Mulch fell out of my hair as I scratched my head in confusion. "How is the Titanic wonderful?"

"It's wonderful because those people have been dead for ages. Merchandising rights should be in the bag. No one's going to give a damn if we put out a musical or a talking doll. Can't say that about KKK. Right, guys?"

Over Hedda's shoulder, I could see Sally coming to the grim realization that she was going to have to think of ideas about how to get fun young families to buy books about other fun young families eating each other. Hedda remained unfazed as she straightened a jewel-encrusted broach on her Chanel suit.

"And Geri, one more thing: don't think I don't know about your little side job," Hedda said as she pierced the pin through her lapel. Sally's eyes darted up at me. Perspiration began to boil out of my skin again. My screenplay. Hedda had noticed my list of query letters. Crap. My mouth opened, but nothing came out. Apparently that was the only part of my body that was dry. Hedda just stuck her finger up to my face. "I know you're quite the little mechanic, but you don't have to fix the copy machines yourself. You know we hire people to do that." She grabbed a paper towel and began to wipe dirt off my blazer.

"Oh, that's not toner, Miss . . . ahh . . . Hedda, it's . . ."

"And you went on anyway without having handouts or even the time to wash up. That shows great love for the company. Great love." Then Hedda bent over and put her face uncomfortably close to mine. Her breath smelled like Dentine and an everything bagel as her eyes stared deep into my dime-sized pupil. "I see the love. The board sees the love. Can you, Geri?"

All I could see was Sally's hand reaching up and smacking her forehead behind Hedda's back. I put my hand over my right eye and with all the joy I could muster, I answered, "Sure thing!"

Then, for one fleeting moment, I thought maybe Hedda knew something I didn't. Maybe the upper echelon of children's publishing was more glamorous and exciting than I could ever imagine. Maybe she would take me under her Chanel-sleeved wing and guide me into the dream job I never knew I wanted. Maybe if I took deep-sea diving lessons, I could learn to hold my breath long enough to ride with Hedda in a cab to downtown meetings. Maybe . . .

Hedda spun Sally and me around, threw her arms around our shoulders and led us out of the bathroom like a coach trying to convince her players to go out on the field and keep getting their asses kicked by the visiting team.

"Come on, ladies. Let's make some magic!"

4

I Saw Mommy Eating Santa Claus

Sally and I followed Hedda out of the ladies room and back into her office. Hedda's office was so uniformly white that on a bright day, Sally and I would put a black coaster on the sofa just so people knew where to sit. She believed that if a woman could have a signature scent, then she needed a signature color as well. The building managers obliged by stripping her office and painting it white to "clear her palette." But after three months and fifty different green swatches between olive and lime, she decided that white would do.

As Sally and I began to situate ourselves on the couch, Hedda started outlining our tasks.

"Sally, you and I can start running the numbers and doing a bit of brainstorming. And Geri?"

"Yes?" I asked before I sat down. For the first time, I felt excited about an assignment.

"Geri, my printer isn't working well. The toner light won't shut off, and the computer support people haven't come up in ages, so would you be a dear and bring it down to the supply room?"

I looked at the monster sitting idle on a small table in the corner. The machine, roughly the size of an ottoman, dwarfed the table it sat on, causing it to buckle in the center.

I cleared my throat. "Your printer is a network printer, Hedda. It weighs quite a . . ."

"You can do it, Geri! I believe in you. What would the suffragettes say, Sally? 'Go, you girl'?"

Sally looked at the machine. The words tumbled out of her open mouth. "It's 'You go, girl.' "

"You go and make my printer work, girl!" Hedda cheered as she chipped me on the shoulder. It was beyond me why the woman who didn't want me to touch a copy machine thought it was within her rights to ask me to carry a fifty-pound network printer down to the basement. But an explanation would get me nowhere.

Sally began to take notes as she watched me unhook the cables from Hedda's printer. She shot me a glance that meant, "If you're not back in ten minutes, I'm calling an ambulance." As I tried to get my arms around the printer, Hedda broke her thought process.

"Oh, and make sure you don't put the printer down. I spilled coffee in the paper tray this morning. If it gets into the body of the printer, it might be cooked for good. And you know how expensive those things are."

Holy shit, I thought. I wrapped the cords around the base, managed to get a decent grasp on the beast and lifted it up. As soon as the printer left the table, I felt as if my spine had broken free from my rib cage and was spearing out of my butt. If I didn't give myself a hernia by the time I made it out the door, it would be a miracle.

But I managed. I hobbled with the behemoth to the elevator.

Berta, unable to tear her eyes from her copy of *Spent Warrior*, called out, "So, Geri, how's the writing going?"

"It's . . . been . . . better . . ." I gasped as I leaned the printer against the closed elevator doors. I hit the call button with my elbow. Once the elevator arrived, the doors opened with the piercing sound of metal scraping on metal. This didn't even fluster the portly man with the Coke bottle glasses who took up most of the space inside the elevator. He diligently read his *Financial Times* while holding two cups of coffee away from his navy Brooks Brothers suit.

Unable to breathe, I choked out, "Please, could you press the basement, please?"

He barely lifted his eyes from his pink paper before he answered. "Sorry. Hands full of hot joe."

The only noise in the elevator for the next few seconds was the sound of my panting. After reading a few stock reports he looked back up at me.

"Looks heavy."

Then I said it. I didn't mean to. I didn't want to. It just came out.

"Eat me."

He paused for a moment to collect his thoughts. "Excuse me? Did you just say what I think you just said?"

"What do you think I just said?" My palms began to sweat as I felt the printer slip. His eyes tried to focus on me through the inch-thick spectacles.

"I think I just heard you ask if I could eat you."

I prayed that the elevator would plummet. The only thing I could think to do was to agree with him. "Why, yes, sir."

He stood for a moment and thought about it. "Weren't you the one who gave that presentation on the Donner party?"

"Yes, sir."

He pushed his glasses up higher on his nose to get a better look at me.

"You think that people eating each other makes for great kids' books?"

I could feel the printer slipping. "Yes, sir."

"Eat me," he said softly to himself. "*Eat Me* would make a great title, wouldn't it?" His voice grew higher in excitement.

"Yes, sir."

"You know what? That's witty stuff!"

My eyes focused on the floor numbers as I counted the moments until we landed in the lobby. A dribble of sweat ran down the bridge of my nose. I tried to wiggle my nose in the hope that the drop would fall, but it only caused my face to itch. Now the urge to scratch engulfed my entire being.

" 'Eat me' is witty! I love it! What's your name again?"

"Geri O'Brien, sir."

He tried to shake my hand, but seeing that my hands were full, he settled for patting me on the back. "Well, Geri, let's get you out of the print shop and into the real world. I'm going to remember your name."

"Thank you, sir."

"Eat me!" he yelled as he bounded off the elevator and into the marbled lobby. With a spring in his step, he greeted everyone with "Eat me!" like he was wishing them Merry Christmas.

Since I'd lost feeling in my hands around the eighth floor, I couldn't hit the button for the basement. I figured if I turned and backed into the wall I might accidentally knock into it with my butt. Instead I leaned flat against the board and triggered all the buttons. The elevator started its journey back up to 37. Floor by floor.

By the time the elevator doors finally opened at the basement, I swore I was about to crap my pants. Doubled over with the printer resting on my pelvic bone, I crawled into the print shop, where a maintenance man stood behind a tall counter reading his copy of *Spent Warrior*. He looked up at me briefly before instructing me to place the printer on the table next to the others.

"What's wrong with it?" he asked as I heaved the printer up into the air. My hope was that it would land somewhere on the table next to the other four dead printers. Instead I missed the table entirely, causing this two-ton missile to explode like a dirty bomb into a million plastic pieces on the floor. Even with the eardrum-splitting crash, Mr. Maintenance Man didn't flinch. We both stared down at the shards that scattered in a ten-foot radius around the floor.

"Well, for starters," I said, scratching my nose, "the toner light won't shut off."

5

A Starr is Born Again

"I told you that 'Eat me' is fucking witty," Maria said through a mouthful of souvlaki.

"You are right and I am wrong," I said, then chugged a glass of homemade Greek lemonade. Fresh lemon pulp burned the back of my throat as I desperately tried to hydrate myself. My polyblend suit didn't breathe, so I felt as if I had been marinating in my own sweat for the past two hours. "No wonder Sylvia Plath stuck her head in an oven. Maybe it wasn't Ted. Maybe she just saw it all coming."

Maria looked at me with a ring of tzatziki around her lips. "Or maybe she decided to bake herself first before she told someone to eat her. Who knows? It's not my problem you don't know what witty is. Trust me, I know. I'm one witty bitch."

I slammed my glass on the table and raised my arm to order another lemonade.

"This was the worst day ever. And it's not even two," I said, thinking out loud.

"At least your job doesn't have the same hazards as mine. On your worst day at my job, you get fucking shot."

The waiter put a fresh glass of lemonade in front of me. I raised it in a toast. "Dare to dream."

Maria and I ate half our lunch before Emmy stormed

into the restaurant. Each Monday, when Maria worked day tours, I would run back to the Upper East Side for a two-hour lunch at the Soupberg Diner. Emmy usually came by for a quick bite between her two periods of study hall to tell us stories about her genius students and how they were planning to save the world. Emmy was not only a fine and respected math teacher but also the best tip calculator two girls with only functional math skills could ever ask to eat with.

As I began to chug my fifth glass of lemonade, Emmy threw herself into the booth next to Maria. Out of breath but very happy, she was flushed from excitement.

"Big news! I'm so happy. I'm so happy. I'm so . . ." Emmy stopped and looked at my face in horror. "What happened to your eye?"

"Nothing. Big meeting. Bad day," I said nervously. "So, what's your news?"

"Oh, yeah. My news. Oh, my gosh, you guys are going to freak out!"

Maria rolled her eyes and continued eating, unfazed. I wondered if Maria knew something I didn't. "Come on, Emmy. Share the joy," I said.

"Well, I was just in Zabar's when I saw . . ." She fanned her eyes as they began to tear. "You'll never believe who. I had to do a double take and . . . well, just take a guess."

"Jude Law!" I screamed.

"No!"

"Brad Pitt!"

"Nope!"

"That hot guy from *The Fast and the Furious!*"

Emmy cocked her head to the side. "Vin Diesel?"

"Vin Diesel looks like my Uncle Pete before the stroke," Maria chimed in.

"No, the other one," I said. "He drove the green car."

"Oh, yeah, he was cute," Emmy admitted. "But no. Better!"

"Cute?" Maria yelled. "Cute? Bulldog puppies are cute. Marijuana legalization rallies are cute. I went to see him in that dopey flick, *Timeline*. That man can turn a row of movie theater seats into a goddamn Slip-n-slide."

"You saw that in a theater? Who did you go with?" I asked, mildly hurt.

"No one. I went by myself."

"I would have gone with you."

"I know. And you would have yammered through the whole thing. Giving your little opinions on the editing or the writing or the acting or some other friggin' thing I don't give a shit about. I just wanted to sit back and relax with my thoughts and my . . ."

"Vibrator?"

"Guys!" Emmy called out. "Back to my news!"

"Sorry, Em."

"It's all right. Now then, you'll never believe who bought me a latte. I'll give you a hint. He's six foot . . ."

Maria took the fork out of her mouth and stared at it. "Bryan Starr."

"But how did you know?"

"The only time I ever saw you get this drunk with happiness was when you thought he was cheating off you in Mr. Presby's English class."

"Well, great, Maria. You just took the surprise out of it," Emmy said, disappointed. I hadn't seen Emmy this excited about a man since, well, Bryan back in junior high. I tried to keep the mood upbeat.

"Did you talk?" I asked.

"We did! And you'll never guess . . ."

"Didn't we reach the verdict in tenth grade that he was a dick?" Maria asked.

Emmy shifted in her seat and focused her entire attention

on me. "We got coffee and talked for almost half an hour. He works on Wall Street. Lives on the Upper West Side *alone*. Smart, handsome and those amazing blue . . ."

"Wasn't he the dickhead who carried a briefcase instead of a lunchbox to school?"

"Let it go, Maria." I said through my teeth.

"Look, all I know is that for ten years, every time that fruit bar accidentally looked at you, I had to hear about it. He never gave you the time of day in elementary school or junior high or high school. Always thought he was the big shit floating in a small pond. He was, is and forever will be a penis."

Maria had a point. Ever since that fateful day in second grade when Bryan smashed Emmy in the face with a red rubber ball during a game of Steal the Bacon, Emmy had been hopelessly devoted. And although we watched him date all the popular girls from every class three years above and below ours, Emmy still held hope that he would one day turn his affections toward her. She came close our senior year, when the soccer coach asked her to tutor him in physics. But even though they spent many a late night in her dad's den talking about everything other than math, the only thing she got from him was his vast knowledge of corner kicks and a rash from wearing too much of her mom's Shalimar perfume.

"We're going out for coffee on Friday," Emmy said.

Maria threw her napkin off her lap and onto the table, signaling that she was officially done. "Shit. Not again."

"I appreciate your concern, Maria. I do. But people change. And can't you just be happy for me? I haven't had a date with someone I like in so long. Please, just be happy for me?"

Maria looked as if she had just eaten all the lemon rinds

at the table. "But is this coffee thing an actual date? Like, are you going to kiss this douche bag at the end of it?"

"Well, no. It's just a friendly cup of coffee. But who knows? Maybe this coffee will lead to another coffee, which could lead to a Saturday brunch, which could lead to a dinner . . ."

"Which will lead to a hand job!" I said. Emmy just smiled and giggled to herself. "I hope it goes great. I'm excited for you."

Maria removed the toothpick from her pickle and dug through her teeth. "Date him hard. Dump him harder."

Emmy reached over and hugged Maria. "I promise I won't let him get to me."

"Just don't let him get to me," Maria warned. "And make sure when he's staring at you with those amazing blue eyes that one's not floating up in his skull like Geri's."

I grabbed a knife off the table and looked at my reflection. One pupil was still the size of a button.

"What? It'll go down."

After we finished lunch, Emmy gathered her books, bagels and homework papers as Maria examined her new round of ammunition. After each bullet was present and accounted for, she put it back on her twenty-pound police belt. Saddled with all the accouterments of law enforcement, it carried a notepad, three-way radio, Nextel, handcuffs, baton and her mini Glock handgun. On a typical cop, the belt looked right at home, with the gun on one side of the hip, baton on the other. But since Maria didn't even reach five feet in height, all the items appeared to be jammed right next to each other, making it nearly impossible for her to sit down. But with her father being a big retired detective in Suffolk County, she was allowed to carry a special issue gun. The Glock was at least an inch shorter in the barrel and the handle, designed for less kickback and a woman's grip. When she first got her piece a few of the officers at the station razzed her about it. Said she must not be strong enough for a real gun, and if it was possible, could she order it in pink? She told them she was considering it because it might make her feel more like one of the guys. Then she would know how it felt to have a three-inch pink appendage that rarely got pulled out.

As we waited with Emmy at the crosstown bus stop, Maria reached in her back pocket and handed each of us a flyer.

"I need you guys to put one up in your lobby. And keep an eye out for this guy."

Under the large bold type that read WANTED FOR ASSAULT was a picture of a gray-hooded head with no face. Emmy turned the picture around in circles like a puzzle, thinking she must have missed something. I scratched my head.

"Next time I run into one of the sand people, I'll give you a call," I said.

Emmy held the flyer up to the sun. "Maria, there's no face on this composite."

"I know. No one could get a decent description of the guy. He covers his face with a nylon mask right before he forces his way into your apartment and robs you blind."

"But all you have here is that the guy is five-foot nine and wears jeans and a black hoodie. You gotta give us more than that. I mean, is he white? Black? Hispanic?"

Maria took the flyer away from me and taped it on the bus-stop pole. "That's the million-dollar question, isn't it, Golden Eye? Right now that guy's sandalfoot with control top. That's about all we got at the moment."

"Has he hurt anyone?" Emmy asked.

"Not yet, but the guys working nights think he's going to.

He's hit five apartments up here in the past two months. Targets women walking into their buildings alone. Usually drunk girls coming back from bars. The last one tried to fight back and grabbed at his face. He stuck a gun in her ear and told her if she ever got a good look at him, he would come back and blow her head off."

Emmy and I stared at Maria in shock. It sounds nuts to say this type of thing doesn't happen in Manhattan, since most people think New York City is the birthplace of violent crime, but the most violence any of us ever saw in our neighborhood was two women duking it out on a sidewalk outside of a Prada sample sale.

"Don't worry. You guys are fine. Neither of you walk around here alone at three in the morning, do you? I didn't think so."

The M79 pulled up in front of us and began to hiss and beep as it lowered its front doors. Still studying the flyer as she got on the bus, Emmy turned back to Maria. "I hope you catch this guy, Maria."

"Someone will. Won't be me, but somebody'll catch him," she said, looking at the flyer. I could sense her frustration as she clutched the baton on her belt. After the bus rolled away, I turned to Maria.

"Do you think the night guys would ask you to help? You know, maybe as a decoy or something?" I asked hopefully.

"Already offered. Said they would consider it."

"That's great!"

"That's a big fat no, Geri. Patrick even volunteered, but they shot him down too." Patrick Kirkpatrick, Maria's partner, weighed about a hundred pounds after a long bath. They worked daylight hours at the 19th Precinct, which happened to be the precinct Emmy and I lived in. The two wanted big arrests so bad, they staged mock attacks on each other just to keep their self-defense skills fresh. But with a protective bigwig father and being the youngest and only girl in a family of five boys, all of whom were cops, the only action Maria and Patrick would get to see would be a drunken brawl at the St. Patrick's Day Parade.

Maria, wanting to change the subject, said she would walk me to the Seventy-seventh and Lexington subway station. She hoped Patrick would be waiting for her at Starbucks.

"While we're talking about jobs," she said, "I didn't get any calls this week."

"That's because I took your name off my résumé."

An exasperated sigh came out as she stopped. "Geri, come on!"

"Maria, I can't have future potential employers call you every time I need a reference. I mean, doesn't anyone at your job notice that from three to three-fifteen you answer your cell, 'Hello, C-SPAN2'? Besides, I think the last one figured it out."

"How?"

"Because when he asked you if I was a good line editor, you said, 'Fucking A.'"

"Oh," she admitted with a smile. "But how else are you going to leave your job?"

"I've been thinking about that. Maybe it's not so bad." We resumed walking as kids ran around us trying to get to the Mr. Softie truck that jingled on the corner.

"Do you like your job?" she asked as she opened her wallet and purchased two red, white and blue Atomic pops.

"No."

"The pay?"

"It's book publishing. It sucks."

"Are you good at it?"

"These kids are going to be sucking on dead puritan finger pops next year. What do you think?"

"So let me get this straight. You have a job that pays you nothing, to do something that you're bad at, that you hate.

"God, when you put it that way—"

"Why don't you just quit? Force yourself into a corner so that you either have to find a film job here or move to L.A. After all, that's what you did last time," she said as she chomped down on her bomb pop. Her lips, like mine, were a not-so-subtle shade of indigo.

"I didn't force myself into a corner. I was let go."

But I wasn't let go. I was fired. Blackballed.

When I first came to New York, I landed my one and only job in television. Upon getting the call from the HR representative at Book TV, a militant literary offshoot of C-SPAN2, I acted as if I'd landed a job as assistant director on the sequel to *Schindler's List*. In my brain, I'd made it. And the position seemed easy enough. If I could work a toaster I could do this. All I had to do was bring a camera into the book readings, set it up and press play. Nothing too hard. The only hitch to this otherwise fireproof job was that the kind people at C-SPAN2 neglected to inform me that the author scheduled to read from his book, *The History of Finches 1745–1806* had a voice so monotonous that it rivaled Valium as a sedative. During the section on the breeding habits of the Gouldian finch, I fell asleep. Unfortunately, this happened right around the time the pivot head on the tripod loosened. The camera slowly panned upward, forcing the whole Book TV viewing public to watch the ceiling of the Union Square Barnes and Noble for an hour. And since the last two rows were filled with publishing assistants who were also getting some shut-eye, no one thought to wake me. The author never bothered to look up until I startled myself awake by yelling out, "Who fired the cake?" during the Q & A. But as soon as I closed the camera case, I found out that the cake wasn't the only one getting fired.

Word of the C-SPAN2 debacle reached far beyond the realms of cable TV. My code name, as I later found out, was Nytol at most of the entertainment temp agencies. I lost hope of ever cleaning that smudge off my record until a quarter of a way down a bottle of Goldschlager, when Maria came upon the idea of her being the newest Human Resources director of Book TV. Putting her number down on my résumé could assure me of always getting a glowing reference on my skills as a production assistant and ward off the idea that I was in any way related to the O'Brien who went narcoleptic on the job.

"Fired, fate, it's the same shit," Maria said. "God didn't want you to be some camera operator . . ."

"Or to stay awake,"

"Or stay awake. You're a writer," she said, throwing her Popsicle stick in the trash. "And you're miserable."

"Miserable?" I asked as I faced her with my freak eye, blue lips and soil-stained suit. "What makes you say that?"

6

Bed, Bath and Beyond

Our bathroom, with only enough room for a tub, a toilet and an extremely hot pipe running down between the two, provided just what I needed to forget about the day's events. Emmy went to bed right after watching *Jeopardy* and had been asleep for three hours by the time I ran my bath. The suit came in the tub with me. I figured it couldn't hurt to put some soap and water on it before it sat in my hamper for three weeks. The pink Mr. Bubble soap did not have the stain-removing power I hoped for, but the lathering action created an enormous amount of foam in the tub. Soon I gave up on the suit and listened to the sizzle of bubbles popping around my face. J. T. sat on the toilet with his long legs propped up on the edge of the tub. He reached into the sudsy water and grabbed my foot. Lifting it over the soapy water, he cocked his head as he examined my toes.

"Your toes are perfectly aligned, you know that?" he said as he ran his fingers along the tips of my toenails. "I've never been a big fan of feet. The pinkie toe always looks mangled. And I can't stand how the second toe is always longer than the big one. I hate that. Mine are like that." He stuck his foot about an inch away from my face. "See?"

"I'm sure they don't look like that in real life."

"Sure they do," he said as he tapped the end of my nose with his big toe. "When we meet you'll see." His foot disappeared back onto the floor as he sat up straight. "When I wear flip-flops I don't look down. I feel like my feet are constantly giving me the bird."

I laughed. "You think I should judge a guy by his feet."

"If you were in love with the man, you wouldn't give a damn what his toes looked like. You'd probably think his freak feet were downright adorable. You might even write a poem about them. 'Ode to My Lover's Snaggle Toe' by Geraldine Agnes O'Brien."

I chuckled as I watched him break into an impromptu poetry slam in my little red bathroom. His face mesmerized me. A perfect face that possessed all the hard edges of beauty. A strong jaw that flexed when he swallowed. Arched and defined eyebrows that didn't look like they were waxed or plucked, and the slight cleft in his chin that seemed to get deeper every time he appeared puzzled. His eyes were the only part of J. T.'s face that looked soft. Always focused and full of wonder. Constantly interested and intent; as if each object he beheld taught him a new way to communicate. I gave myself a mental pat on the back. I picked well.

I was nine years old when J. T. whistled his way into my life. Every Sunday, after ten o'clock mass at St. Patrick's Church, my dad and I would drive across town to visit my grandfather, Poppy, on the farm. These visits started with Dad and Poppy reading the local paper in silence over a cup of coffee. Then, after they polished off a half dozen hot dogs, the two would spend the afternoon and a better part of the early evening hunched over a busted tractor or a rusty potato combine. Normally, I would climb into the seat of Poppy's largest tractor and observe two masters at their craft. Dad would only let me watch. He'd talk me through the process of oil changing or putting in new spark plugs with a wink and a smile. Poppy thought I should take a more active roll and would call me over to help when he needed a small hand to reach in where his enormous Irish farm paws couldn't fit. This always pissed off Dad. He'd yell at Poppy, saying that if the gears slipped, I would be lucky not to lose my whole hand. Poppy would just brush him off as he always did, stating that a one-handed girl is less likely to hitchhike and that, in time, I would save a bundle on gloves.

One Sunday when Poppy and Dad were tackling a rusted lawnmower, I decided to save my fingers and play hide-and-go-seek in the rye field behind the barns. On the far edge of the field, right before the rye turned into woods, stood two enormous apples trees. From a distance, the trees looked like a couple taking a stroll along the shore. I could never climb one of the apple trees. It was older, and its lowest branch was still too high for me to reach. So I scurried up the other. Once settled on a steady limb, I closed my eyes and counted to ten. As I pressed my face into its bark, I told the universe that when I opened my eyes, my mother would find a way to let me know where she had been hiding for the past year. But when I hit the number ten and looked up, I saw someone else. Sitting on a branch in the un-climbable tree was a boy. A lanky blond twelve-year-old wearing white pants and a white T-shirt. He appeared calm and pleasant. As if he had spent his entire life up in that tree waiting patiently for me to see him. A breeze rustled the leaves around us as we sat bobbing in silence on our respective branches.

Wanting him to leave, I figured if I covered my eyes again and counted to a hundred, he would be gone. But when I turned around the second time, he was still there. Only this time he sat a few branches over from me. I cleared my throat.

"Hi. You need to leave."

"You sure? I came all this way," he said as he bit into a Red Delicious. His puzzled expression somehow remained on his face as he ate.

"Yes. I was hoping you'd be someone else."

"Like who?"

"My mom."

"Oh," he said, looking rejected. "Her." He took another bite and looked out into the field. "Well, Geri, if you ever want to talk, just whistle." He turned and looked at me. His hard blue gaze made me jump. "You can whistle, can't you?"

"Sure. Now leave please," I ordered.

"You can not."

"Can so."

"Prove it. Whistle," he goaded.

I puckered up and blew, but I just wound up spitting all over the front of my green corduroy dress. This sent him into a fit of laughter.

"I said whistle, not drool all over yourself." He chuckled. "Blow out. Like this." He pursed up his lips and did an imitation of a Bob White quail that was so good, it caused birds to cluster in a nearby tree. "See? It's easy."

I kept trying as I watched him hop from branch to branch toward the ground. Once he landed, he looked back up at me. "Now, don't leave this tree until you know how, okay? That will be our call. If you ever need to talk, just give a whistle."

"Okay," I answered as I watched him walk toward the woods. As he left, it suddenly dawned on me that he might have the information I needed. I quickly climbed out, on my limb and tried to whistle. Nothing came out, so I just yelled.

"Hey, you! Whistle, whistle!" The boy turned around and walked back. I looked down through the branches at his hard but youthful face. "Do you know where my mom is?"

He took another bite of his apple and extended his arm. His index finger appeared to be pointing directly at me.

"She's there."

I turned around to see if she was behind me but saw nothing except the open rye field shifting in the wind. I turned around and found his hand still extended, indicating her whereabouts. I traced the direction with my finger, but it stopped right on the patchwork tabby cat embroidered on the front pocket of my dress. After examining the pocket, I found nothing but a rub-off tattoo. I pulled it out to show him.

"This is Popeye. See?" I explained, pivoting the tiny red square around so that he could see from all sides. "It's a prize I got in a Cracker Jack box." I took another look back inside my chest pocket. "She's not there."

He tossed his half-eaten apple up for me to finish. "Yes, she is," he said. "Keep looking. You'll find her."

I caught the apple and took a bite. I could feel disappointment start to crawl through me like a fever. But as I chewed, it suddenly stopped. Maybe all hope was not lost. Maybe he could take me to Mom. Maybe this was a sign. I wanted to call out to him again, but by the time I swallowed, he had already disappeared into the pines.

For the rest of the afternoon I sat in that tree, determined to get some sound that resembled a whistle to come out of my lips. And fifteen apples later, I could do it. That evening when Dad found me sitting up in the tree holding a brown apple core, he asked why I was whistling like a blue jay. I wanted to tell him about the boy. The disappearing boy in white who could bring Mom back. But I didn't. Something in my chest told me not to. Like the tattoo nestled in my front pocket, I wanted to keep him close. I wanted to keep him a secret. That boy existed only for me, and only I could make him come out. And sometimes he came without me ever having to make a sound.

But as I got older, I needed to find a face for him. Picking a face for a long-term imaginary friend turned out to be very tricky. You don't just pick one as you would a novel at an airport or a pair of shoes. Like any lasting relationship, you can't base your choice solely on looks. Over the years I found that the best faces came from anonymous, non-actor types with minimal facial hair and a sense of classic style. Athletes worked better than news reporters. Baseball players better than basketball. Outfielders better than infielders. Left fielder better than center. Models worked better than rock stars. Writers and politicians were out of the question. Reality show stars could do in a pinch, but only if they got voted off in the first two weeks. But never actors, no matter how tempting. You don't want someone who will most likely get a face-lift and fake tan at the first whiff of a failing acting career.

The other problem with actors is that you're apt to find out about their real lives. This totally ruins the fantasy. Take face number three, Jude Law circa *View From Another Room*. I got sucked in by this quirky blond Brit and then, boom, in walks *The Talented Mr. Ripley* and his numerous kids with his numerous gal-pals. Imaginary friend face gone.

After *Enemy at the Gates*, I needed to find a face that I would only see occasionally, like in a commercial or on a billboard. One that couldn't be linked to a woman, a man, Paris Hilton or a murder. I almost gave up hope until I got the worst case of shingles my doctor ever saw on a person under the age of sixty. While waiting in his office, perusing the February issue of *Town and Country*, I came across an advertisement for a herpes medication. Staring up at me from the page was the most handsome blond male model I ever saw, shushing down the mountain with a woman who looked elated that her herpes outbreak wasn't bursting through her snowpants. The advertisement's heading read WHISTLE YOUR BLUES AWAY. WIN A TRIP TO WHISTLER RESORT AND SPA. I ripped the page out of the magazine and stuffed it in my bag. In my head it made perfect sense. The boy I knew was all grown up and saying hello.

The only thing I knew about this model was his initials: J. T. His name was something that sounded like Joshua Tenor or Taylor. I couldn't remember because I hadn't read enough of his biography in *Glamour* magazine's "Hottest New Faces" article to find out. Occasionally, he would pop up on a billboard in Times Square or on the side of a bus in an advertisement for Ralph Lauren. But other than those few sightings, he's lived with me. And he wasn't going anywhere. Not if I had anything to say about it.

"When is that?" I asked as I rubbed a bar of soap over the stain on my lapel.

"When is what? When do I wear flip-flops? Usually at the beach or when I shower at the gym . . ."

"No. When am I going to find that someone?"

"With or without snaggle toes?"

"Either."

"Well," he said as he searched the bottom of the tub for a scrub brush. "That depends on you, really." He pulled the yellow loofa brush above the surface and began scrubbing my heels.

"On me?"

"When you are ready, he'll come and get you."

"Jesus, I've *been* ready!"

He pointed the brush at me. "I'm J. T. Not J. C., remember."

"What will he look like?"

"Can't tell you that."

"Then how will I know he's the right one? Am I going to recognize him? I mean, will he look like you?"

"Or like a handsome neighbor who lives—" He pointed down at the water.

"At the bottom of the tub?"

"Come here." He grabbed my calves and slid me closer to him. Wiping some of my wet, matted hair away from my face, he bent over and looked me right in the eye. "When love comes walking into your life with its long, hairy toes, you will know."

"You see, that's where you're wrong. I won't know. People say that all the time, but I just know I'm not going to have a clue."

"Yes, you will."

"But remember when I believed Poppy invented butter? I thought that was true with my whole heart. And what about when I was certain the Mets would win the World Series against the Yankees? And when I thought George Michael could never, in a million years, be into guys."

"Okay, so maybe you might not recognize it right away. But you will certainly hear it. Something deep inside you will hear that bell. And when you do, that will be your cue, Geri Bean, to wake up."

But I was awake. Even after the hot bath I couldn't fall asleep. I spent the first hour of insomnia watching the nudists who lived on the fourth floor across the street hang wall art. Since I wasn't particularly fond of looking at their naked fifty-something bodies or their choice of watercolors, I decided to rotate my futon mattress. The unforgiving firmness of a futon tends to be hard on the spine. Harder yet if the mattress dips on one side from hundreds of nights of singlehood. The level side didn't provide any more comfort as I spent the second hour watching the iron curls on the fire escape burn shadows into the white of my walls.

Back in my bedroom in Southold, every night seemed unique. What with the moonlight, the trees, the shadows and the wind, each night created a different canvas on my walls. But in the city, each night felt the same. Cars rushing and barking up the street replaced the wind. Sirens, horns and car alarms replaced the birds. The only light came from the streetlight. The moon only hit the tops of the buildings. The glow from the city seemed to push its light back, never allowing it to make its way to me through the bars.

I debated whether or not I should turn on Book TV when I remembered Emmy's dating book tucked in my messenger bag. For the next two hours I powered through Kelly Cox's, *The Love You Always Lose*. I didn't know what made Ms. Cox the authority on how to hunt and trap a male within three dates, but I figured if I couldn't manage to get a man to introduce himself to me after making playful eye contact with him for two hours at a bar, I probably could use some of her pointers.

She divided the book into six sections; each date having three "Do's" and three "Don'ts." Ms. Cox's credibility skyrocketed as I read the "Don't" sections for each date. I realized that I committed all nine with reckless abandon. "Don't swear," "Don't get drunk," and "Don't ask where this is going" have been known to happen before the salads arrived on the first date.

Although I didn't consider meeting Todd at Doc's to be an actual date, I figured it couldn't hurt to keep Kelly's advice in the back of my mind. Maybe if I followed her plan, Todd would forget all about his high school sweetheart and fall madly in love with me. And then maybe I would drop my rule about not dating anyone who drove a foreign car and fall madly in love with him. And after I pulled myself away from writing query letters, I would write Kelly a letter thanking her profusely for her insightful tips. And then she would read my moving testimonial and publish my success story in the second edition of her book, along with a picture of Todd and me cruising in our new Jeep.

Then I thought, who the hell am I kidding? This mattress will never be level.

And Todd will never buy American.

7

The Don'ts and Really Don'ts
of Dating

"How about another Black and Tan there?" the Irish bartender asked while drying a pint glass. I drank my first beer at Doc's in record time while faking interest in the soccer game playing on the television hanging over the bar.

The crowd that Thursday night consisted mostly of the leftovers from Happy Hour. Small groups of three to five men and women clustered in the corners as they screamed over U2 songs with smiles plastered on their red faces. The bartenders disconnected the jukebox so they could play *Rattle and Hum* all night while watching the game. The match between Ireland and England had been going on for over an hour. Although I liked the bartenders at Doc's, I secretly hoped England would win. The last time Ireland won a soccer game, they played House of Pain's "Jump Around" for three hours on loop. And with that racket, I would never remember how to apply the rules and regs of dating with Todd. Who, at that point, was fifteen minutes late. I decided not to get upset for at least another fifteen minutes. A half-hour delay must be factored in due to his car.

"I'm good, thanks," I answered. Four more sips and I would officially be breaking "Don't #1"—"Don't get drunk." I tried to focus my attention on the small men in green and red kicking the ball when I felt the warmth of a face pop up next to mine. The clean scent of Zest cut through the smell of Guinness as he placed his arms on either side of me at the bar.

"She's been patient. Set her up for another round," Todd said with a smile. "Make mine an Amstel Light."

"Amstel Light?" I questioned as he slid on to the stool next to mine.

"Watching my figure," he said as he lifted his shirt and patted the place on his stomach where his beer gut should have been. My eyes spent a second longer staring at his lower stomach/groin area and I could feel myself start to blush. I'm sure "Don't stare at his dick within the first five seconds of your date" was a given and didn't need to be stated in the book. I turned my eyes back to his face as he smiled. "Come on. Let's move somewhere less crowded."

When we moved, I noticed that every set of female eyeballs was fixed on us. Every woman in the place was thinking the same thing: "Why is he with her?" I wanted to scream out that we weren't together, but I figured I might as well enjoy the idea that other people thought I was capable of going out with a cute guy.

"You take all your men here, Geri?" he asked as he placed our beers on an oddly intimate table in the corner. "Or is this reserved for only marriage material?"

All my men. How sweet, I thought. He obviously knew nothing about me.

"Marriage material drinks Black and Tan. Light beer drinkers are cheap and easy sex."

"Well, looks like we'll be calling it a night soon." We clanked our mugs, then sipped our beer. Over the rim of the glass I saw Todd looking at me. Not casually looking but examining. His brain seemed to be processing my face. He cocked his head to the side as his eyes drifted over the upper half of my body. Suddenly I became very aware that it was Thursday and the panties I was wearing had the word SUNDAY embroidered on them. I tried to shrug off the feeling that I was being sized up as I didn't want to turn manic and run to the bathroom with a needle to pull out the embroidery on my underwear. After all, this wasn't a date. Just a nice friendly drink between neighbors. Between me and a good-looking neighbor. One who'd just left an eight-year relationship.

"So you double as a mechanic when you're not promoting great children's literature. That's a very attractive quality in a woman."

"Oh, sure. I've gotten many a man by knowing how an engine works. It's a great thing to know. Especially when you live in a city and don't own a car," I said, crapping on my God-given talent and my self-esteem simultaneously. "If yours wasn't such a heap, I'd probably forget everything I know." As soon as I said that, I wanted to take it back. Kelly Cox had now interrupted the soccer match on television to remind me that "Don't # 6" was "Don't ever, under any circumstances, insult a man's anything. Especially his car." Even if it sucks like Todd's did. It's like saying he has a small penis or doesn't know the rules of football. I inadvertently slammed my drink down on the table, causing it to splash back up on me.

"I didn't mean that," I said, wiping up my spill. He chuckled. Apparently, my nervousness amused him.

"It's okay. I know it's a piece of junk. But it's the only way I can get you to spend time with me."

"Very funny. You're rebounding, remember?"

He sat up defiantly. "That's right. I am. And love will never touch my heart again. At least for the appropriate eight months it will take to get over her."

"Eight months?"

"That's what my dad told me. Says it takes one month for every year of a relationship to get over the person," he said as his eyes trailed away. He took another, considerably longer gulp of Amstel. "By this time next year, she'll be history."

Wow. I was impressed. So this was the formula men worked out. Eight years to eight months. By the way it came out of his mouth, it sounded as if he had been repeating this formula to himself every morning. I could imagine him waking up in his boxers, stumbling to the huge calendar on his rejection refrigerator and making a big *X* on the date. *Yes, sir. Only seven months, two weeks and six days to go.*

"Good luck with that. I'm still trying to get over Colin Farrell and I just bumped into him for a second at Krispy Kremes."

"Very funny, Ms. O'Brien," he said. He wiped his mouth with the back of his hand. "So, tell me: Your dad's a crack mechanic. What about your mom? A comedian? No, wait, a model who sits on top of cars trying to get men to unload all their dough on a Rolls-Royce."

Maybe I should have eaten before I started to drink, because without thinking, I broke the number one "Don't" rule of date number two—*"Don't talk about anything too personal."*

"My mom was a bitch." And with that, the flirt flew out of the room.

Now, most men would have shifted nervously in their seat, looked uncomfortable and immediately changed the subject. Todd, to his credit, reached for my hand. Normally when the subject of my mother came up, I would ignore it or say she'd passed away. Maybe because he was my neighbor or maybe because he appeared to care, I found I had no energy to bullshit.

"I'm sorry," he said as he stroked my knuckles. "I shouldn't have asked that. You don't mention her and I should have taken that as a hint."

He was right. I didn't. I didn't even have a photo of her out in my apartment. But there was one. I kept it at the bottom of my sock drawer. A black-and-white picture of her at a barbecue. In the picture I'm wearing nothing but a diaper, slung over her shoulder as she laughs at someone who is out of the frame. In the far right corner of the picture is my dad, standing over a grill, cooking burgers and smiling at me. I imagine that if my face were visible, I would be smiling too.

"Oh, God, Todd, no. You're really sweet but I should be the one who's sorry. You're the one who needs to drown his sorrows," I said, trying to change the subject. "Come on, neighbor. You're a free man. Let's get you good and drunk."

He held up his mug defiantly in the air. "To bitches!"

"Can't get us down!" I cheered.

We chugged our beers and slammed them on the table. If only it was that easy.

For the next three hours we talked about everything. From our first kisses to the most embarrassing moments in gym classes, nothing was off limits. And the more we talked, the more it seemed that Todd and I had known each other for longer than just the time we were neighbors. We both loved the old Abbot and Costello reruns that played on Channel Twenty after school. We both claimed to be four-square champions of the fifth grade. And his two best friends from home, Matt and Al, sounded like male versions of Maria and Emmy. In the middle of his story about his dad walking in on him dancing naked to The Cars' "Magic" the first few chords of "Jump Around" hit the air.

Soon all the barstools were being pushed aside so that people could jump up, jump up and get down. I began to shout over the music as I looked at the crowd.

"You don't have the urge to strip now, do you?" I shouted. I went for my beer and noticed that Todd wasn't looking at the businessmen and women throwing their mugs in the air but instead right at me.

"Maybe," he answered.

Feeling good from the three Black and Tans, I asked, "What are you smiling at?"

"You," he shouted. "You have a gorgeous smile."

"Do I remind you of Ric Ocasek?" I asked, laughing. He leaned over across the table.

"You want to get out of here?" he asked.

His low whisper somehow cut through all the noise in the bar. My face began to burn as I felt myself start to flush. I waved my hand in front of me, hoping he wouldn't notice.

"Sure. It's getting hot in here anyway," I said. We gathered our things and headed out of the bar, past all the soccer fans and out of the House of Pain.

The two-minute walk home lasted another hour. We decided to get some ice cream before Sedutto's closed its doors. Todd ordered butter pecan (a flavor I thought had been discontinued after the Depression) and I bought a cup of vanilla with rainbow sprinkles. We sauntered back to the building, enjoying the night air and the view of the rows of beige, mustard and brick walk-ups that lined our street. We settled on our front stoop and faced each other, occasionally taking scoops out of each other's cups.

"I didn't think anyone under the age of fifty-five ate this," I said as I sampled his flavor.

"I didn't think anyone over the age of ten put rainbow

sprinkles on anything," he answered as he wiped a sprinkle on my nose with his spoon. I removed the offending sprinkle and geared up to ask the big question I had been dying to ask all night.

"Okay. I think I know you a bit . . ."

"You know my johnson fell out during a gym class when I was ten. I think you can ask me why we broke up."

I was struck a bit dumb by his perceptiveness. "All right. Why did you and Cassie break up?"

"She cheated on me with a guy at work."

"At the salon?" I said. "But I thought . . ."

"Yeah, me too. They ain't all gay."

"Ouch. I'm sorry."

"Well, it wasn't just him. She said I was crowding her. I guess after eight years I might have been," he said as he scraped the bottom of his container.

"Was she crowding you?"

He stopped eating and looked up at me in thought.

"I don't know. Maybe we were crowding each other. We were all either one of us knew. Dad says it's not about hearing wedding bells or feeling your heart skip a beat. It's about knowing your path. I thought she was it."

"Maybe it was just the one of least resistance."

"Possibly. She said she needed to see what was beyond the world of Todd. I guess I just wasn't enough," he said with his gaze low. I hunched over and tried to get him to look me in the eye.

"You know, that world doesn't seem so bad to me." He looked up at me. Each feature on his face seemed to react separately. First his eyes sparkled, then his head rose, then a smile crept across his face.

"Okay, you. I spilled my guts. What about you?"

"What about me? I'm not in a relationship."

"Why not?"

"'Cause I'm not a relationship type of gal." It sounded nice. Better than, "I can't seem to get anyone I like to like me back."

"Again, why not?"

"Not good at them. Shit, Todd, if I have to read books on dating, then I'm probably no good in a relationship." Great, I thought. My secret's out. The mother of all don'ts. The don't that's such a don't you don't need to say it. DON'T ADMIT YOU READ BOOKS ON DATING.

Todd slowly sat up in interest. "You read books on dating?"

"Yeah. I did. Just one."

"Before tonight?"

"I happened to finish it before tonight, but it wasn't for you. . . ."

"You read a book for me?"

"No!" I couldn't stop smiling, despite the hole I was sinking in. And the closer he came to examine my nervousness, the nicer the hole felt. "This isn't a date."

"Why not?" he asked as he shifted his body over to mine. "You read a book on it, so why not make it a date?"

"Because I bought my own ice cream!"

"Let's just try to pretend, then." His face crept up so close to mine, I could feel his breath on my cheek. I couldn't tear my eyes away from the empty cardboard cup that I was starting to shred into a hundred nervous pieces.

With an insecure adolescent crack in my voice, I asked softly, "Hay . . . ow do we do that?"

"Well, I bought you a few beers. That we'll count as dinner," he said as he tucked some loose hair back behind my ear. "And then I walked you home . . ."

"But you live here too."

"Still counts. And now I'm going to give you a good-night kiss." His hand reached beneath my chin and tilted my face toward his.

"Todd," I whispered. "I think I'm going to be sick."

"Trust me. It's the sprinkles."

Kisses can be funny. The last man I'd kissed had such a bad overbite that we constantly bashed teeth each time we dove in. But Todd's lips were unsettlingly familiar. As if we'd kissed each other a million times before. The lip pressure, the slight play of the tongue, the gentle sucking that was intimate yet not slobbering felt, in a word, perfect.

After a few moments we pulled apart and looked at each other in mild shock. Todd kept his hand around the nape of my neck.

"I hope you don't think I'm easy," I blurted.

He laughed as he kissed me on my forehead. "Geri, if there is anything you are not, it's easy."

All of a sudden I got scared. Was the forehead, Grandpa-style kiss a signal that the kissing portion of the evening was over?

"Then can you kiss me again? I mean, if you want to? On the lips?"

Surprised by my directness, he answered, "Does the book allow it?"

"Fuck the book."

Just about the time Kelly Cox was setting herself on fire, his grasp tightened behind my head and he pulled me toward him. This time our hands and arms got into the act. In the middle of a madly inappropriate public display of affection, I heard it.

PING PING.

My head jolted back in shock as I stared at him.

"Did you hear that?" I gasped.

"What? What did you hear?"

"Nothing. It's nothing," I said as I dove back into his face. And then again:

PING, PING, PING.

I pulled back and asked Todd breathlessly, "Did you hear it?"

"No, but I can smell it," said the man from Apartment 19, who stood over us holding a basketball. He had been waiting for our facefest to end so he could walk out of the building. We both jumped up, spilling out apologies.

"Oh, my God, I'm so sorry," I said.

"We didn't hear you, man."

"Mmm hmm," the man grunted as he walked past. Todd and I just stood there quietly looking at each other before breaking into a fit of laughter. Two days prior I was standing here fixing his car. Tonight, I was making out with him. God, I love New York.

After we walked into the building and up the stairs, we stopped on Todd's floor. I felt a pull to keep going up the extra flight to my place. He looked surprised as I kept climbing the stairs.

"Can I walk you to your door?" he asked.

"I think I'll be fine from here on." We exchanged a long smile before I walked up the remaining steps. I heard his lock catch and felt the rumble of his door shut under my feet. Todd was safely inside.

Every inch of my skin hummed as I fumbled my way through my dark apartment. The digital clock on the DVD player read 1:14. I took off my clothes, slipped into an old T-shirt and crawled into bed. Staring at the iron bars, I couldn't quite pinpoint the feeling in my gut. Just as I began to whistle for J. T. to help me out, I heard a clicking noise against my window. My body shot three feet in the air before landing on the floor. I did the army crawl over to the window and noticed a wooden handle tapping on my pane. I opened the window and looked down the fire escape. Below stood Todd, holding a toilet-bowl plunger.

"Hey, I didn't want to go to the front door and wake up Emmy," he whispered loudly. "But I was wondering . . ."

"If you scared me to death? The answer is yes."

"Sorry. I just wanted to say I had a really nice time tonight and that I'd like to come up and see you sometime."

I immediately wanted to turn into an uber-dork and do my best impersonation of Mae West, but thankfully, I held back. "Sure. I'd like that."

"Good night, Geri. Sorry for scaring you."

"Good night, Todd. Sorry for being scared."

I closed the window and slipped back into bed. Just then, I noticed that for the first time since I could remember, I could smell bread baking in the bakery next door. I figured I'd either just recovered my sense of smell or I had never been up this late and sober enough to notice. Tucking the sheets under my chin, I kept imagining him lying in bed. Six feet below me. Breathing in. Breathing out. *And he's been there the whole time.*

"J. T.," I whispered. "J. T., come here. I'm awake now."

8

Expiration Date

For the next month, whenever I found myself alone at a copy machine or enjoying a quiet moment in a bathroom stall, I wondered if the clouds had passed Emmy, Maria and me by for good, or if the three of us just found ourselves sitting in the eye of a hurricane. Things were not just looking up but coming together.

Emmy began meeting Bryan three afternoons a week at a coffee shop around the corner from her school. Bryan looked every bit like the Wall Street trader he was. Tall and handsome, with a mildly metrosexual shaggy blond haircut and more money than he could possibly know what to do with at twenty-seven. Bryan enjoyed teaching Emmy the ins and outs of the stock market. For someone who proofed math textbooks in her spare time, she reveled in Bryan's enthusiasm for numbers. Both loved their jobs and the goals they hoped to achieve. Emmy believed that one of her students would cure cancer. Bryan believed that one of his hedge funds would allow him to retire at thirty-five. And although the two never kissed, Emmy remained certain that it would come to pass. Even Maria's constant eye-rolling at the mention of his name had stopped.

Maria didn't have much time to worry about Bryan since the East Side burglar had begun to step up his game.

She and Patrick spent their days chasing leads and following the trail of the faceless criminal. He became the NYPD's Public Enemy #1 after he outran the cops twice and then managed to double back and steal their hats. Since Maria and Patrick's shift was during the day, they mostly stood outside the doorways of the apartment buildings he robbed. They knew the guys who worked the night shift would probably be the ones to catch him, but that didn't dissuade the two from devising elaborate plans on what they would do if he struck during the lunch hour. On the afternoons when the Seventy-seventh Street subway station appeared calm, Maria and Patrick took turns hurdling the turnstile and sliding down the handrails. In just two weeks, Maria could make it from the Pick-a-Bagel on the corner of Seventy-seventh to the end of the subway platform in less time than it took the average person to find their wallet. If the creep so much as walked out into the light of day, Maria would be ready for him.

As for me, after our unofficial "date," Todd and I slipped into a comfortable routine that made the vast array of disappointments and rejections in my past fade from memory. Every evening was delightfully the same. Todd would come up at eleven o'clock to watch the late-night news. He said he wanted to make sure Emmy was fast asleep, as well as give me time to write my query letters. When he arrived, we'd stretch out on the couch and watch the nightly shooting gallery, followed by a rerun of *Cheers*. But before the beginning credits would roll over the old pictures of the Boston bar, we would be engaged in a healthy make-out session that would eventually progress to my futon. His strong frame sprawled over mine. The weight of his body would cause my legs to part so he could hold himself up. Our hands and hips fell into rhythm as we reached for each other under our clothes. His hips pounding into mine caused his jeans to become tighter and warmer with every rub. The smell of his breath became as familiar as my own.

Every time I heard his knuckles rap on my door, my heart had me lurching to my feet. On two occasions, I actually skipped to the door.

On this particular night, the other man in my life decided to chime in.

"Geri! I haven't seen you in ages. You haven't been home in a month!" Dad said on the other end of the phone. Normally on weekends I would take the bus back to Southold, but since Todd and I had begun hanging out, I'd decided to stay in the city. I wanted to make myself available for the possibility of doing something with him on a Saturday or Sunday. Todd didn't seem to be around very much, but I didn't want to take any chances.

"I know, Dad. It's just that I met someone and I was sort of hoping that . . ."

"A boy? And who is this young man?" Dad asked. "And more importantly, what does he drive?"

"He's my neighbor, Dad and . . ." I was interrupted by his incredibly loud laugh.

"The one who owns that brown bomb in front of your building?"

"That's the one."

"Well, at least I don't have to worry about you forgetting what I taught you. How long have you been seeing this character?"

"Well, we're not really seeing each other. He just got out of a long relationship and we're just hanging out."

"Do you let him kiss you?" he asked matter-of-factly.

"Dad!" Normally fathers and daughters don't get into these waters, but since I was raised by a single father from the age of eight, the topics of boys, Barbies and tampons were fair game.

"I'm just saying you're not 'hanging out' if you're kissing the guy. I hang out with Fat Marty from the shop. You don't see him trying to snuggle with me."

"We're just enjoying each other's company. Let's leave it at that."

"You like him?"

Just then I heard a knock at the door. "Yeah, Dad, I do," I admitted.

"Well, tell him I hope he takes better care of my little girl than he does his car."

"I will." I ran over to the door and looked through the spy hole. On the other side was Todd, holding up his license with a stern look on his face.

"Police. Open up."

"Dad, I gotta go. I'll come home next chance I get. Promise," I said as I unlocked the door.

"Make it soon. I need some help with the Muntz. I trust your eyes better than I trust your grandfather's. Yesterday he thought an old ten-speed tire was a fan belt. When it broke apart, he threw it on the ground and cussed for fifteen minutes."

"He just wanted to show it who was boss," I said as Todd walked in.

"Well, he's not going near the Muntz until he gets some glasses. But I'll let you go. And remember, I love you, Geraldine."

Looking right at Todd, I answered, "Love you too." I hung up the phone as Todd glanced around the apartment.

"Was that one of your boyfriends?"

"Actually it was a man."

"You mind telling me who? You know, it's not very nice

to tell one man you love him while another is standing in the room," he teased.

"That was my father. Besides, I am bound by the rules of the book never to say 'I love you' to a guy first. I think it's rule number 3 for date number 3."

"Why?"

"Because saying 'I love you' to a man scares him and gives away your power. So Kelly Cox says."

"Oh, does she now?" he said as he turned off the television. "So, if you did love me, you wouldn't say it? Even if you really, really felt like you did?"

Instantly I felt my face turn hot and probably a not-so-subtle shade of pink. "Nope. Against house rules." I couldn't move as I watched him turn off the standing lamp. He slowly walked backward into my bedroom.

"Then how would I know you loved me?"

"I . . . I don't know," I stammered.

"I guess you'd have to show me, now wouldn't you?" he said as he stretched out across my futon. His long legs were still able to dangle off the edge.

Fuck, I thought. I wished I watched more soap operas. I had no idea how to be sexy. I took a deep breath and jammed my hands into my jean pockets. "I guess."

"How? How would you show me?" For a moment the only sound in the room was my audible gulp. Then he sat up in bed and pulled me toward him. His clean smell made my head spin. "Would you write me a poem? Or maybe sing me a song?" His hands reached toward my face.

I wracked my brain for a perfect, honest, sexy and appropriate answer. Be honest, I thought. Just be honest. Honesty is hot.

"I'd probably install a new muffler on your car so people couldn't hear you coming." *Great answer, Geri. You're a tool.*

He pulled me on top of him as he lay back on the bed.

"Maybe I want you to hear me come."

Oh, God, I thought. Game time. It was on.

Our mouths reached for each other as our hands did the big land grab underneath each other's shirts. I raced through my mental sex checklist.

Shaved armpits?

Check.

Shaved legs?

Check.

Shaved panty area?

Check.

Box of condoms?

Check.

Have they expired?

Check. Really, check now!

He sucked on my neck as I reached over to my underwear drawer and grabbed the small black bag of tricks that held three condoms and an ancient tube of KY Jelly. I knocked the tube out of the bag, as I couldn't quite remember when I'd purchased it. By this time the KY would probably act more like an adhesive than a lubricant, so I figured it would be best to skip it entirely. I couldn't read the expiration date in the dark so I held the condom about an inch away from my eyes. At that moment, Todd popped up briefly for air.

"What are you doing?" he gasped.

"Nothing," I said as I kissed him. When he caught sight of the condom, he sprang up in surprise.

"What is that?" he said, pulling back from me.

"What?"

"That!" He pointed to the condom in my hand, looking as though I were holding a hand grenade rather than a rubber.

"What?" At this point I wanted Kelly Cox to come in and explain why the appearance of a Trojan during foreplay should cause an abrupt halt in the action. All the blood that pulsed in my erogenous zones suddenly b-lined to my head. My temples started to throb.

Todd couldn't even look at me as he sat in the middle of the bed. "Geri, we can't have sex."

"What?"

"I mean, I thought maybe you could give me a hand job."

"*What?*" Still clutching the condom, I knelt on the bed with my shirt unbuttoned, completely confused. What in the hell was happening? He'd displayed all the signs that he wanted to have sex. It seemed as if we had been priming ourselves for this moment for weeks. And every man wants to have sex. Right? What single man would turn down a half-naked woman holding a condom? But as much as I wanted to know the answers, my mouth wouldn't let me ask the questions. It became increasingly clear that I didn't need to read books on dating. I needed a semester abroad.

"Geri, I think . . ." he started to say as he hastily buttoned the front of his shirt. "I think I'd better watch the news at my place."

He didn't even bother to put his shoes on before making a break for the front door. I watched, stunned, as he tried unsuccessfully to find the correct sequence to unlock the three deadbolts. Each failed attempt caused him to yank the doorknob with such force that I figured it was only a matter of seconds before he would rip the door off its hinges. When it finally popped open, it smashed him in the forehead. He stumbled only for a moment before scurrying out of the apartment. A little thing like a concussion wouldn't stop him.

The blood that had rushed to my head now drained into my heart, making it feel more like a brick than a functioning organ. I looked down at the condom still lodged in my hand. I checked the date: 2/14/01. It was no good. Even before it was ever opened.

I tossed it into the wastepaper basket, then heard a familiar voice come from behind me.

"Remember this," J. T. said. "There's a distinct difference between being afraid and being a coward." I turned and saw him standing next to the window, picking his teeth with a toothpick. The shadows from the fire escape swirled around his face.

"What's the difference?" I whispered.

"Why don't we let Todd show you that?"

A stiff breeze blew through the window, causing the curtains to billow and fall. The room suddenly smelled like rain. It was only the eye of the storm, I thought. The peace was over. The wind was picking up.

9

Stepping In It

Todd's inability to perform not only caused me a sleepless night but also caused me to take my morning shower without even reaching for the bar of soap or the shampoo. I also used Emmy's Ben Gay on my teeth rather than my normal tartar-control toothpaste, then put on the same same clothes I'd worn to work the day before. Fortunately, I missed Emmy in the morning so I didn't have to explain what had happened, or rather, what hadn't happened, with Todd during the night. The bars of my fire escape, which I'd stared at all night, gave no clue to Todd's actions. Nor did cracks in the ceiling plaster. Nor did the headlights of the M103 that was about to hit me on the corner.

"Geri! Watch where you're going!" Max cried out as I took a step in front of the uptown bus. The shock of hearing his voice startled me out of my fog. I never saw Max in daylight hours. After stepping back onto the sidewalk, I turned to see him in front of a corner shoe shine shop with his black bowl in one hand and an enormous raspberry hamantaschen in the other. "How did you not see that bus?"

"What bus?"

"That one!" he said as he pointed his pastry at the bus rolling away from the curb. The bus slid past my field of vision with an advertisement sprawled on its side. The ad featured the man I'd modeled J. T. after. Lying in the middle of a wheat field with his legs akimbo, J. T. wore a white T-shirt, khakis and a wry smile, with a stalk poking out from the corner of his mouth. The caption underneath read SOME HAVE IT. SOME DON'T.

"Thanks, Maxie. I owe you," I said as I rifled through my wallet. Finding no cash or coins, I tossed what I thought was my MetroCard into the bowl.

"No thanks required, kid. Just watch where you're stepping."

Max shooed me off as I hustled my way down into the station with the rest of the morning crowd. Halfway down the stairs I realized I'd given Max my Subway sandwich card, which still had two sandwiches left until the free six-inch sub kicked in. I ran back up to make the switch. But when I got back to the top of the stairs, he was nowhere in sight.

Once I forced my way onto the train and found a couple of inches of room to move, I opened my messenger bag to touch my wallet for the seventh time that morning. When I looked inside, I noticed Kelly Cox's face smiling up at me. I didn't remember leaving the book in my bag, but suddenly it dawned on me that this was a sign. If anyone possessed the answer to why a man would turn down sex, it would be Kelly. I rifled through the pages until I hit the last chapter, "Finishing." I flipped right to the back, and my eyes landed on the second to last paragraph:

"These rules are tried and true. Any skimping, scrimping or skipping; any cutting of corners; any breaking of even one of these rules will ultimately lead to the failure of your relationship. Men are not hard to figure out. I have done that for you. If you don't go by my guidelines or are upset with your

outcome, it's probably not men you need to figure out
but yourself.

"Happy dating. Happy loving. Happily ever after."

I slammed the book shut. Kelly's author photograph
peered back at me through the gaps between my fingers.
Her bright, hopeful eyes seemed to laugh at me. Holding
the book inches away from my face, I shouted, "I hope
you die alone, you prissy douche bag!"

Then I slapped the photo. I'd never hit anything in rage
in my life. Dad always told me if there was any hitting to be
done, he would be happy to step in and do it for me. But it
felt so good, I slapped it again. Then I thought, I can take
this bitch, so I slammed the book against the wall of the
subway car. Rage pulsed through my arms as I repeatedly
smacked Kelly's happy headshot against the map of the
subway and then against an advertisement for a law firm
specializing in divorces. As I raised the book over my
head, ready to pile drive Mrs. Marriage into the floor of the
6 train, I looked up to notice everyone staring at me from
the opposite end of the subway car. They huddled together, heads cocked to the side, looking at me in the same
way they would if they'd just seen a penguin or some other
harmless wild animal waddle onto the train: with mild fear,
curiosity and complete disbelief. Great, I thought. I'm what
the police call an EDP: an Emotionally Disturbed Person. I
had to think fast in order to get out of this with any kind
of pride.

"Cramps!" I yelled.

When I got to the office, I hadn't the energy or focus to
turn on my computer. No one was in yet, so I just sat and
listened to the hum of the computers, printers and photo-
copy machines on the floor. When Sally arrived, she found

me sitting quietly at my desk, looking at a dark computer screen, still holding Kelly's book.

"Geri, I know you don't have a huge wardrobe, but honey, you've got to give people a day or two to forget."

"Sally? Are these rules right?" I asked as I handed over the book. The action itself made me feel completely ignorant. Handing a dating book to Sally was like handing Suze Orman a *Complete Idiot's Guide to Balancing a Checkbook*.

"This stuff is for people who were raised in a barn," she said as her acrylic tips skipped through the pages. She glanced back up at me after realizing that comment wasn't far from the truth. "I didn't mean you. Sorry. But rule number three, date number three is a given, although I personally would keep it going to date number eighteen. Unless he doesn't keep kosher. At least that's what Mom says. The rules for date number two are just plain good manners, and if you ever utter the word 'love' to a man, even if it's 'I love this movie' or 'I love how my legs look in this skirt,' you'll see the skid marks on the street instead of his underwear." She handed the book back to me. "Why are you asking, Geri? Geri?"

I started to cry.

Sally grabbed my shoulders and pulled me into Hedda's office. She put her arms around me and tried her best to be consoling.

"You told him you loved him, didn't you?"

"No, Sally. Worse. He didn't want to sleep with me."

Her voice suddenly dropped an octave. "Oh."

"Why? Guys never shoot down sex. Right?"

"Not with me. I mean . . . Oh, sweetie, he's probably gay."

"No, he's not. It's like he's like this unbelievably super, super man, and I'm just a walking chunk of sexual kryptonite." The tears kept coming as Sally reached into her bag for something to wipe my face.

"It's all right. Look, you're pretty. And if you wore foundation, you could be a knockout. Maybe it's just nerves.
Maybe you remind him of his mom. Maybe his penis bends
to the left and he's embarrassed about it. Talk to him. I'm
sure he won't make the same mistake twice."

"Okay," I uttered through a sniffle.

Just then Hedda came barging into her office. She flew
past Sally and me without so much as a glance. I prayed
she wouldn't see my tears as she dropped a burgundy
Berkin on her new printer.

"Sally, make sure you remind me to get my driver a bottle
of new cologne. He stinks like cod. I don't know what the
son of a bitch eats, but people will start thinking I get driven
around by the goddamn Gorton's Fisherman." She reached
into her desk and pulled out an emergency bottle of L'air du
Temps. As she spritzed it all over her hair, she noticed the
tears. "Geri? What is going on?"

"I'm fine, Miss Jove. I just needed a minute. It's nothing."

"Call me Hedda. And it's not nothing if you're producing
tears. Now tell me. Why is my best girl crying?"

I was trying to formulate a quick-and-easy fib when Sally
jumped in.

"The guy she really likes couldn't do it."

"Does he bend to the left?" Hedda asked as she demonstrated with her index and middle finger.

"No. No. He . . . wouldn't do it," I corrected.

"Oh!" Hedda yelled happily. "That's easy. He's gay,
sweetie! Welcome to New York! It's bound to happen at
some point. My second husband's gay. Gay and fabulous.
After that fact came to light, we became inseparable. Divorced but inseparable. Now we shoe shop, look through
International Male together . . ."

"No, Miss . . . Hedda, he's not gay. I think I just scared
him off . . . somehow."

Hedda straighten up and shot Sally a knowing look.

"Sally, could I have a word with Geri, alone?"

Sally gave me a quick hug before leaving the room. Hedda and the onslaught of her signature scent wafted over to me.

"Geri, this is a personal question. Forgive me. But . . . you know what I was just saying about my driver? That business with the cod. Are . . . you . . . as a woman . . . down there?"

"Hedda! Yes. I'm . . . it's all fine and pretty." At this point I wanted to call Maria and ask if she wouldn't mind stopping by the office before work and shooting me in the face.

"Look, you might be trying too hard. Geri, love is like when you step in dog shit. It only happens when you aren't paying attention." Hedda took the wipe from me and tried to dab the tears away. My eyes began to burn as I realized that Sally had accidentally given me a wet nap instead of a tissue. Since I'd never seen Hedda act this motherly toward anyone, I tried to hold back a scream as she unknowingly dabbed alchohol into my tear ducts.

"Thanks, Hedda. I'll be okay."

"You'll be better than okay. You'll be great. Forget this guy. Go out with your girl friends. You'll see that this big city is teeming with men. All you need to do is keep your eyes open. Some are good. Some are great. Some are even golden. But some, dear Geri, are golden retrievers. Just make sure to avoid their shit."

10

Skating in it

"Watch out for the dog crap!" Maria yelled back to me as we bladed past the Central Park boathouse. Maria managed to hop right over the little pile of poop while I just lifted up one blade and rolled on past.

Summer had finally started to emerge around us. After seven o'clock, when traffic is banned from the park, there was finally enough sunlight for the three of us to hang out in the bandshell and practice our in-line skating moves. Emmy popped off to the park early to set up our trick cones and talk with a few of her students. This gave Maria and me sufficient time alone for her to comment on my situation with Todd. I figured it would take about ten minutes. Not like the cumulative fifty-two hours Emmy and I had spent on dissecting the male brain. In Emmy's quest to find a logical explanation of why Todd had bolted while at the same time sparing her best friend's feelings, she came up with everything from Todd's being so completely in love with me that he feared he would have a premature ejaculation to his retroactively giving up sex for Lent. After talking herself in circles, Emmy finally settled on the fact that he wasn't good enough for me and that I could do better. The same answer I'd gotten from Hedda and Sally. The same fact that my head and heart wanted to believe, but somehow couldn't.

"What did you say, exactly?" Maria asked as she braked at the hot dog vendor.

"Nothing," I answered as I dug through my suit pockets. I found a penny and figured it couldn't hurt to throw it into the Angel of the Waters fountain. "I just kind of sat there stunned."

"So you actually said nothing?"

"I think I said, 'What?' but he didn't really give an explanation. He just got up and left."

"Perfect!" she yelled as she threw her wristguard–protected hands in the air. "There's mistake number one."

"Well, what should I have said?"

"The two little words every man wants to hear."

"You're big?" I answered as I handed money over to the vendor.

"No. Fuck me."

The vendor almost dropped my hot dogs back into the dirty water before he handed them to me. As we rolled over to fountain to sit, I leaned toward Maria in hope of keeping the volume down.

"Maria, I don't think I would like the first night with the man I want to father my kids to start with, 'Fuck me.' "

"No. You're right. It should have been 'Fuck me, chump.' That would have been more appropriate."

I started to eat my dog smothered in sauerkraut and what I hoped was caramelized onions, and thought that if Todd would only explain, I wouldn't be having this brilliant exchange. But he never came up. He never even called. I couldn't muster the heart or nerve to pick up the phone because I thought the conversation really needed to happen in person. For the past four nights I took the garbage out late and checked to see if there was light coming out from under his door. Every night his apartment was dark.

"Look, Geri, between my brothers and my job I know a thing or two about men. One of them being, don't ever ask a man to explain himself. In bed or otherwise. He can't. It's physically fucking impossible for him to do it. If you ask Todd why he won't nail you, it's only going to freak him out more." Maria took a bite of her hot dog and looked up at the crossword puzzle the airstreams from the planes taking off and landing at LaGuardia and JFK made in the sky. With a mouth full of dog she continued. "Truth is, guys don't know why they do what they do. That's why they get married. Most of the guys I know need someone to tell them what to eat, when to fuck and what color the downstairs bathroom rug is going to be. I'm sure your Todd's no different. I bet he doesn't even know why he got spooked." She swallowed half her dog in one big gulp. "That's probably why he hasn't called you. He's trying to conjure up some lame excuse that sounds decent to you and halfway true to his friends."

"Really? You think?"

"I know. And when this happens again . . ."

"There's not going to be an again."

"Geri, when two people want to have sex with each other, there's always an again. And when that time comes, and if you want him to do you right, then don't give him a choice. Don't ask him why. Don't look at him like a puppy lost at a carnival, hoping he'll change his mind. Give him orders. Look him right in the eye, grab him by the balls and say with conviction, 'Fuck me, soldier. Now!' "

I had to get up and move. If I sat there any longer, I didn't know if I was going to laugh or throw up. "That's beautiful, Maria. Thanks."

"Just trying to help," she said as she crumpled her napkin. I tossed the penny into the fountain. I watched it as it landed with a soft *plop* and shimmied down to the fountain floor. Maria reached in and winged a quarter at the angel's head. It smacked the angel's face with a loud *ting* and ricocheted into the lake twenty feet behind it. We both watched as the quarter skimmed the surface of the lake before disappearing beneath it. She looked at me and smiled.

"Watch out, Gere. That shit's coming true."

We continued to blade our way under the bridge and over to the bandshell, the one area of the park where you can see people practicing six or seven sports-on-wheels without anyone smacking into each other. As we bypassed the figure bladers, the skateboarders and the little kids learning to skate backward, we saw Emmy talking to a handful of her students. One of them I recognized as Shoshanna, a punked-out Filipino teen who Emmy loved to brag about. The girl's head looked like a Benjamin Moore paint sample strip for the red family. She was hell-bent on working at her mom's salon after graduation even though Emmy thought she had the smarts to solve the world's energy crisis. Shoshanna was goading Emmy as we rolled up to them.

"So who's this guy?"

"I don't know who you're talking about," Emmy said as she tried unsuccessfully to stifle a smile. Emmy bent over and placed the orange cones down exactly six feet apart. Shoshanna pointed to Maria and me.

"You guys want to tell us why Ms. Kozak can't stop smiling every Wednesday after fifth period algebra?"

Maria and I stood there silent as Emmy jumped in. "I just love logarithms. And if you're ever in the middle of an earthquake and a seismograph is nearby, then you will love them too."

The gang of kids gave up and began to walk away.

Shoshanna stayed behind and waited until the group walked out of earshot.

"You're not fooling me, Ms. Kozak. I saw that blond hottie waiting for you outside after school."

"That's my brother."

"Want me to be your sister-in-law?"

"You don't want a long-distance relationship when you're at MIT," Emmy answered, unfazed, as she finished putting down the cones.

"I told you, I'm going to be a color technician!"

"That's great. You'll earn some nice pocket money in the dorms that way."

Shoshanna just shook her multitonal head and began to walk over to the rest of her friends. She shouted back to Emmy, "You know how hard it is to get this kind of red to keep its shine for eight weeks?"

"You know how hard the quadratic equation is to say in one breath?" Emmy retorted. Shoshanna turned around, put one foot in the air like a dancer and held her nose.

"X equals negative B plus or minus the square root of B squared subtract four A C all over two A. Try challenging me next time."

"Massachusetts is beautiful in the fall. Send me a postcard."

Wearing a smile, Shoshanna ran to catch up with the group. Maria and I stood there as if we'd just watched an Indian film without the subtitles. I felt another rush of admiration for Emmy and her determination to educate the young until Maria chimed in.

"I hope she doesn't get pregnant. Teenage girls are sluts nowadays."

"Maria! My students are not sluts."

"Nah, they're just luckier than we were back in school," I said as Emmy and Maria took turns side-surfing through the cones. I sat on the bench and tried to get a ketchup stain out of my mustard-colored polyester suit pants.

"Speaking of lucky," Emmy said, "Bryan just asked me to the Knickerbocker for an informal company dinner."

"Is this the 'date' we've been waiting for?" I asked.

"Well, yes and no. He said I'm his date, but I should bring a friend. And Geri, I'd like to know if you would come with me."

"I'd rather give myself a pap smear," I answered.

Emmy looked shocked as she pleaded, "Why not?"

"Because I can't think of anything I'd enjoy less than being the third wheel on your first date with Mr. Perfect."

"Come on, it's just one night."

"Yeah, Geri. Would it kill you to try and get a piece of stockbroker ass?" Maria yelled.

I looked down at my cheap suit and thought out loud, "Who'd wanna sleep with me?"

Emmy skated over to me, flushed. "Come on. It's not about that." She bent toward me and whispered, "You want a nice guy. You don't want a one-night stand."

Maria rolled up to us and whispered, "Yes. Yes, she does. We all want to fuck."

"Well, I don't," Emmy answered as she straightened up defiantly. "I want to be in love and to make love. With Bryan."

"Geri, you want . . . wait, let me rephrase this . . . we need you to have a good fuck. Or lovemaking session or whatever you want to call it. You haven't been laid in like, what? Two years?"

That comment seemed magically to shut off all the noise in the park. All movement stopped as I felt the eyes of the other parkgoers bore into my head. My ears felt like they were filling up with fluid. I thought maybe I was suffering from a case of vertigo until Emmy broke through.

"Geri is just choosy. She could have guys anytime she wants. She just chooses love over meaningless sex."

This made Maria laugh so hard she knocked over three cones.

I unfortunately concurred. "No, Emmy, abstinence actively recruited me in 2006. Anyway, I don't really exude sexuality. Guys, at least the kind of guys who will be at this dinner, don't look at me and think, 'I want to see her naked.' They think, 'I got to pick up my dry cleaning. I left it there over a week ago.'"

"Better than me," chimed in Maria. "When they see me, guys think 'Screw the pig, make it squeal.'"

Emmy plopped herself on the bench, disheartened. "Then will you go with me for moral support? Just keep an open mind. Maybe, if you put your heart into it, you'll meet the man of your dreams."

"Emmy, I don't think picking up a friend's potential boyfriend's Wall Street friend involves that organ."

Maria smiled at us. "Then why don't you put your vag . . ."

"I'll go. But for you only," I answered. Emmy sprang up and did a big looping circle for joy. Emmy's happiness was always contagious. Then I thought, maybe she's right. Maybe it will be cool. Maybe I'll stop thinking about Todd for two seconds and actually enjoy myself. Maybe I'll have the time of my life.

11

A Night at the Knickerbocker

Maybe if I pretend to have an attack of infectious diarrhea, Emmy will take me home. Maybe gas. Maybe acid reflux. Embarrassing dandruff? My mind couldn't come up with excuses fast enough and we hadn't even started on the soup.

Emmy, Bryan and I sat on the fifty-yard line of an enormous dining table at the club, The Knickerbocker. Bryan not only looked every bit as handsome as Emmy had described after their coffee dates but also possessed a charm that seemed to make all the men in the room want to be him and all the women want to be on his lap. He wore a dapper charcoal Brooks Brothers suit with silver bull-and-bear cufflinks that sparkled in the candlelight. He was in the middle of telling some utterly fascinating Wall Street yarn, which riveted all the men at the table and made all their obnoxiously thin dates stare at his mouth.

". . . and I thought this massive man was going to kill me, but he just bent over and said, 'You mean the Chaikin Oscillator?'"

The punch line caused the entire table to erupt in laughter. Except for two. Myself and Emmy. Because as apparent as it was that Emmy and I had no idea what Bryan was talking about, it was even more apparent that the story was intended to impress the woman who sat directly across from Bryan. An amazingly beautiful Swedish woman named Ingrid. She'd just started working at his office as an underwriter. She could have easily been a model if she didn't have such a hard-on for monotonous insurance jobs. Her green eyes offset her long chestnut hair, which cascaded over her toned, self-tanned shoulders. She traced the rim of her glass with her middle finger, stopping ever ery so often to dip it in the water. She gave Bryan a long mischievous smile that either meant, "Your story was a sweet attempt to entertain me," or "Guess if I'm wearing panties."

Emmy leaned in toward me. "What is a Chaikin . . ."

"I don't know. Just laugh when they laugh. I got to pee," I said as I sprang from my chair. The moment we arrived at the Knickerbocker Club and I took one glance around the crimson-wallpapered room at all the married men at this function, I'd decided to get myself a quick date with Mr. Alcohol. Four champagnes later, I had practically carved a path to the beige marble ladies room.

As I sat down in the stall for the fourth time that evening, I recognized a familiar smell that made me want to eat a package of cheap Chinese noodles. Marijuana and Downy fabric softener. After I finished, I looked into each stall to find the smell's origin. When I got to the last stall, I gently pushed open the door to see a teenage bathroom attendant sitting on the last toilet. She held a joint in one hand and a roll of toilet paper stuffed with dryer sheets in the other. Instead of jumping up with apologies and snuffing out the spliff, the attendant just sat there and looked up at me with bloodshot eyes.

"No one ever leaves the table during the bisque," she said as she took a firm drag off the joint.

"If they wanted to get away from stories about Cayenne operators they would."

Her face puckered as she tried to talk without exhaling. "Chaikin Oscillators. I overheard him telling it. It was funny." She held the toilet paper roll up to her mouth and exhaled through the roll. The smoke filtered through the dryer sheets causing the air to smell like a bag of weed after it went through a delicate tumble dry. She closed her eyes and inhaled the scent. "Ahhh. Now that's April fresh."

"Like springtime at Snoop Dogg's house."

"Want some?" she asked as she held up the joint and the roll of Charmin.

"No thanks," I said. "I'm kinda drunk."

"Well, can you do me a favor and watch the tip jar for me? I don't want anyone stealing my singles."

"You think this crowd would do that?"

"You kidding? I always put ten of my own bucks in there to start. On a good night, I walk out of here with three."

"Fair enough." As I made my way back to the primping area of the ladies room, I heard the door close and Emmy's light footsteps patter inside. She threw her cute button clutch in front of the mirror as she stared at her reflection.

"He notices me about as much as that stuffed antelope head on the wall," she said in a huff.

"It's an ibex!" the attendant yelled out from the back of the bathroom.

Emmy looked at me, puzzled. I just shook my head. "Don't ask."

"Geri, what am I going to do? She's gorgeous. No, she's not gorgeous, she's stunning. And interesting. And smart. And single. And works next to him day after day after day."

"Please. She might have perfect legs and highlights, but she can't be perfect everywhere."

Emmy turned to look me square in the face. She could barely contain her anger. "Geri, she has a degree in massage."

I put my hand on her shoulder. "You're screwed."

As many humiliating crushes as I'd had in my life, I thought I would rather live them four times over than trade places with Emmy. Even with Todd going AWOL, at least I'd never seen him with another girl aside from his ex. Another girl who looked as beautiful as the Skankasaurous Rex who appeared to have just swooped down and dug its talons into Emmy's man. Emmy seemed to be handling the knowledge of Ingrid's existence with more composure than I would have. But as I watched her dab on her clear lip gloss, I could tell she was losing hope. Halfway through the application, her bottom lip began to quiver and she stopped.

"Who am I kidding? I'm a math teacher. I look like a math teacher."

"I think you're beautiful. And smart. And interesting. And so does every kid on the Mathletes team at your school. Besides, if it makes you feel any better, none of us have dated since the last election. Well, except Sally, but she's a virgin, so it doesn't count."

Emmy closed her purse sadly. "I'm sorry I brought you here, Geri. I know you don't want to be here. *I* don't even want to be here."

"Hey, anywhere with you is cool with me."

Just then Ingrid came into the ladies bathroom and sauntered right up to Emmy. Her strides were long and deliberate as her hips rocked like a metronome from side to side.

"Oh, Emelia."

"It's Emily. Well, Emmy."

"Emmy, I was talking with Bryan and he mentioned that you work in a school." Her eyes sparkled with curiosity, as if she didn't know whether Emmy worked as a custodian or perhaps painted the inside of classrooms.

Emmy answered matter-of-factly. "I'm a teacher."

"Back in Sweden, I did volunteer work at schools, teaching International Sign Language. Maybe if you don't already have a program in your school, I could start one? Yah?"

The liquor wouldn't allow me to control my sudden obvious eye roll. As Ingrid and her gooey, lubricated accent went on, Emmy looked as if she had been kicked in the stomach by an ibex. "Yeah . . . sure. That would be neat," Emmy choked out.

Ingrid clapped for joy. "Wonderful! I will make sure I get in contact with you through Bryan. He can be our man in the middle. I will make sure to have lunch with him tomorrow to discuss. Good?"

"Yeah," Emmy said. The word was barely audible.

"I look forward to talking to you later." Ingrid solidified their camaraderie by giving Emmy a kiss on both cheeks. Emmy walked away, wiping her face like a five-year-old who'd just been kissed by an aunt with a mustache.

With the attendant still occupied, I stayed behind and watched Ingrid brush her tresses. As she brushed her hair, her eyes peered into the tip jar. One long finger pushed the money around until she could see the coins at the bottom. I stared at her hand until she stopped.

"I collect the state quarters," she said.

"Don't we all."

"You must be the publisher."

"Writer. I write film scripts. Well, I wrote a film script. I only work for a publishing company."

"Really? Back in Sweden my father's best schoolmate was Ingmar Bergman."

"Back on Long Island my father's best schoolmate was an alcoholic named Fat Marty. They called him that because . . . because . . ."

I couldn't continue. My voice seemed to trail off as my eyes began to drift over Ingrid's languid arms. As she arranged a fashionably loose knot on the top of her head, I couldn't help staring. There it was: the absolute perfect flaw. She held up her bun in a gorgeous French twist and checked her profile from each side. "Up or down?"

"Definitely up," I said, stunned. "I gotta go."

I pulled a five-dollar bill out of my pocket and threw it in the tip jar. On my way out, I heard the attendant walk back into the primping area. From a distance I heard her say to Ingrid, "In this country, all our fives look the same."

I bolted into the dining room and right into the waiter refilling the water glasses. I tried to apologize as I wiped the front of his white waiter's coat, but he just shooed me away. While I was looking like a Keystone Kop, Ingrid sashayed past me to the table, leaving me unnoticed in the wake of her beauty. I broke away from the waiter and scurried to my seat with the quickness of an eight year old who's just heard the record scratch to a stop in musical chairs. When Bryan caught sight of Ingrid, he chivalrously shot up out of his seat and smoothed the front of his tie. He waited until she was seated before he sat back down.

Emmy looked at Ingrid in shock and whispered, "How can she look . . . better?"

"Wait," I said as a man brought Ingrid up to speed with the conversation.

"So Ingrid, how big are men in Sweden?"

"Depends on what you're talking about. I don't have much experience with Swedish men." She cocked her head and looked at Bryan. "I prefer American men in that department."

All the suits at the table began cooing as she kept her gaze locked on Bryan. He held back a smile as he pushed his napkin back on his lap. Probably to hide a spontaneous boner. Emmy stared at her soup in the hope that no one would notice her eyes beginning to tear.

I yelled out over the table. "Big as in height or girth?"

Ingrid broke her gaze with Bryan and looked at me, perplexed. "I don't understand."

"Well, are they big this way?" I asked as I raised my hand in the air up over my head. "Or this way?" I threw my arms in either direction, accidentally knocking into the same waiter filling a water glass.

"Oh, no. They are big this way."

A noticeable hush filled the room as Ingrid lifted her arm. Like the majestic American bald eagle stretching its wings, Ingrid's arms floated high above her head, exposing a luxuriously long, black, curly thatch of underarm hair. All of the women at the table immediately looked down and away from the toupee lodged under Ingrid's armpits. They began to blink some sort of high society Morse Code at one another as they tried to stifle their gasps. The men appeared disgusted, throwing their napkins off their laps and onto the table in a disappointed huff. The man who sat next to Ingrid actually spit his bisque back into the bowl.

The only two who didn't appeared to have their wet dreams shattered were myself and Emmy. She took her napkin and dabbed the corner of her eye, catching the tear that never had a chance to fall. She looked at me and mouthed the words "Thank you." Her dream of Bryan was spared another night.

"I thought Swedes were like that," I said. "Great soup. Is that cilantro?"

By the end of dinner no one wanted to speak to me. I tried to make myself scarce as Emmy and Bryan talked quietly on the piano bench in the lobby. The two began to giggle as Bryan taught her how to play chopsticks. In the middle of the last glass of champagne that the bartender would serve me, I looked up at the ibex staring down on all of us from the wall. Gazing at its glassy black devil-may-care eyes and pointed horns, I whispered a little prayer. Out of all the expensive suits, furniture and taxidermy in the Knickerbocker, I hoped Bryan would come to realize that he was sitting next to the only priceless piece of work in the room.

Armed with my crystal flute filled with the most expensive glass of anything I would ever drink, I decided to explore the other rooms. As I walked down the dimly lit hallway, past the portraits of old, fat, rich dead people dressed in green velvet, I felt a strange pull toward a doorway at the end of the hall. The warm welcoming smell of burning wood guided me into a tiny sitting room where two crimson, leather-studded chairs faced a crackling fire. Over the mantel hung an oil painting of a man who bore an uncanny resemblance to Max. The date underneath read 1843. I leaned against the doorway and chuckled out loud. Just then I noticed a man sitting in one of the chairs. He began to turn around to get a look at me. I, however, knew who he was just from glimpsing the back of his head.

"I can't imagine you in a place like this," I said as I swirled the drink around in my glass. He slowly stood up, unfolding his 6-foot, 3-inch frame. Wow, I thought, J. T. really looks great. Only he wasn't wearing his usual white suit. His wore khaki pants similar to the ones I'd seen him wear in the bus advertisement. And the rich royal blue shirt that he'd unbuttoned slightly below his collarbone seemed to match the exact shade of his eyes. His hair appeared shorter on the sides and a touch darker than I'd last imagined. I blamed the bisque for the slight inconsistencies.

"I like the blue. Looks good on you," I said, taking another sip of my drink.

But J. T. didn't say anything. He just stood there with his brow furrowed, looking at me as if he didn't know who I was or how I got in the room. After a few moments, he finally spoke. "Thank you."

We stood in silence, facing each other, examining each other, soaking each other in, but neither of us moved. I wondered if it was the expensive champagne or the pot contact high from the bathroom attendant that caused me to have such a clear vision of J. T. Whatever it was, I needed to bottle it and take it with me. Even as I heard Emmy call out to me from down the hall, I felt like I could reach out and chip him on the shoulder.

"Geri! We're leaving!"

I set down my empty glass on a nearby table and gave him one last smile. "See you around," I said as I shoved my hands in my pockets. The puzzled expression was still on his face as he watched me exit the room.

When I entered the lobby, I saw Emmy in the middle of a sea of Bryan's coworkers. Her face beamed as Bryan bent over and gave her a slight kiss on the cheek. Catching sight of me, she waved me over with a smile, her bag happily clutched to her chest. As I walked past the money men shaking each other's hands, with their wives exchanging little waves, I turned and looked back up at the frozen ibex. Giving him a quick smile, I gave credit where credit was due.

Thanks, Buddy, I thought. You pulled the evening out of the crapper for me too.

But I spoke too soon. Buzzing still from Bryan's attention, Emmy fumbled with her keys as we entered the first doorway of our building. She was so excited that she couldn't locate the correct key on her chain. I was so drunk I couldn't steady myself without the help of the wall.

"I can't believe he wants to see me again! I know I'm one step closer to being asked out on a date. I can feel it. Oh Geri, I owe you, big time," she said as she unlocked the entryway door.

"You got me through ninth-grade algebra. It was the least I could do," I said as I stumbled into the entryway. All I wanted was to get into my bed and put down my spinning head.

Emmy kept analyzing Bryan's every word until we reached the first flight of stairs. When I heard the familiar double clicks of the front door lock opening behind us a sudden wave of sobriety hit me. Another person had walked into the foyer and a cold breeze blew up my back. My ears registered the gait immediately. With the first few strong steps I knew that if I looked behind me, I would see something I desperately didn't want to see. The female voice that sounded warned me that it was going to be even worse than I'd imagined.

"Hey, Geri," Todd said, his voice sounding an octave higher than normal. "How've you been?"

Taking a deep breath, I turned around slowly to confirm my nightmare. From the flight below he looked up at me with an expression like someone who's been punched in the gut, or maybe had his shorts pulled down in gym class. His eyes seemed to plead with me, trying to tell me more than what his mouth could say at that moment. My whole soul wanted to run down the flight and cup his face in my hands. I wanted to throw my mouth on his mouth, then nuzzle my cheek into the beautiful space behind his right ear. But the subtle stink of her breath mints kept my feet planted on the stairs.

Cassie stood behind him. Unfazed and unaware of my presence as usual. By the look of it, she seemed to be everything I wasn't. Ultrafeminine and impeccably groomed. Her hair seemed to gleam under the harsh yellow lighting of the hallway. She wore the kind of form-fitting black dress that doesn't allow for underwear. Shifting her weight from one ankle-breaking stiletto to the other, she dug through her rhinestone clutch while holding an *Annie Get Your Gun* playbill. After a fruitless search, she tugged Todd's suit sleeve.

"Can I have the keys, hon?"

"Hon"? Why was she calling the last man I went to bed with "hon"? My expression upon hearing this endearment must have been one of shock or disbelief because when I looked at Emmy, all she could do was tiptoe up the stairs. I looked back at Todd, whose gaze never wavered from my face. It seemed as if we were looking at each other from the opposite sides of prison bars. Only I couldn't tell which one of us was in jail.

He cleared his throat. "I came up to see you the other day. Wanted to see if you might be interested in going out with a group of us for a beer."

He was lying. Lying to me in front of my friend and whoever Cassie was to him. Even drunk, I knew when I was being taken for a fool.

"Really?" I said with surprising coolness. "I've been around. Every night, actually." Wow, that sounded desperate.

Then he began to stutter. "I don't really remember what night it was," he admitted. "I think . . . maybe . . . maybe it might have been last week . . ."

Emmy looked down on me from the second-floor landing and waved me upstairs. She probably thought that in my inebriated state, I would start a fight in the hallway or throw up on him. Both of which seemed like great ideas. Instead I pursed my lips together, ripped my eyes off Todd and followed her up. I didn't answer Todd or wish them a good night. I wanted them to have an awful night. A horrific night. I hoped the musical sucked and I prayed she was looking for her crabs medication.

When Emmy and I walked into the apartment, she asked if I wanted to talk about it. Too embarrassed, I told her I'd rather just go to bed. But when I shut off the light and rolled into the dent in my futon, my thoughts spun faster than my head. Seeing Cassie explained it all. He probably never came up because there wasn't a reason to come up. Explaining yourself to someone means you want them to understand you. Wanting them to understand means that you give a damn about them. The answer became painfully simple. He'd pulled a Rhett Butler; Todd didn't come up because he just didn't give a damn. Only he didn't care to wait a thousand pages to tell me or stick it out through a civil war.

I had been in love plenty of times before. I'd hurdled each disappointment with surprising agility. When I walked in on Timmy Taggart, the love of my life in ninth grade, kissing Suzy Motts behind the stage at the Halloween dance, I got over it by the time we bobbed for apples. When Kevin, my college boyfriend, asked to see other people, I cried for two days, then forgot his phone number in four. But a horrible feeling began to set in. This experience with Todd didn't feel like the ones with other boys. It wouldn't be forgotten by the next dance or solved by a few nights out with the girls. It felt cold and disorientating; as if I'd just found my way home in an ice storm, only to be told I wasn't welcome inside. This had happened once before. I just couldn't believe that anyone other than my mom could make me feel so bad again.

12

Heart-Shaped Rocks

Since I didn't have to worry about my weekend plans, I grabbed my notebook and a seat on the Jitney to Southold. Once on board, I settled in with my composition book, preparing to work on a newer, punchier version of my query letter. The bus hadn't made it out of the Midtown Tunnel before I fell fast asleep on the shoulder of the nun who sat next to me.

Two hours later, after I slept through Queens and the strip malls and outlet shops that cover most of Long Island, I woke to see rows of grapevines whipping past the window. We had officially driven past the end of the Long Island Expressway. Where Route 25 comes back to reclaim its rightful position as Main Road. Where vineyards and sod farms have room to stretch out over the open acres between the sound and the bays. By the time I finished apologizing to Sister Mary Eunice for drooling on her habit, we pulled up at the bus stop in front of the savings bank in Southold. From my window, I could see my dad standing on the corner waiting for me, anticipating my arrival like the first time I stepped off the school bus when I started kindergarten. Wearing a free T-shirt some motor oil company had sent him and his favorite John Deere hat, he waved before I even had a chance to disembark. In sixth grade, I would have been embarrassed at the sight of my six-foot, seven-inch Herculean father waving at me like an excited kid from the side of the road. At twenty-six, I would be disappointed if he stayed in the truck.

"How's my girly-girl?" Dad cried as he gave me an enormous bear hug.

"Fine," I choked out. Being in his linebacker arms made me want to sob, but I kept it together. I tried to blink away the tears before I looked him in the face. "Told you I'd be home to help you with the Muntz," I said.

He held my shoulders away from him and peered down into my eyes. "You okay?" he asked with less excitement. I nodded my head *yes* until I saw Poppy walk across the street holding a steaming pizza box.

He handed the pizza over to Dad as he scooped me up. "You better have one of those for your ol' Poppy."

"Hey, Pops," I gasped under the weight of his arms. The only man I knew bigger and brawnier than my own father was his father, Poppy. With his gray hair and handlebar mustache, he looked like a biker bar Santa who only made toys for good little girls and boys who could bench press 250 pounds. Emmy thought that the reason I didn't date in high school was because every boy in town was terrified to get on the bad side of the men in my family. Until I realized that I could pluck the hairs between my eyebrows, I believed that too.

We hopped into the truck and I sat crushed between Poppy and Dad, holding the pizza box all the way home. Pulling up the driveway and hearing the gravel crackle softly underneath the tires, I realized how happy I was to be back in the country. When Dad opened the garage, my lungs took in the familiar smell of motor oil, gasoline and fuel injector fluid. This elixir caused the thought of Todd to waft completely out of my brain. With the pizza on the roof of the old pickup, I pulled out a slice as I watched Dad and Poppy take the nylon cover off the Muntz.

Dad began to apologize. "Sorry for the lame dinner, sweetie. If I had known you were coming . . ."

"He would have ordered Chinese," Poppy interjected.

"But we wanted to get the Muntz out soon. The weather being so nice and all."

"It's okay, Dad," I said as I chomped down on my slice. I stopped chewing when they pulled the cover completely off. For a moment I lost my breath. The three of us looked at the car in silence. After all these years, she still could take our breath away.

Dad let out a sigh, wiped his brow and said the same thing he does each year he takes the winter cover off.

"Damn, you are pretty."

And he was right. Before us sat the finest piece of American-made machinery since the washing machine. A 1954 mint green Muntz Jet with white walls so thick you needed to use a horsehair brush to clean them and a chassis so long that it almost didn't make it in the garage. The backseat looked like a hundred cow's tongues were lined up in a row and stapled one right next to the other. The blood-red interior never seemed to fade and the chrome shone even if there wasn't a light in the room.

Dad walked over to the dinky cassette player in the corner and hit play. Elvis's "(Marie's the Name) His Latest Flame" filled the garage. This was the most important rule of the garage. Before Never walk in the house with grease on your hands, Never touch an air conditioner hose and Put the micrometer back where you found it, comes house rule #1. Always, in the presence of the Muntz, play Elvis. Dad's reasoning: a girl's got to know who her daddy is.

It's true. The car came from Elvis. Back in dad's army days, he got stationed in Friedberg, Germany, in the Thirty-second

Armor Regiment right along with Elvis Aaron Presley himself. As the story goes, he asked Dad to drive him off base to
see this young American girl who'd just arrived in town for a
visit. On their way, their jeep ran into a ditch and began to
smoke. Elvis apparently freaked as he told Dad that he
couldn't be late to see Ms. Beaulieu. He told Dad he would
give him anything if they could just make it to the hotel before lights out. Well, Dad, being the spry mechanic he was,
jimmied up the engine so tight that they made it to the hotel
with a half hour to spare. He said that Elvis was so thankful,
he took his badge number and said if they made it out of the
army, he'd send him a thank-you note. Dad told him that
having the bragging rights to getting the King out of a ditch
was thanks in itself. He never saw Elvis after that day, but
when he got Mom's next letter from home, she said that a
man had showed up and left a mint green convertible in the
driveway. She included the note from Mr. Presley, thanking
Dad. Mom told the man that she didn't know what Dad had
done, but that they certainly couldn't accept such a gener-
ous present. The man told her not to bother trying to give it
back as Elvis believed in always thanking the boys in green
and that he didn't drive anything but Cadillacs.

I hummed happily along to the song as I watched Dad
and Poppy rotate the white walls. Poppy broke my happy
home bubble when he shouted from behind the car, "So
Geri, I bet your new boyfriend says the same thing when
he sees you walk into a room."

My appetite vanished. I dropped my crust into the box.
With one look, Dad could tell I didn't want to talk about it.
He deflected Poppy's remark without missing a beat.

"She doesn't want to talk about boys with you, old man.
You just concentrate on that wheel rim. Try not to nick it
this time."

Poppy shot up from underneath the car. "Nick? How

about I nick you in the teeth, you doorknob? When have I
ever in your little lifetime . . ."

"I'm going for a walk," I interrupted. "Need to work off
my pizza while there's still some light out. I'll be down at
the beach."

"Women," Poppy said. "Always watching their figures."

"You just watch my rims."

"You can just watch my fist thump down on your skull."

I bounced out of the flatbed and slipped on my ratty
Tretorns that still sat in the corner of the garage. Walking
down the driveway and onto the road that led me to the
beach, I could still hear the sound of those two bickering.
Their voices didn't fade until I hit the wisteria in the Mil-
freds' garden three houses down.

Our road got quiet after dinner. Only a couple of cars
passed me on the five-minute walk down to Goose Creek
beach. Usually, I would recognize at least one of the drivers
just by the make of the car. They would give a quick toot
and a wave. Some would even stop and roll down the window for a chat. Normally they'd ask what Dad was up to or
when I thought Poppy would put out his first pints of straw-
berries. But since I hadn't lived in Southold for the past four
years, tonight no one blew their horns or so much as looked
up from the road as they drove past.

I didn't care. The evening reminded me of early summer
nights when my Mom, Dad and I used to throw all the dirty
dinner dishes into the sink, make ice cream cones and walk
down to the beach to watch the sunset. I usually fell behind.
My only concern was catching all the rainbow sprinkles that
dripped off my cone. Trying to suck up all the dessert that
dissolved in my hands, I lagged behind long enough to
watch Mom and Dad walk together. When it looked like
there weren't any cars coming, they would meander hand in
hand to the center of the road. The only thing separating

them was the double yellow line. They stretched their arms wide, as if they were walking past something that was big enough to separate them, but not so big that it would cause them to lose their grip on each other. When we reached the part of the road that had an elevated curb, Mom would jump onto it gracefully and pretend to be a tight-rope walker. She held her ice cream cone in the air like a torch while the other hand's slender fingers meshed loosely with Dad's. Dad wouldn't even move out of the way of the oncoming cars if it meant he had to drop her hand. He wouldn't dare let her fall into the abyss of the Hamans' manicured lawn. But no matter what road we took to the beach, whether it was the road with the curb or the shortcut through the woods, they never lost their grip on each other. This night, as I walked past the Hamans' house, I jumped onto the curb with my hands stuffed in my pockets. I had no sense of impending doom. No hand reached out to balance me. I felt no need to reach out for one. I would not go spiraling out into the un-known, no matter how much I wanted to.

When I walked onto the beach, I took off my Tretorns and headed down to the water's edge. Each mussel and jingle shell pinched the skin under my feet. I winced through the pain, refusing to believe I had city feet. You could always spot the summer people from Manhattan when the Good Humor truck pulled into the beach. They looked like they were stomping to bluegrass music as they jerked their feet up in pain each time they stepped on the oyster, clam, jingle and mussel shells that covered the bay beaches. Those people had city feet. The locals were the ones who walked unfazed over the burning noon black-top without so much as a flip-flop on.

I searched the beach for some flat rocks for skimming but settled for a handful of slipper shells. The water lay still as the sun glowed larger and lower by the minute, causing the pinks and purples that surrounded it to morph into streaks of blue and indigo. But as magnificent as the sun's display might be, I prefer the moon. The sun rises and sets so dramatically. People get up for it, plan their day around it, protect themselves from it and bask in it. But the moon is patient. All day it waits behind the haze of blue in the sky for its turn to arrive. It fades in and out with little or no fanfare. Its light is cold. But it's there.

Right about the time I was making my shells bounce across the top of the water, the moon slowly came out to define itself against all the colors that the sun splashed over the sky. I sucked in the salt air and stretched out my arms to the moon, not really knowing why. Not caring if I looked ridiculous. I didn't know if I was proclaiming that I was here on the shoreline or if I was just reaching out, waiting for something to step up and hold me. Nothing but a stiff breeze came off the water to lash around my hair.

As I looked down over the smooth stones, I noticed a flat, heart-shaped rock. Upon closer inspection, I saw a scratch on its surface that appeared to be in the shape of the letter *T*. I looked around the beach to see if I could find Maria or Emmy hiding behind the sea grass and giggling at their practical joke. And for a moment, I thought I would put it in my pocket and take it to Todd. Tell him how ironic I thought it was that I'd found this on my shore and that he should keep it in case he needed something to throw at his car.

But instead I heaved it into the water. I figured a heart-shaped rock would be the closest I would ever get to actually holding Todd's heart or any other organ of his. And the probability of me ever getting close to him again would be as likely as that rock finding its way back to shore in my lifetime. I grabbed my shoes, dumped out the sand and began to storm back up the beach. The best I could hope for was that someone, someday, would find my heart-shaped rock washed up on the shore, wipe off sand and seaweed and say, "Geri O'Brien, I think this belongs to you."

For the rest of the weekend, I found myself on the receiving end of a funnel and oil pan while listening to Dad and Poppy argue over who had a better swing: Mike Piazza or Topper "Apeman" Goldsmith from the class of 54. In the class D division baseball finals, Topper hit one so far out of the baseball diamond that it was rumored to have landed in the creek two hundred yards past the school grounds. After hours of bickering, the two came to the consensus that although Topper might have gone pro had he not lost his thumb at his mother's ice cream parlor, he would never have gotten a close enough shave to carry off Mike's goatee.

At the end of hours of working in, on and under the car, Dad and I decided to take it out for a spin. We dropped the top, popped in *Blue Hawaii* and took the Muntz out for its first ride of the season. People out for their evening walk noticed the car and waved at the beautiful green gleam that purred down the street. Most of my childhood was spent in the middle of the backseat, sans seatbelt, looking at my dad driving proudly with his two girls. He'd have one arm slung over the passenger side as Mom's head rested on the red leather. She would smile up at the sky, her dark curls bouncing in the breeze. Every so often she would tilt her head and smile at Dad, who just sang along to whatever Elvis song came out of the new cassette player he'd installed.

This time, I sat in the passenger seat. My short curls never quite hit my face, but they were growing puffier by the minute in the wind. Dad took his usual route around Southold. We passed the old potato farms that had turned into Pindar, Lenz and Raphael vineyards. Miles of neat rows of green grape vine wrapped around wire had just sprouted with the first buds of Gewürztraminer. We drove past Krupski's farm stand, where the summer help was pulling in unsold pots of impatiens. Past the front of our brick high school and the soccer fields Maria used to play on, which always smelled like freshly cut grass. And finally past Jockey Creek, where Topper created a myth that still lives on in my dad's garage. On this ride, as I took in the sights of the town, while Dad hummed along to the song, pretending that my silence didn't bother him. Once we drove the car into the garage and turned off the engine, neither of us made a move to get out. We finished listening to "Can't Helping Falling in Love," and then Dad finally spoke.

"You wanna talk about it, kiddo?"

"Nah," I said, fidgeting with the shiny silver lock on the glove compartment. "Nothing to talk about."

"Then you want to tell me about that neighbor of yours you're so fond of?"

"Let's just say he wasn't so fond of me."

Dad just huffed in objection and disbelief, the way he normally did when I got rejected by a boy he could beat the crap out of. "Well, then something's seriously wrong with him. But you should've known that from the start. After all, he doesn't buy American."

"No. I'm just not his type, Dad. I'm not . . . put together."

"You look together to me. Your fingers are on your hands. Your toes are on your feet. Got ten of each."

"No, Dad, I mean I'm not pretty enough. I swear too much. I don't care about my breath. Musicals make me sick . . ."

"Wait, wait, wait," Dad interrupted as he turned to face me. "You listen to me, Geraldine Agnes O'Brien. You are the spitting image of your mother. And your mother was the most beautiful woman I or anyone our graduating class ever laid eyes on. Jesus, I never showed Elvis a picture of her because I was too damn scared he'd try to steal her."

He was right: I was the spitting image of my mother.

A strong German woman with soft, dark features. Except that my mother knew how to make herself look like a movie star. In her senior high school portrait, she resembled Marilyn Monroe when she was Norma Jean Baker. The kind of girl men wanted desperately to have on their arm. Growing up, people always reminded me of the resemblance. A trait I used to be proud of. After she left, I never touched a bit of makeup or let my hair grow longer than my shoulders. I knew with a bit of help, I could have her face. I was just terrified that with that face, I'd get her heart too.

"Well, I'm not her. I can't just charm people the way she did. Maybe if I could twirl my hair around my finger or look normal in a skirt, I would stand a chance of winning someone like Todd."

"Someone like Todd? You talk about this guy as if he's the second coming. What makes him so special?"

This question made me think. What made him so special? We hadn't really dated. He never bought me dinner other than pizza. Flowers would be out of the question. He never even asked what my weekend plans were. So what made him so special? I scratched my neck.

That was it. It was the way he casually reached over and scratched the back of my neck during the news without wondering if I itched there. I remember resting my head on his leg and feeling his hands rub my neck while he concentrated on the recap of the Yankees game. Every so often I would look up at him. This would break his concentration and he would peer down at me and smile. I couldn't remember a time when I'd felt so comfortable. So present. I didn't want to be anywhere in the world other than where I was at that moment. I was exactly where my heart wanted me to be. Lying in his lap, watching the news. My mind cleared and I turned to Dad.

"He wasn't afraid of me," I answered as I wiped a tear from my face. "At least I thought so. Now he's terrified."

Dad pulled out a red handkerchief from his back pocket and handed it to me. "Well, did you do anything to scare him?"

I pulled out a rubber during foreplay, I thought, but I couldn't tell Dad that. Still, my answer was honest. "I don't think so." My words were muffled by the handkerchief as I blew my nose.

Dad chuckled to himself and slapped his oil-stained Levi's. "Well, if you didn't do anything, then he's either chicken shit or in love with you." He got out of the car still laughing to himself. I followed him out of the garage and into the house, completely confused.

"He's not that," I said as I followed him into the kitchen.

"Not what? In love or terrified? Is either so shocking?" he asked as he dug through the freezer. "You want a creamsicle?"

"No. I mean yes."

"Is that no, you don't want a creamsicle or no, he couldn't possibility be scared to be in love with a beautiful, smart and handy young woman like yourself?"

"Possible? No. Popsicle? Yes."

Dad passed me a creamsicle that was still smoking from the cold. He unwrapped his halfway before taking an enormous bite. "Geri, I sat in a tank on the border of West Germany and Czechoslovakia next to a seven-foot border guard who wore a green felt cape and walked a German shepherd that looked like it'd never been fed. That fear pales compared to what I felt when I asked your mother if I could drive her home from the Halloween dance." Dad shook off a shiver. I couldn't tell if it was from the ice cream or the thought of asking Mom out. "Sweetie, trust me. You only beat feet if you think you're going to lose something. Your dreams, your limbs, your kid or your heart. Only three of them are decent excuses to run."

I just stood in the kitchen, digesting this statement as I watched my father lumber down the darkened hallway into the family room. He plopped into his favorite worn leather recliner. Still contemplating what he'd said over my creamsicle, I called out to him. "Did you ever run? For the wrong reason?"

"Sure I did. Every man does at some point or another," he said as he reached behind his back for the remote that he always sat on. "But you stop once your get your wits about you. Always do."

The glow of the television lit up the dark room as canned laughter from an old episode of *All in the Family* filled the silence. My reply was so soft that no one but a ghost could hear. "She didn't."

That night, as I lay in my twin bed in my childhood bedroom, I looked past the old Duran Duran poster I'd never taken down to the crimson and gold velvet curtains that Mom put up in my bedroom on my seventh birthday. Dad always felt they were a bit gaudy for a kid's bedroom, but Mom would say that velvet curtains made houses feel like castles and girls feel like queens. But really the only thing they were good for was blocking out all the sunlight that came in through the windows. On the afternoons when Mom never left her room and just stared up at the valances bordered in gold cord, I imagined she felt like anything but a queen. Those days I would sit at the end of her bed, telling her stories I made up about princesses and fairies, hoping I would hit on something that might spark a smile and jolt her out of bed. That never worked. When I got to the happily ever after part, she would say my story was lovely and ask if

I would just give her some time alone. I would leave the room but would stop just outside the bedroom door. I hid behind it until I could hear her breathing steadily in sleep. When I was sure that the little pills with the *V* etched in them had knocked her out, I would creep back onto the bed and stroke her hand. With each stroke I repeated a rosary of wishes, the Hail Mary of which was, "Please God, make her be happy here."

I lay in my bed and let out a quiet whistle. Within seconds, J. T. appeared from behind one of the curtain panels and took a bow. His normal white blazer was replaced by a white T-shirt. I guess he dressed down for the country.

"And for my next number, I'd like to recite, 'Ode to a Grecian Urn,'" he said as he ran his hands over the embroidered fabric. "Why don't you get rid of these?" he asked.

"Don't have anything to take their place," I replied. This was the pat answer Dad always gave when I asked him to redecorate. From the olive carpeting that never looked clean to the coffee table that took up way too much space in the living room, anything that Mom had found a place for, Dad didn't want to move. All the artifacts in the house were exactly where she'd wanted them. Too bad she never had a clue where to put the people who belonged in it.

J. T. crawled onto the bed and held my hand, stroking each knuckle with the pad of his thumb. He finished my thought. "Do *you* know where you belong?"

"No," I whispered. "I thought I did for a minute, but now I'm not so sure."

J. T. put my hand down and stretched his long frame out next to me. He placed his head alongside mine as we looked at the curtains. "Maybe it's time you start thinking about taking down things that block out so much light," he said softly in my ear. "And figure out where you do belong."

13

Pick A Sign, Any Sign

For the rest of the weekend at home and through the entire bus ride back to the city, the question J. T. had posed looped through my head. Where *did* I belong? What move, if any, could change everything? Instead of working on my new-and-improved query letter, I let my mind race. I knew that living with Emmy wasn't the problem. The location of the apartment might be the answer. But even if I found another place, getting Emmy to move would be almost impossible. And even if I could persuade her, I didn't know if I was ready to leave the only common ground I shared with Todd. I kept shifting from one area of my life to another, hoping some easily changeable aspect would float to the top and present itself. Nothing but the same problem appeared. My job. Nothing would change in my life unless I left my job.

During my Monday morning commute, I took Poppy's advice. "If you can't change it, give it to God. He figures crap out." So that's exactly what I did. When I got on the subway, I found a car with a few empty spaces to sit—provided in large part by a street violinist who kept poking commuters in the face with his bow during his truncated version of "Devil Went Down to Georgia." Looking up at an advertisement for Dr. Zizmor's new back-to-work chemical peel,

I wrapped my hands around my MetroCard and posed my question to God.

"Please, Jesus, Mary, Joseph or God—or whoever is taking requests now—I need your help. I want to retire from a career of scaring children into eating all their vegetables. I don't want kids to grow up thinking that Joan of Arc is famous for being in a kid's burger meal. I don't want to be known as the woman who said that women's right to vote won't sell in the big markets like cannibalism. Please Jesus, Mary, Joseph or God, give me a sign. If I can't get some form of film job because of my history, then please tell me where I can start over. Where should I be? Where do I belong?"

The train let us out and I made my way up to the street. It smelled like rain, but the sun strained its way through the clouds, causing a few of its rays to beam over the buildings. When I turned the corner onto Madison Avenue I only needed to look ahead of me to see that my question had been answered. I rubbed my eyes in amazement. It had only taken a New York minute for Jesus, Mary, Joseph or God to rally.

There, on the block where I worked, was a film shoot.

Up and down Madison Avenue, flatbed trucks sat loaded with baby klieg lights, stands and film equipment wrapped in sound blankets. Grips and gaffers were pulling out rain tarps as people huddled on the corners, hoping to catch a glimpse of a famous actor. A security guard let me through the barricade after I showed him my building ID. As I walked slowly past the workers, my eyes scoured the scene, absorbing all the mechanical excitement of the set. One of the burly gaffers stepped down from a lighting truck with yards of cable coiled over both his shoulders. He made a quick stop at craft services to grab a bagel, which he held between his teeth as he walked. I hustled up to him, hoping to get my verbal résumé in before he could take the bagel out.

I tapped him on the shoulder as I walked alongside him. "Excuse me. Hi. I was wondering if you guys needed an extra hand?"

"Whaaaa?" he said through the bagel.

"You know, thought you might need some help. Looks like a pretty big shoot," I said as we both ducked under the boom microphone. "I could help you carry some of these cables. I know I don't look like much, but people around the office call me farm strong. But I might just seem strong because the women I work with have long nails and they don't like to lift anything that they can't grab by their palms. But I know how to operate most sound and sixteen-millimeter equipment. Nagras, Bolexes, even an Airre. And I know how to work on engines. Cars, trucks, lawnmowers. Possibly a semi, although I've never tried. Antique cars aren't a problem unless they're foreign and made before Nineteen thirty-two. You might not need that sort of help now, but it's good to know . . ."

He stopped and turned to me. With a full mouth he started to speak. "Wah, quid, we whad eh." I took the bagel out of his mouth. "Nah, kid, we got it under control."

"I know what I'm doing. I studied film in college and I . . ."

"No, really. That's okay. We're all set here," he said as he turned and continued on his way. I looked down at the slimy cinnamon raisin bagel in my hand. I called out to him.

"Sir! Excuse me. You still want this?" I asked as I held up the half-chewed bagel. "No sense wasting something perfectly good."

I must have looked pretty pathetic because when he looked back at me, he let out a huge sigh. He trudged back.

"Look, there's a tech list at the mayor's office. If you want to help, you can check that out. And my name's Ralph. If you see a posting for 'Commercial—Chunky Soup,' say I referred you. I don't know if it will get you far. I'm no Scorcese. But it's a start."

He might as well have been Scorcese. My spirits lit up immediately. "Thanks! Thanks a lot, sir. I mean Ralph. I mean Mr. Ralph." I leapt forward and gave him a hug, which nearly sent him tumbling backward from the weight of the cables. After steadying him, I jammed the bagel back in his mouth and ran up the street. My feet barely touched the sidewalk. When I reached the front of my office building and looked up at the big gold letters that read JUNIOR VARSITY PUBLISHING, I sucked in my breath, puffed out my chest and said defiantly, "Kismet."

The elevator, although packed with the normal cast of characters, felt less like a crush and more like one enormous hug. I made my way out past Berta, the receptionist.

"How's the writing going, Geri?"

"Wonderful, Berta!" I said with a spring in my step and a goofy grin on my face. Then, like clockwork, Howard the mailroom man came through with his cart.

"Hey, Geri! Always on time. Like the sun!"

I inhaled his cologne and stepped past. "Thanks, Howard. And by the way, you smell great."

He blushed. "Why, thanks, Geri. I don't think I've ever seen you this happy. You in love?"

As Daisy kiss-ass Dickinson walked by on the way to the company crapper, she stopped short to hear my reply. I answered, "Why, yes. His name is Ralph."

Sally hadn't arrived at work yet when I got to my desk. I switched on the computer and began to address my resignation letter. While typing the words, "I regret . . ." I felt a hand land on my shoulder. I quickly minimized the screen as Hedda's face and scent came close to my ear.

"I need to see you in my office," she said with none of

her normal morning cheer. I followed her in and looked at my watch. I had no idea what she could want this early. With two cups of Starbucks on her desk and her computer already booted up, she appeared to have been at work for quite some time. She closed the door after me before she made her way behind the long glass desk.

"Have a seat," she said as she picked up the phone. "I need to finish up this call."

My mind raced through possible scenarios. Maybe I wouldn't have a chance to quit. Maybe I was getting fired. A hard lump formed in my throat as my rent check burned into my mind. I couldn't get fired again. If I did, then I would never land a job at Dairy Queen, let alone a production company. What would I tell my dad? What would Emmy do? Rubbing my sweaty hands on my knees, I listened in to her conversation, hoping to pick up a clue.

"I told you before. Kids were your brilliant idea; you keep them," she said as she opened her second venti mocha and dumped three packages of artificial sweetener into it. She put her hand over the receiver and mouthed, "Only be a second," then continued in a stern voice. "Kids are noisy, whiny and smell like shit most of the time. And I'll tell you this, I'm not buying another stinking old goat to take care of them. You can give them away or put them up for adoption, I don't care. I'm sure someone in the country will love to take care of them and give them a home. They can play out in the grass; shit in the yard; do whatever the hell kids like to do. I bet they'll friggin' love it. Are we understanding each other here?"

Blood drained from my face as I looked over at the photograph of her two sons lying face down on a pile of papers. I gulped loudly. She slammed down the phone.

"Goats," she said as she threw her hands in the air.

"I asked them to bring in one adult goat for the book signing and they brought in a stable of kids. The handler took off. Now the vendor wants us to help him get rid of them."

My eyes inadvertently rolled back in relief. Relief that didn't last very long as she folded her arms over her chest and took a hard look at me. "I've been meaning to have this conversation with you for a while now, Geri."

I stuttered. "Funny you should mention that. I was going to ask you . . . or rather tell you . . ."

"How long have you been with us?"

"Five years. Give or take eight months and fifteen days."

"Before you speak, I want you to know that some of us on the executive side are on to you. We've noticed the level of work you've been doing here."

"I can explain, Hedda . . ."

"We were all aware of the Book TV incident and were willing to overlook it. To be honest, we've overlooked many things with you. But we, mostly I, have decided that we can't overlook certain things anymore. It's not good business. And we are a business, first and foremost. And unless everyone is on board, we are going to sink."

"I know. And this is a great business. But I think . . ."

"Geri, we want you as part of our management team."

The words hung in the air like a fart in a steam room. Her face cracked a smile as my eyes bugged and my mouth opened to let out a silent scream. "Excuse me?"

She got up from behind her desk and walked over to me. "Your ideas have been nothing short of stellar. We have seen you shed your television skin only to find your niche here in children's publishing. Maybe your falling asleep at the camera was fate's way of sending you to us. Where we think you belong."

The room started to spin. My mouth seemed to be completely devoid of saliva and my right eye began to twitch.

Hedda leaned over, causing her perfume to wrap around me like fog.

"There will be a pay raise, of course. A large one. Well, large by publishing standards. A small window office, fifty shares of stock and this." She slipped something small and shiny out of her Chanel suit pocket and handed it to me. In her hand was a gold American Express corporate card with my name on it. "Sorry for being presumptuous. I just wanted you to see it before you accepted."

My shaky hand reached out and took the card from hers. I ran my index finger over the shiny surface. *So this is what my name looks like embossed on faux gold plastic.* The sound of her voice became hollow and distant, as if she were calling out to me from the top of an empty stairwell.

"I've seen a great change in you, Geri. And I must say, I like it. I want you more immersed in this company. So? What do you say?"

I looked out the window. The first drops of rain started to nick the glass. The sky grew black; within a minute it would pour. Somewhere out there is my dream of making movies, I thought. Somewhere, out there was Ralph. Somewhere out there, Ralph was getting wet. I looked back down at the card.

Somewhere out there, Ralph is running the risk of getting electrocuted.

When I returned to my computer I maximized my half-assed attempt at a resignation letter. Sally, now at her desk, looked up at me while munching on her bacon, egg and cheese.

"You okay? You look like you're going to ralph."

The cursor flashed on the *t* at the end of the word *regret*. Instantly enraged at myself, the fates, Jesus, Mary, Joseph and God, I slammed my hand down on my keyboard.

"Damn it!"

14

No Idea

As my new corporate card sat with the bartender keeping our tab, shot glasses bounced off the table and into our mouths at the darkened bar called *No Idea*. The bar's name alone made it the perfect spot to celebrate my promotion. After adjusting to the shock, I called Emmy and Maria from my new office and invited them to meet Sally and me for a celebratory dinner. Maria declined as she was called onto a late shift. After I told her my news, a long pause ensued before she said, "Good luck with that." This came out with the same enthusiasm as "You failed the Bar" or "You have genital warts."

Emmy's response was considerably more enthusiastic. She arrived at the bar, full of cheer and optimism, with an appropriate Hallmark card and a gift. The card was printed with glitter lettering that read, "Reach for the Stars," and there was an adjoining gift of a brown speckled rock paperweight engraved with the word COURAGE. I didn't quite get how a courage rock worked, as I normally didn't get my strength from a ten-dollar chunk of jasper, but Emmy instructed me to rub it anytime I felt insecure. I thanked her for the thoughtful gift and figured by the end of the week, the rock would probably just read RAGE.

Sally had already downed her fourth Kamikaze shot by

the time a waitress with a sprawling tribal tattoo on her lower back brought us another round of drinks and a side of mustard. Rightfully indignant and half in the bag, Sally seemed to be talking more to her shot glass than to Emmy and myself.

"Imagine that. You go in to quit and bam! Hedda makes you management. Me? I have to wait until someone dies. But not Geri. Geri just waltzes in and they give her a window office." Sally waved her arms in the air to call the waitress back for another round. "I can't think of anything more ironic. Well, except the fact that my hair always looks the best right before I go to bed."

Looking down at the swirling flecks of gold in my Goldschlager, I couldn't help thinking of Ralph. I wondered if he would look for me in the coming weeks. Wondered if he would be disappointed when I never showed up. Wondered if he ever finished that bagel.

Emmy leaned over to catch my eye. "Geri? You okay? You don't look very happy with your decision," she said as she took a sip of her cranberry and seltzer. "What were you going to do when you quit?"

"I was thinking maybe I could get something in film again."

"But you tried that before," she said.

"I know. Thought maybe there was a statute of limitations on screwing up. I mean, making movies is a big business. They always need production assistants," I said hopefully. "The money isn't that great, but . . ."

"Great? It pays nothing to start. And you would have to spend long hours outside, which would take away from mailing out your screenplay. And you'd have to look for a new job every six weeks. And all they ever do is eat from those tables on the street, and you hate eating al fresco."

"But I'd be doing what I love. I think."

"Now you love money!" Sally exploded. "And stock options and business cards with the little red and gray J. V. pom-pom in the corner," she added sadly. "And company cars that take you to company dinners."

"Well, I think it's wonderful," Emmy said defiantly. "Your promotion might be the best thing that's ever happened to you."

"You think?"

"Shitballs!" Sally yelled. "Geri, don't you realize you will never have to take a typing test again? You've graduated!"

"To what? Corporate yes woman?"

"Then why did you take it?" Emmy asked.

"I asked for a sign," I said as I stared at Sally dipping fries into her beer. "I guess I didn't want to wait any longer."

"Well, if that was your sign, then waiting was worth it. Take Bryan and me, for instance. It took years, but now it seems as if it could all pay off."

Sally perked up and pointed a soggy fry in my direction. "I agree, Emmy. What have I told you, Geri? Waiting is always worth it."

"A sign is one thing. Or waiting for a particular man. But intercourse, Sally? Come on. Your virginity is a technicality." I began to eat my ten-pound burger, just happy the subject had finally switched from my soaring publishing career. "And I hate to be the one to burst your illusion, but sex isn't all that."

"Well, if you're such an expert, how come you're not dating?"

"Besides the fact that there are about as many available men in Manhattan as there are parking spots?"

Emmy, unflinching in her optimism, pulled out her mother's wisdom as the sign for FLASH 'EM FRIDAYS—LADIES DRINK FREE FOR A PEEK loomed in the background. "It's like Mom always said. Every time a woman says that there are no good guys out there, a nice man somewhere complains . . ."

". . . that there are no good girls," Sally and I chimed in. We all took a sip of our respective drinks quietly, then collectively uttered the word, "Bullshit."

"Well, I still think waiting is worth it. I'm going to tell my husband on my wedding night that I . . ."

"Only blew guys for ten years?" I answered.

"Still a virgin, baby. Still a virgin."

"Remind me again what your definition of losing one's virginity is?" I asked.

"When a man puts his pee-nee in you." Sally demonstrated this by thrusting her right index finger in and out of her left hand.

"But if you had oral sex, then technically his 'pee-nee,' as you call it, *has* been in you," I replied.

"But he didn't break the hymen."

"But your hymen could have broken in gym class," Emmy said.

"Or it could have disintegrated by now."

"Very friggin' funny," Sally said as she twirled around the salt shaker.

"And what about other parts?" I continued.

"What other parts?" Emmy asked.

"Well, by Sally's definition here, she could take it up the pooper and she would still be a virgin."

"Oh, no. She wouldn't be," Emmy said, shaking her head. "Would she?"

Sally wiped her mouth with her napkin, put it gently on the table and leaned in with her elbows. "Kids, a man could strap on a dildo, put that inside your vagina while his penis was in your butt and you'd still be walking out of the room with your virginity intact."

My burger became suddenly unappetizing. "I don't know if you'd be walking."

Emmy's expression was a mix of horror and enlightenment, as if Sally had just stumbled on a way to prove quantum physics by using the tip calculator function on her cellphone. "That's . . . so . . . gross. . . ."

"That's life," Sally said as she salted the inside of her thumb. "And it's not as gross as you think."

Emmy and I almost puked in unison. Sally, unfazed, raised her glass. "On that note, let's have a toast."

"To anal sex?" I asked.

"No. To you, Geri. Other than myself, it couldn't have happened to a better girl."

"May all good things come to those who wait," Emmy added.

"To the refrigerator door," I said before we all knocked back our drinks. Our waitress came back with my gleaming new corporate gold card peaking out from under a leather bill folder. I checked the tip math with Emmy and signed my name. The waitress did a double take on the bill.

"Wow, thanks, Ms. O'Brien."

"Don't thank me. Thank Junior Varsity Publishing," I said as I put the card back in my wallet. "It's where dreams go to die."

"You keep on writing, girl," Emmy said as she patted my elbow with pride.

The waitress and I answered in unison.

"Of course I will."

Walking out of the dark bar and into the early evening night, Emmy and I steadied Sally as she carefully placed one drunken foot in front of the other. Sally reassured us that her puking in the bathroom was more a result of bad mayonnaise than seven shots of limy alcohol. By the time we got to the end of the block, Sally turned a soft shade of pea green and couldn't continue.

"You want to go back to the bar and throw up some more?" Emmy asked as she held Sally's shoulder.

"No, I just need to rest," Sally answered weakly. She stopped and put her hands up to steady herself against the large windows of the Gramercy Park Tavern, one of the most fashionable and expensive restaurants in all of Manhattan. The stylish couple eating their escargot on the other side of the glass looked at Sally in silent terror as she stared down at their plates.

"Are those snails?"

Then it hit. A pounding spray of vomit exploded out of Sally's mouth all over the restaurant window. Inside, mayhem ensued. Like good friends who've just witnessed the most embarrassing moment of another friend's life, Emmy and I stood motionless in shock and held in fits of laughter as Sally wiped her mouth on the sleeve of her Burberry raincoat. Before I could dig through my gift bag to find some tissue paper to absorb the puke, an attractive Indian waiter ran out of the restaurant with a handful of cloth napkins. He patted down her face as she appeared to tear up in embarrassment.

"Are you okay, miss?" he asked. Sally nodded shyly that she was. "Did you come with friends?" he continued.

"No," she whimpered as she shot us a glance not to come over. "I think I ate some bad mayonnaise."

"Poor thing. Let me call a cab for you."

As Sally was lovingly cleaned up by the hot Indian waiter, Emmy and I walked a safe distance away.

"I hope he's not upset when he finds out her ass isn't a virgin," I said.

Emmy turned toward me and whispered, "How does she

do that? If it were me, I wouldn't be able to show my face below Fourteenth Street ever again. She winds up getting a date!"

"It's the nails," Sally answered as she walked up to us, wearing a pout. "I hate you both. And his name is Habibe." She held up a spew-drizzled napkin with his phone number on it.

"You are the luckiest girl alive," I said.

"No thanks to you." Sally tried to slap me on the shoulder but missed. Instead she hit my bag, sending the card, my rock and my wallet out into the street. As Emmy, Sally and I scurried into the road to retrieve my belongings, I noticed the courage rock had landed near the intersection. I ran out into the street to grab it just as a black town car came screeching to a halt a few feet from me. The smell of burned rubber rose from the wheels as I slowly looked up. An angry bald man stuck his head out the driver's window and yelled, "You trying to get yourself killed, lady?"

"Sorry," I said as I stood up, holding out the courage rock as evidence of my stupidity.

"Sorry isn't going to get you out of a body bag. Watch where you're going."

As the car slowly began to drive past me through the intersection, I noticed a set of eyes locked onto mine from the half-open tinted window in the backseat. I could only make out part of his face, but the blue of his eyes and the blond brows were undoubtedly J. T.'s. I couldn't help smiling as the car drove past. I remained in the intersection until the car and its passenger drifted out of view. I even held my hand up to wave good-bye. Emmy's voice and a loud horn behind me knocked me out of my haze.

"Geri! The light's changing! Get back!"

I ran out of the street and hopped back onto the curb.

Emmy looked at me in shock as Sally tried to rub a large puke stain out of her coat.

"Why did you run out there? You could've been killed!" Emmy reprimanded.

I just smiled at her and handed her the rock. "How else was I going to get my courage back?"

15

Green Means Stop

The next morning, the morning of my first real day of being a manager, I woke up the same way many other up-and-coming young executives do—hung over. Soaking wet from night sweats with a headache that felt as if my brain had drained out through the back of my skull onto my pillow, I lay in bed and wondered if the last twenty-four hours had been some sort of bizarre dream. *Did I really make a contact on a film shoot? Did I get promoted? Did Sally throw up on the windows of Gramercy Park Tavern?* I propped myself up on my elbows and looked out of my window.

Is that Maria?

I rubbed my eyes and crawled to the window ledge. Past the swirling bars of the fire escape and the hanging philodendron, I looked right into the window of the nudists' apartment across the street. Only this morning they didn't look like a couple of old happy hippies sipping their morning green tea. They looked concerned. And so did the cops who were standing in the middle of the room. Maria walked over to the window and turned her flashlight on and off repeatedly in hopes of getting my attention. I waved back, signaling that I saw. As the woman explained something to Patrick, using sweeping hand gestures, Maria stuck her pinkie and thumb out by her face, mouthing the words, "I'll call you."

I crawled back into bed and threw the blanket over my head. "Oh, God," I thought. "This can't be good."

By the time I got in to work, my headache had moved down from orange alert to yellow alert, courtesy of six Advil and showering with my mouth open. Neither Berta nor mailroom Howard had heard about my promotion until Daisy Dickinson barged through the door.

"Geri! You're moving into a window office. Are you guys making room for more filing cabinets?"

"I got promoted, Daisy," I answered, wanting to smack her.

"Really?" she said as she cocked her head in disbelief. "I didn't know anyone had left the company. Who are you replacing?"

"Your mom," I wanted to say but cut the insult short. "Nobody."

"Really? Is Sally pissed?"

Desperate to escape the backhanded insults, I said, "I have to run."

The door to my new office had already been opened when I walked in. I stood in the doorway and surveyed my new domain. Clean, tidy and smelling like cat. I spent the first two hours in my new digs sniffing around, trying to detect the source of the odor. The previous occupant, a contracts director, used to bring in her cat on half-day Fridays during the summer. She would head to her summer share on the Hampton Jitney with her tabby in a carry-on. Rumor had it the cat was terrified of the stapler and it must have pissed somewhere in the room to show its displeasure. I wouldn't blame it, though. If I was getting dragged to Quogue in a Le Sportsac, I would too.

As I crouched on the floor with my nose to the rose-colored carpet, Sally walked in with a stack of papers, looking almost chipper.

"Can I get you something? Like a chair and a clue, perhaps?"

"No. But you can get me a can of Lysol and a Bloody Mary."

"Very funny. By the way, two things: One, I told that guy from the restaurant I'd call him around lunch. Can I use your office?"

"Sure," I said, getting up. "Sally, aren't you hung over? I had half as many drinks as you and I feel like shit."

"Me? I never get hung over. I feel great. Must be my intact hymen soaking up all the alcohol. And secondly, pick up your phone. Someone's on line two."

"Okay. Thanks," I said, crawling up to my desk to get to the phone.

"It's the flashing green light. Remember, I'm not your friggin' secretary. If I have to pick up your line, I'm going to say you can't answer the phone because you're too busy giving someone a blow job."

"Great. They'll think you're on a coffee break," I retorted as I picked up the phone. "Hello, this is Geri."

"Hey, Geri, it's me."

There was no need for him to say who it was. By the hairs that raised on my arms and the sudden twitch of my lower intestine, I knew who was on the other end of the line.

"Hi, Teah . . . Todd," I sputtered schizophrenically. Sally, halfway out the door, abruptly stopped her exit and turned on her heel. We both stared at each other with the same openmouthed expression. "Give me one sec," I spat as I hit the hold button. While I held my hand over the receiver, as if he could still hear me on hold, Sally and I began a rapid-fire analysis of the situation.

"What do you think he wants?" I asked.

"I don't know, what do *you* think he wants?"

"I don't know. That's why I'm asking you."

"Ask him."

"I can't."

"Sure you can."

"He won't talk to me."

"He's on the phone."

"I don't know how to sound."

"Are you happy?" she asked, forcing a fake smile, as if I needed an example of what happy was.

"Yes?"

"Are you pissed?"

"Yes?"

"Sound aloof."

"What does aloof sound like?"

Sally ran her hands in the air quickly, looking for an explanation. "Hung over!"

"Okay. Hung over. I can do hung over." I took a deep breath, pulled my hand away from the receiver and pressed the button. All the lights on the phone suddenly went out.

"Shit!" I yelled. "I just hung up on him!"

"That's not aloof. That's evasive," Sally replied.

"Shit! Shit, shit, shit," I repeated as I stared at the phone, hoping that uttering the word *shit* would make him call back. "What did I do?"

"Hitting the hold button twice disconnects the call. Don't worry. He'll call back."

"No, he won't. I know he won't. Guys never call me back. I screwed up . . ."

"Geri?" Sally interrupted.

"What?"

"Line two's blinking again," she said, pointing to my phone.

"What? Oh." I hit the button and tried in my most professional voice to sound hung over. "Junior Varsity Publishing, this is Geraldine Agnes O'Brien, Marketing Manager. How can I . . ."

"Geri, it's Todd."

"Oh, Todd. I'm sorry. First day with the new phone," I said as Sally walked out of the office with both fingers crossed, mouthing, "Good luck."

Todd sounded sweet as he replied, "Don't lie. You hung up on me. And you can do it again. Just let me ask you something first."

I giggled to myself. Damn it, he was adorable. Even over the phone. "What is it?"

"Well, first, how are you?"

"Good. Busy. I got a promo . . ." Before I could finish bragging, Hedda barged in to the room.

"Jesus Christ, it smells like cat piss in here!" she hollered.

"Wait . . . Todd . . . hold on." I put my hand over the receiver, not willing to run the risk of losing him again on hold. "Hedda, can I help you?"

"Come by my office when you're done. I want you to help Sally move my desk around. Too many UV rays are hitting me in the late afternoon. Figure I might save a few years and a few thousand dollars on surgery if we feng shui my office. And make sure you call maintenance about this smell."

"Sure," I answered, praying that Todd hadn't heard that. Hedda promptly left the room, leaving the office in a fog of L'air du Chat.

Todd stifled a chuckle on the other end of the phone. "Cat piss?"

"If she thought the smell was bad, she should see the hairball that's stuck in my printer."

As I listened to Todd let out a full-blown laugh, I forgot how hurt I was. This felt comfortable, I thought. This felt fun. But then Cassie's face came to mind and the image of her holding that Playbill. This felt fleeting.

"I wanted to talk to you. In person. Will you be home tonight?"

"Yeah."

"Can I come up?"

I didn't know what to say. I desperately wanted to see him, but in the way we used to be with each other. Somehow I knew this night wouldn't end with us in my bed. Or would it? "Sure," I answered shyly. "Come up late."

"I know. After Emmy's asleep."

"Yeah."

"You'd better get going."

"Yeah," I said sadly, wishing even this prosaic conversation wouldn't end. "I've got some furniture to move."

"Remember, lift with the knees, not the lower back."

"Thanks for the tip."

"See you."

"See you," I said. I didn't hang up the phone. I just sat there and let the phone rest in the crook of my neck as I looked at the little green light, waiting for it to go out.

16

Like Father, Like Son

After hours of e-mailing during a completely unproductive work day, Sally and I came up with three distinct conclusions: 1) Don't buy a new outfit, which would turn into a visual reminder of the night I got my heart smashed. 2) Don't cry. 3) Move bowels at work, not at home. The front door faces the bathroom.

I also prepared many mini-speeches. My personal favorite started, "You know how many men would have given their eyeteeth to sleep with me that night?" The question being rhetorical as I, myself, had no idea how many men would have given a filling, let alone a prominent tooth, for the chance to go to bed with me. Other than a guy named Sparrow, who had a hopeless crush on me in high school because I didn't laugh at him when he got an erection looking at nude paintings in art class. The truth was, I didn't notice because I was too busy daydreaming about what my hand would look like if I were Anne Boleyn and had six fingers. Had I known he was sporting wood, I probably would have laughed my butt off. But my grinless expression doubled for tenderness in his head. He liked me for two years. Until a girl who only listened to The Cure moved in from Yaphank. Then I went from art to history. But in a pinch, I thought he would still have sex with me. He and any men with either a sex addiction or a fetish for polyester pantsuits. But the mini-speech still sounded good and could pass for the truth, if only in theory.

The rest of the day raced by. It wasn't until the clock hit 10:00 that each minute seemed to crawl. By the end of the 10 o'clock news, I just sat on the couch and stared at the clock on the DVD player. I didn't tell Emmy about Todd's call. I knew she would stay awake to discuss all its different possible meanings. By the time the eleven o'clock news ended, I'd almost worked myself into a panic. Deciding I didn't want to be stood up in my own home, I started to get ready for bed. It wasn't until I was about to put on my old T-shirt that Todd knocked softly on the door.

My heart leapt into my throat as I looked through the spy hole. There he stood. No smile, just looking down at the floor as if any contact would be too intimate, even through a hole one centimeter in diameter. I opened the door and he walked in; his hand rubbed the back of his neck as he quickly looked around the apartment.

"Emmy asleep?" he whispered.

"Yeah," I said. "Let's go into my room."

We walked the two feet from the living room into my bedroom and closed the door. Feeling awkward, since the bed took up the entire room, I sat down on one corner. Todd just stood.

"Look, I can't stay long, but I wanted to explain about the other night."

"Please do," I answered coolly. Inside, I gave myself a high five for not sounding completely sad.

"It's not that I didn't want to. I totally did. I just couldn't . . . I just didn't want to hurt you."

"Hurt me?" I rolled my eyes and whispered, "Todd, I have

had sex before. I might be rusty, but in a minute I would have gotten used to . . ."

"No, not physically hurt you. I mean, I didn't want to hurt you when things didn't go anywhere."

Ouch. That did hurt. "You mean you were just using me to get over Cassie?"

"No, I wasn't. Well, maybe at the start. Shit, this is all coming out wrong," he said as he tried to pace in the two-foot space between my bed and the closet. "Geri, I just wanted to protect you."

"Rolling around with me on my bed is protecting me? Protecting me is fighting off a mugger or giving me sun-block in July."

Then he flipped the script. "You know how many guys would have given their left nut to have had sex with you that night?"

All I could do was stutter. Sparrow's name flew out of my head and I couldn't think of one.

"Look, Geri, I like you. My God, I do, but everyone knows you don't fall in love immediately after you get out of a relationship. It doesn't work that way."

It was then I realized why I read books on dating. I obviously had no idea that love kept such a tight schedule.

"My dad's right. It takes time to get over people. He told me that he had a similar situation with my mom. He got out of a long relationship with a girlfriend and said he felt like he fell for the next girl that came along. But he knew it couldn't have been right, so he passed on her. Then bam! In came Mom."

"So what's the deal with Cassie?"

"Cassie wants to make another go at it."

"But she cheated on you!"

"She made a mistake. She's human. And even though

we had our problems, we know each other. Our families grew up close together. My dad and her dad are close. Their offices are on the same block."

As I looked at his expression, I noticed a distinct droop. He'd thought of excuses to stay in the relationship, but not one real reason. I took a deep breath and asked what I needed to know.

"Are you in love with her?"

Then he took a deep breath and looked down. "Geri, we've dated a long time . . ."

"I didn't ask how long you've dated. Are you in love? Do you hear bells when she walks in the room?"

He looked up at me with tired eyes. "It's like Dad says. It's not about bells."

My bottom lip began to quiver. I bit down hard on it as my eyes drifted toward the floor. I wanted to shake him and let him know that I heard bells each and every time he walked through my door, but I didn't. He'd made up his mind to be with Cassie before he would even give me a chance. This fact became clear right at that moment. And in realizing it, I thought I would feel my heart crack in half. But it didn't. He wasn't breaking my heart. He was strangling it.

Todd sat on the bed next to me and rested his chin on my shoulder. "I miss you. More than you know."

I could smell his shirt as his breath grazed my ear. I thought if I just turned my head toward him, our lips would be touching. He waited for my reply. All I could do was look at my feet and pray the tears that I felt crawling up in the corners of my eyes wouldn't spill over while he sat there. He leaned in and pressed his lips firmly on my cheek. He gave me three soft kisses and pulled away. My gaze never broke from the floor as he got up and stood in front of me. He waited a moment but knew I wasn't going to look up or make a motion. The temperature in the room dropped as I sat there frozen, unable and unwilling to look at him.

He walked out of the bedroom. A second later, I heard the front door open and shut. When the sound of his footsteps faded in the hall, a tear broke free from my eye and rolled down the cheek where he'd placed his kiss just a moment before. I whispered to myself, hoping the words would carry themselves downstairs, past his ears and into his heart.

"I miss you too."

16

I Spy

The next morning Maria called the apartment and told Emmy and me to watch our butts and take cabs home after eleven o'clock. The East Side burglar had tried his luck with the couple across the street and gave the woman such a scare she'd never walk around the apartment naked again. It was the second time the burglar had brandished a gun, and Maria thought it was only a matter of time before someone got shot. I decided not to tell Dad; he worried about Emmy and me enough already. But Maria's mom must have gone in for a tune-up and spilled the beans, because the next day I received two tire irons in the mail with a note: "One by the door, one under your bed. Love, Dad."

Between Todd and our friendly neighborhood thief, I became as sensitive to sound as a blind man with no sense of smell. Every slam of the door, every thump, every loud laugh traveled up through the hall and the floorboards to echo in my ears. I assumed that due to Jesus, Mary, Joseph and God's cumulative inability to seal my broken heart, they'd granted me a psychotically keen sense of hearing so that I would know when to exit the apartment. After two successful weeks of dodging Todd and his ex-ex, I gathered that the all-powerful foursome had given him the same gift as well.

This superpower worked wonders in the morning when I left for work but became murder at night. Each thump made me cringe. I couldn't discern whether I was hearing him not bolt out of the room for sex or just throwing his gym bag on the floor. Realizing that pillows around the head lend themselves more to suffocation than quiet and that cotton in the ears makes the sound of my breathing annoyingly loud, I bought one of those sound machines. With the sirens and street noise of Manhattan overlying the subtle sounds of *Rain Forest II*, I drifted off to sleep feeling like I'd wandered into a bad section of the Amazon.

Emmy knew something had happened between Todd and me, even though I never told her about our conversation. I normally fell asleep after the late shows, but those weeks I was in bed before her. As soon as I walked into the apartment, I couldn't seem to keep myself awake. I passed on any dinner she would cook for a bowl of Cap'n Crunch. I blamed my sleepiness on my new job and my lack of appetite on breathing in cat-piss fumes all day. But after losing all feeling in the roof of my mouth due to the abrasive cereal and the night vision in my left eye from malnutrition, I accepted some of Emmy's chicken a la king.

"You feeling better?" she asked as she handed me a bowl.

"Define better."

"Well, better enough to go out with me?"

"You, yes. You and Bryan and his band of merry money men, no."

Emmy just smiled as she kept dishing it out. "Well, it's not going to be just Bryan. It will be you, me, Maria and Sally in the newest, hippest, hottest club in Manhattan. His work buddies will just happen to be there."

"Where?"

"Spy."

My eyebrows rose in surprise. Spy, the most fashionable bar of the week, appeared daily on Page 6's sightings and gained major press when a woman lit her pubic hair on fire just to get the bouncer's attention.

"Are we going to have to burn our beavers?" I asked. "They don't let just anyone in."

"No, silly. We'll be on the list. All we need to do is show up," she said, as if she crashed trendy New York bars on a regular basis. "It will be fun, Geri. And it will be good for you to get out. Just put on your dancing shoes and a smile. We'll blend right in with the crowd."

Emmy's statement couldn't have been further from reality. The truth was eloquently stated by Maria when the four of us got out of a cab and looked at the line of beautiful people waiting to get in.

"Holy fucking fuck," she muttered, dumbstruck.

"I heard they have a VIP lounge that even Jeter couldn't get into," Sally said as her eyes eagerly explored the row of models/socialites waiting on line. They all tapped their spiky heels while chatting on rhinestone-studded cellphones. "You think we'll see any celebrities?"

"You think they'll see us?" I answered as I tried to dislodge a piece of cereal from between my teeth with my fingernail.

Maria patted me on the back. "That's the fucking spirit, Geri!"

Emmy searched the line but couldn't find Bryan. "Everyone must be inside. Let's go to the door. Bryan said he'd leave our names with the bouncer."

Emmy bounded up to the bouncer, who sat directly in front of the entrance to the bar. His enormous frame only allowed for one butt cheek to fit on the bar stool. Looking completely bored and unimpressed while picking his teeth with a toothpick, he drummed his finger on the clipboard that rested on his lap.

"We're on the list. Under Starr," Emmy said, all smiles.

The bouncer didn't even look down at the clipboard. "I don't see it."

"Oh, I'm sure it's there. Hold on. Sally, can I use your cellphone?" Emmy asked.

Sally dug through her bag and gave Emmy her phone. Emmy opened the flip phone, causing the numbers to light up and the phone to play a tinkling synth bell version of "Like a Virgin." Emmy held the musical blue flashlight up to the clipboard. "See? Starr. Party of four."

"Oh, yeah. Starr. Four. Can you please shut that phone off?" he said rolling his eyes. "And there is a dress code."

"Dude, I'll have you know I just bought this at Old Navy. It doesn't get fresher than this," Maria said as she gave him a wink.

He hopped off his stool and unhooked the velvet rope. "Go ahead. Quick."

As I was about to walk past him, I stopped short. "You got another toothpick, buddy? I could really use one. Got a chunk of Capt . . ."

"In. Now!"

After a short walk through a dark hallway and forking over thirty bucks a person to a Kate Moss look-alike, the four of us emerged through a heavy velvet curtain into the main section of the bar. We stopped as soon as we broke through. We all looked up at the magical mirrored room filled with cascading lights and loud trace music. The main floor was open, with a few model types walking around carrying trays. Small intimate tables surrounded the floor with a second-tier balcony that overlooked the whole scene. Large video screens blocked our view of people up there, but we assumed they could see us. After a moment Maria spoke.

"Welcome to the merry old land of Oz, bitches."

Bryan suddenly appeared next to Emmy, holding a blue drink. "Emmy! Glad you could make it."

Emmy's face twinkled as bright as the lights tumbling off the spiral staircases. "Hey, Bryan! You remember Geri and Maria, right? And this is Sally, Geri's co . . ."

"Let's go to the bar. There are some people I want you to meet," he said as he escorted Emmy over to a group of businessmen clustered in the far corner of the room. Emmy followed Bryan while giving us a smile and a shrug. The three of us just surveyed the territory.

"I feel like I should be wearing a green beret and selling cookies," Maria said as two drag queens began to examine each other's fake breasts.

"I'd rather be taking GREs right now," I admitted.

"Come on. Let's get some drinks." Sally grabbed our shoulders and led us to a free stool at the bar.

"Rounds?" asked Maria. "I got first." She plunked her enormous man-wallet on the bar.

The unsettlingly handsome bartender, who was also picking his teeth with a toothpick, slowly made his way to us. "What can I get you?"

"Sally's favorite. Three Kamikaze shots, please."

"We're not allowed to make those shots here," he answered.

"This is a bar, right?" Maria retorted.

"Not that kind of bar."

"How unfucking cool of me!" Maria said as she threw her arms in the air. "Make that a round of blow job shots, then. Sally likes hers with extra cream. And if you got a fresh can of Reddi-wip, be a peach and give it to Geri here first. Whip-its get her geared up to breakdance."

The bartender just stared at Maria. Pulling the toothpick

out of his mouth, he complied with as much enthusiasm as a man taking a laxative. "Three Kamikaze shots. Coming right up."

Waiting for our drinks, we turned and continued to people-watch. At the other end of the bar, Sally and I noticed Emmy standing next to Bryan but talking to a short, bald businessman. Bryan had his back to Emmy as he sipped from a stirring straw in the stunning Ingrid's highball glass.

"Is it me or is everyone here shiny?" Maria questioned.

"Is that the arm-pit hair girl? God, she's really gorgeous," Sally said. "Everyone here is really gorgeous."

"And shiny. Definitely shiny."

The bartender set down three enormous shot glasses filled with the light green concoction. "Three shots for the three lovely ladies."

"Excellent!" Maria cried as we all grabbed a glass. "To troop Three-fourteen." As soon as the liquor hit the back of our throats, the bartender spoke up.

"That'll be thirty-nine dollars."

Each of us spit the shot back into the glass and handed it over to the bartender. Even more disgusted, he wiped his hands and said, "This one's on me."

We each picked up our respective glasses again and began to sip and savor our thirteen-dollar shots. Meanwhile, Emmy broke free from Mr. Suit and headed back over to us. "So? What do you all think?"

I looked over at Ingrid smoothing down the front of Bryan's hair, then over at two high waitresses making out with each other. "This isn't you," I admitted.

"This is history," Maria said as she tried to stuff her wallet in her back pocket. "That round and admission cost more than my outfit."

"Guys, please. I know we paid a lot to get in, but can you stay for just an hour more? Then I promise I'll leave with you."

Maria shook her head. "I don't know if I can last. No one's even dancing."

"They don't have a cabaret license." Emmy pointed to the signs around the bar that read NO DANCING.

"Obviously. This music is going to put me to sleep."

"Guys, please. Just an hour," Emmy begged. She looked back over at Bryan, who now was running his fingers through Ingrid's bangs. "Maybe less."

"We'll be fine," I told Emmy. "You go get your man." Emmy smiled tentatively as she headed back to Bryan. I turned my attention to Sally and Maria. "Well, ladies. Let's make the best of what we got."

"What have we got?" Sally asked as she gingerly sipped her shot.

I opened my wallet and pulled out the shiny gold card. Waving it slowly in front of Maria, I continued. "Free drinks all night. Courtesy of Junior Varsity Publishing if you, Miss Maria, for one night only . . ." I pointed my card up to the DJ booth overlooking the floor.

"Oh, no," she said. "I can't abuse my position like that."

"I'll abuse mine if you abuse yours. Just think, Vodka Collinses, Baybreezes . . ."

"White Russians?" she asked, looking at me with hopeful eyes.

"You can fight osteoporosis all night long if you want to."

"I'll talk to the man."

"Bartender!"

Maria made her way up the spiral staircase to the DJ booth. From our vantage point, Sally and I could watch as the conversation took place. After a moment the DJ produced a CD and a new Madonna song played softly in the background. Maria looked down at Sally and me. I cupped my ear as Sally gave the thumb's up signal to turn up the volume. Maria turned back to the DJ, who appeared to be ignoring her. She reached for the microphone, and soon the entire bar heard her.

"Hey, I know you. Don't you work at the Dollar Store on West . . ."

Suddenly music roared throughout the bar. Sally and I made our way to the open area that served as the dance floor with our drinks. Maria soon joined us, and I handed her a White Russian. Everyone around the bar stood at the edge of the dance floor, too embarrassed to step on, yet too intrigued to look away. The three of us just danced like idiots, knowing that this was the only way we common folk could have any fun. I walked over to Emmy and yelled over the song for her to join us.

"Come on!"

"I can't," she said, looking over at Ingrid.

"Screw Bryan! Screw his friends! Come dance with us!"

"Hold on." Emmy turned around and poked Bryan on the arm. "You wanna dance?"

"You kidding?" he said without even taking his eyes off Ingrid's cleavage. Ingrid laughed out loud as she pointed to Maria and Sally.

"That's not how we do it where I'm from," she cooed. I could see Emmy's fury boiling as she turned to me.

"In a minute."

I walked back to the dance floor to join Maria and Sally, who at this point were do-si-doing in circles. I curbed the urge to walk back and dump a drink on Bryan. I figured if I did that, Ingrid would probably just suck it out of his suit.

"Is she coming?" Sally yelled.

"Nope. She's holding back," I answered.

Maria stopped dancing. She looked past me and pointed. "I wouldn't be so sure about that."

Time suddenly stopped. For one brief, shining moment, we were back on the basketball court at half-time. In the far corner of the open dance floor stood Emmy. Leg extended, toe pointed, chin held high and one hand propped in the air, signaling to all that she was about to take off. Maria and I had sat through many a half-time dance during which Emmy showed off her seven years of gymnastic camp. Now, in the hippest bar in the borough, we were about to witness it again.

"Holy . . . fucking . . . shit," Maria said as the straw fell from her mouth.

"What's she going to do?" Sally asked.

Then, with arms pumping by her sides and legs gunning, Emmy barreled down the dance floor. She lunged into a round off and pounded out three back handsprings into a back tuck. Sticking the landing, she nonchalantly looked back over her shoulder at Ingrid.

"That's how we do it here, bitch."

Maria almost knocked Emmy's legs out from under her as she tried to prop Emmy on her shoulders. And with Emmy's flip, the entire bar rushed onto the dance floor. She had done the impossible. With a gaggle of people raising her up in the air in praise, Emmy had found a way not only to break the ice in the coolest club in all of Manhattan, but also the spell Ingrid had on Bryan. If only for one more night.

Eight or nine drinks later, while I was sandwiched between two crossdressers, a cute, scrappy guy tried to cut in. Yelling over the music, he asked, "Who are you?"

"I'm not sure anymore," I said, thinking I sounded hip.

"I don't know either, but I'd like to find out. Can I buy you a drink?"

"Sure," I yelled. "I think I've blown my credit out of the Spy." Then I became lucid. I thought to myself, stupid joke. Shut up, Geri. Just shut up.

We made our way off the crowded dance floor and up to the bar. His name was Nathan. He had sandy brown hair and a smile that made one side of his mouth curl up. After a minute of introductions, we wound up in a heated debate about the joys and beauty of early filmmaking.

"So, I took my love of beautiful women and emulsion to the next logical step: photography."

"Pornography?" I asked over the music.

"No, photography." He laughed. "Someone once told me if it can be written or thought . . ."

". . . it can be filmed. Stanley Kubrick. Sorry to finish your sentence."

"How did you know I was going to say that?"

"Former film major. Future scriptwriter."

"Very cool," he said as he sipped his drink. "Another artist."

I smiled to myself. Each sip made me find Nathan more and more attractive and pushed Todd further and further out of my field of vision. After all, Nathan and I could understand each other. We were artists. Souls on a common journey of expression. Not an artist and a chiropractor, but real kindred spirits. Maybe he would see the beauty in me. Maybe he wouldn't run away from the idea of having sex with me. This could be good. This might allow me to fall asleep without fake waterfalls and tree frogs.

Then the bartender handed me my gold card and the tab. I looked at the total in shock.

"Five hundred dollars?" I choked out.

The bartender reached over, took the bill and ripped it in half. "Taken care of if you and your cop friend put in a good word about the cabaret license."

"You got it," I said.

Nathan just looked at me in amazement. Suddenly I felt as beautiful as the woman taking our cover charge. "My God, who are you?"

By three o'clock Emmy, Sally, Nathan and I stumbled out of the bar and onto the street, where Maria stood in fighting stance, showing off her self-defense moves to the bouncer. Sally walked into the street with her arms waving in the air for a cab. While our group said good-bye to our new friends, Nathan handed me his card and planted a kiss on my cheek. Afraid I would say something completely ignorant, I just smiled and waved back. The girls piled into the cab as I looked down at the card.

NATHAN FERRY—PHOTOGRAPHER. Geri Ferry, I thought. That sounded stupid. But I'd get used to it.

Just as I was about to jump into the taxi, I heard a man hail a cab. His voice seemed to cut through all the street noise and the base thumping out of the club. Looking over the roof of the taxi, I noticed a cab pull up in front of him. Wearing jeans and a faded red Atari T-shirt, he looked even better than I'd last imagined.

"Hey!" I called out in my drunken haze. He stopped as he was getting into the cab and looked over at me, puzzled. Our eyes locked as I smiled wide. "Red suits you."

J. T. rested his arms on the roof of the cab and looked at me. His face sported the same look of curiosity as that night at the Knickerbocker. He didn't appear to recognize me, but from the way he was studying me, I knew I must have registered somewhere in the back of his mind. His smile was not at the ready as it usually was, but for that moment, I didn't care. Seeing him so clearly felt great. He wouldn't take his eyes off me, even when his cab driver leaned out of the window and yelled.

"Hey, buddy, you going or staying?"

"Geri!" Sally called from inside my cab. "Let's go. I gotta pee."

I looked back over the roof at J. T. and smiled. "See you around."

My drunken mind tried to take a snapshot of his face. I wanted to picture him again like this, but I knew that in the morning I wouldn't be able to keep the image as clear as it was tonight. I hopped into my cab as the girls leaned in to discuss Nathan. But before I answered their questions, I opened up the window and looked into the driver's side mirror. Even as our car turned the corner, he still stood outside his taxi, craning his neck to catch a glimpse of us driving away. Maria brought me out of my trance.

"Let me guess, he's a proctologist," Maria said.

"A teacher!" Emmy yelped.

"A fluffer," said Sally. We all looked at her strangely.

Producing the card, I handed it over to the jury. "A photographer."

The three let out a collective scream of joy.

"So when are you going to see Ansel Adams next?" Maria asked.

"This weekend. He invited me to a gallery opening for one of his friends. Isn't that cool?"

"Well, don't fuck it up."

"Maria!"

"I'm just saying, don't do what you did the last time."

"Maria's right," admitted Sally. "Don't tell him you just got a mole removed."

"Or that you just bombed the apartment for silverfish."

"Or swear," pointed out Sally. "You tend to swear a lot when you're nervous. Guys don't like it when girls swear."

"Okay, okay. I got it," I said. "I'll be someone else for the night."

The three of them relaxed back into their seats and collectively sighed. "Good."

17

Free Gift

Two days before my date with Nathan Ferry, Photographer, Sally and I headed to Victoria's Secret for "provisions." I rarely visited the chain lingerie store since I normally bought my underwear in bulk at a wholesale club, but Sally figured that I might act a bit more sexy on the outside if I had lace on the inside of my butt cheeks.

Pouring over the satin-lined tables of pink thong panties and second skin demi-bras, Sally and I began the awesome task of finding my new dating underwear.

"This is so weird," I said, picking up a nice set of cotton briefs. "Normally I buy my underwear in packs of ten."

Sally walked over to me, pulled down the safe cotton boy shorts and gave me a black mesh thong. "My first rule of dating: Don't buy your intimate apparel where you buy a ten-pound jar of mayonnaise."

"But nobody sees them. Besides, that way I can put off doing laundry for two weeks."

"That's exactly why nobody sees them," she said, ushering me to the changing room. "Try on this sexy combo. It will be perfect unless you're going strapless. Are you going strapless?"

"I haven't thought about it, to be honest."

"Well, you'd better think about it before you buy black

underwear. You want him to see it *after* the clothes come off, not before. You want to be a Stephanie. Not an Annette."

"Huh?"

"*Saturday Night Fever?* Didn't you see the movie?" she said, exasperated. "You want to be like Stephanie, Tony Manero's dancing partner. He thinks this woman is such a class act that he changes the whole scope of his life just to impress her. Not like tacky Annette. The girl's so desperate to get laid by him that she actually hands him condoms. You don't want to be her."

"Yeah, right. Who wants to be that girl?" I mumbled as I tried on the lingerie. Maybe Todd thought I was an Annette. Maybe he considered me so desperate, tacky and presumptuous for owning condoms that he wouldn't think of sleeping with me. But then I thought, who gives a crap? It's the dawn of a new date, and even if I looked like an Annette to Todd, maybe I could look like a Stephanie to Nathan. And in time, Nathan would look like a Todd to me. Then we could look like Paul and Joanne, Ron and Nancy or Sigfried and Roy to everyone else. Looking at myself in the mirror, I examined my chest and said to Sally, who waited outside, "I think this makes my boobs look like my earth science teacher's."

Sally yelled over the door, "It's called form and shape. You're probably not used to it."

"No. It gives me torpedo tits."

Sally opened the door a crack and looked in. After looking at my breasts, she concurred. "Yeah, you could take out a few U-boats with those. Try this one. It's gold, so it won't be visible under your clothes."

"Thanks," I said, closing the door.

"Geri, this might be a good time to have the talk."

"What talk, Mom? I already know where babies come from."

"No, I mean do you have a good razor?"

"It's summertime. I shave my legs."

"I'm not talking about your legs. I'm talking about your vagina."

I quickly opened the door and dragged Sally into the fuchsia-and-white-striped changing room. "Sally!" I tried to whisper.

"When was the last time you mowed down there? I mean, these panties and those hand job instructions we downloaded will do you no good if you look like Sasquatch."

"May I remind you I *did* have a boyfriend at one time. I'm not completely oblivious when it comes to . . . maintenance."

"I'm just saying guys nowadays are weird when it comes to hair down there," she said as she politely looked at her nails while I changed. "Guys are human, like you and me. I mean, anyone will go downtown to Chinatown just as long as they can be sure they're not eating dog when they get there." She looked up at the new gold bra, which adored my breasts. "That's the one."

"Ya think?" I said, looking proudly at my rack. I had to admit, everything looked in place and at attention. "How can you tell?"

"Because you're smiling."

After changing and grabbing the matching panties, I paid for my purchases. I told Sally I wasn't woman enough to pull off a thong. We came to the understanding that even though thongs were sexy, it would not be sexy if I spent the evening trying to root my underwear out of my butt. We walked out of the store and up Third Avenue toward the Fifty-ninth Street subway station. We tried to run through my faults and foibles before she caught the W train back home to Queens.

"Now, I promise that I won't say anything weird," I reassured her.

"And you'll curb your cursing."

"And I'll attempt to curb my cursing. If there's food there, I'll wipe my mouth with a napkin and cut my meat with a knife. And I'll shave so that he doesn't think I'm the Yeti."

"You'll do great, Geri," she said, smiling, "I know you will."

"I think he's cool. I mean, maybe you and Emmy were right. Maybe if you wait long enough, it happens. Maybe this is my New York minute."

"Your what?" Sally asked as she dug through her purse to find her MetroCard.

"My New York minute! The minute I can go from Upper East Side obscure to ultra famous because one Thursday, Harvey Weinstein eats bad Mexican food, gets the runs and it just so happens that *my script* is sitting in the trash can next to his toilet in the company men's room. He knows he's going to be there a while so he picks it up, reads it and bam! Next thing you know, my screenplay is in a bidding war between Miramax and Paramount. That's my New York minute."

She stood there motionless in the middle of the sidewalk with her hand in her purse, looking at me as if I'd just told her I was going to marry her dad. "You can't tell me that you really believe that crap.

"Of course I do! I have to! I'm an artist! Hell, the New York minute is why I didn't move back home after the whole Book TV fiasco."

"You're telling me that you're banking all your dreams on the hopes of someone having to take a dump?"

"Maybe not a dump. He could also be passing a stone or something."

"Well, that's great. Let me know when your minute

happens. Maybe I'll be famous because someone had bad sushi." We continued our walk until we arrived at the subway entrance. "Look, good luck, hon. Just a hint—I know you're both 'artists' and what not, but don't tell Nathan about this theory of yours until later. Much, much later."

"I'll be sweet and quiet," I said as I mimed zipping my lips.

"We'll talk Monday," she said as she walked down the stairs. "We'll compare stories about our men."

"Got another hot date with Habibe?" I yelled down.

"Third one this week," said Sally.

"We like him?"

"We like him a whole lot," she said as she smiled wryly. I gave a wave as she disappeared into the station below.

Standing on the corner of Fifty-ninth Street and Third Avenue, I looked up at the sleekly fashionable windows of the almighty Bloomingdale's. Pushing my way through the revolving door, I walked into a wall of scent and color. The black, beige and white of Burberry scarves and purses greeted me on the left, while on the right rich girls fought with their moms over what Juicy bag would go with their school uniforms.

Politely declining the six women who wanted to spray me down with the new Herrera experience, I found myself drawn to the makeup counter at Estée Lauder. I looked down at the color easel on the counter. Small samples of lipstick and eye shadow stared up at me in every shade from wine cup to emerald stone. I might as well have been looking at the periodic table of elements. I had no idea how any of this made women pretty.

Just then a pang thumped my chest. *She* would have known. She could make her face glow with the simple stroke of a blusher. I had no clue. And she didn't stick around long enough to teach me. If Nathan found his art in beautiful women, if he took pictures of models all day, then how would I ever compete? Being cute, drunk and entertaining at a bar with my friends was one thing. Being a beauty to make a man forgo all others was another. As I put my finger in a pot of Bois de Rose lipstick, I thought my mom would have been able to help me with this. And she would have done it years ago, so that by this point in my life, I would've been an expert.

Although I rubbed the lipstick into my bottom lip, I didn't have the courage to look in the mirror. I was too afraid that if I kept going, her face would be the one looking back at me. I reached for a tissue and began to wipe my lips. Then I realized I would need it for my eyes, as they'd begun to tear. When I turned, I caught my reflection in the mirror and noticed that I'd rubbed lipstick into my eyes. It was then a dashing older woman with perfectly coiffed hair and flawless skin walked over to me.

"May I help you, miss?" she asked elegantly. Her name tag proudly held her title: Miss Ava—Beauty Consultant. "We have a wonderful free gift going on right now."

"No, that's all right," I said, embarrassed at the mess I had made of my face. "I was just trying something out. But it didn't work."

"Of course not, darling. That shade of pink is far too old for you. You need something more like Juicy Fig. That's what all the young girls are wearing. Come here." She grabbed a Q-tip, broke it in half and rubbed some lipstick on the end. She held my chin in her hand as she applied the lipstick with the accuracy of a surgeon. "Then a little gloss in the center of the lip—," she said as she tilted my head toward the mirror. "Beautiful! Just like our fragrance."

I didn't have time to shut my eyes before I caught a glimpse of myself in the mirror. Instead of being freaked out, I had to admit that I liked what I saw. The color made my teeth look two shades whiter and my lips a half an inch thicker than normal.

"What sort of shadow do you wear on your eyes? Our free gift has an amazing shade of orange that would make the blue in your eyes just pop."

"Nothing," I admitted shyly.

"Why?" she asked in shock. Her hand actually went up to her chest to catch her breath.

"Because I don't know how. And I don't like makeup."

"But you've found your way here to Estée Lauder. Something in you must want to see how beautiful you can be."

I wanted to tell her that the only thing I knew about makeup was what I'd read in my mother's Mary Kay catalog on the toilet. And since they didn't have a counter and I once saw a bottle of Youth Dew on my mother's dresser, I figured this was a safe place to start. But I decided to confess the real reason, no matter how stupid it sounded. "Well, you see, I have a date. And he works around pretty girls . . . well, models really . . . and . . ."

"Say no more!" she said as she held up her hand to silence me. "Come with me."

And like a good general teaching the young soldier the maneuvers of a battlefield, Miss Ava decided to school me in the various ways to apply war paint. She escorted me over to a tall swivel stool in front of an enormous lit mirror. First she patted my face down with makeup remover. She had no need to do this, but I liked the feeling of her hands pressing my skin so I kept silent. During the application she informed me of all the beauty tips a young woman should know. Tips passed down to her from Miss Lauder herself while waiting on a bathroom line at the Four Seasons. Rule number one being always put the same moisturizer that you use on your face on the back of your hands. Apparently the hands give away age just as much as the neck and eyes. Then after a few minutes of smearing foundation, powdering and lining my eyes and mouth with pencils and polish she examined my face closely for any missteps. She swiveled me toward the mirror.

"Now that's a beauty."

Afraid to look right into the mirror, I kept my eyes locked on hers, still frightened to see what or who would be looking back at me. Miss Ava smiled encouragingly and nodded to the mirror. Looking at my reflection, I was amazed at what I saw. It wasn't my mother. It was me. My lips, my eyes, my cheekbones, only better. It was as if Miss Ava had animated my face, allowing each feature to express its own emotion. My eyes smoldered while my lips formed a pout. I couldn't help smiling proudly. After she gave a slight nod of approval, her gaze drifted up to my hairline.

"What are we doing about your hair for this event?"

"I don't know. I can't do much. It's just short and wavy."

"My dear, the average head has a hundred to a hundred-fifty thousand strands of hair on it. That means there are a hundred to a hundred-fifty thousand ways to do it." She leaned over me and called out over the floor. "Monique! We need your expertise." A moment later a stunning Somalian woman walked over and gave Miss Ava a quick kiss on each cheek.

"Moni, darling, we have a young woman here who has an extremely important date to go on and we were thinking about hair."

Monique's hands instantly dug through my scalp as she flopped around my curls. "What are you wearing, child?"

"I'm not sure," I admitted sheepishly. "Does it matter?"

"Matter? Child, everything matters! If you're going for a forties style we can give you finger waves. If you're wearing

Pucci, then we go slick. Classic, we can soften the top and curl the back . . ." She stopped, exhausted at the idea of naming all the different alternatives. "Come with me."

Monique grabbed my hand and guided me toward the Fredric Fekkai station on the floor. I looked back to Miss Ava for permission to go. She just nodded her approval and yelled out after us, "Bring her back here when you're done. I need to see the final result."

For the next hour I became a baton in a Bloomingdale's beauty relay race. From makeup to hair to dresses and shoes, each specialist worked his or her magic. Apparently, Miss Ava had called four different departments, instructing them to leave me better than they found me. After purchasing a pair of pink strappy sandals that were not only 50 percent off but made my feet look downright edible and an elegant sheath dress modeled after the one Claire Danes wore at the last awards show, I made my way back to the counter that started it all.

"Well, missy. You ready to meet the man of your dreams?" she asked as she handed me a bag of goodies.

"If I can re-create this, then yes, I will be ready," I said as I happily took the bag. I pulled out my wallet to pay for her services, but she just pushed my hand back the way Poppy always did when I tried to pay for Sunday breakfast at the local greasy spoon.

"You just make sure you leave an impression. And pass the beauty tips along."

"I'll try, Miss Ava," I said as I gave her a hug. "And thank you so much for all your help."

"That's my job, deary."

"You know," I said thoughtfully, as if I were talking more to myself than to Miss Ava, "I never thought anyone in a store like this would pay so much attention to me."

"Well," she said, rubbing some lotion into her hands, "it's

funny. When I saw you, I just got an overwhelming feeling that I should help you. It was like someone was whispering in my ear, 'Go help my daughter.'"

My heart dropped. "Excuse me?"

Looking over at another shopper, she said, "I mean you remind me of my daughter in Chicago. Must be a mother's intuition. And speaking of Intuition, I need to go to the third floor to help with our fragrance promotion. Good luck."

"Thank you. Thank you again," I said as I watched her leave in a whirlwind of perfume. I made my way out of the store, stunned and choked up. But as I walked the twenty blocks back up to the apartment, I kept it together for the honor of Miss Ava, knowing that being grateful meant I would smile at every man, woman and child I made eye contact with, my rose-dusted cheekbones held high.

When I turned the corner of Seventy-eighth Street, I saw Max struggling to push his baby carriage of precious possessions. He must have hit a sidewalk sale or a street fair, because his carriage looked in danger of toppling over. I walked up to him and tapped him on the shoulder. He turned around in surprise.

"Why, hello, Miss Hepburn. I loved you in *Roman Holiday*," he said sweetly, wiping his brow with a piece of newspaper.

"Thank you, Max. Here." I handed him a five-dollar bill and the free sample bottle of face cream. "This is for saving me from a bus."

He disregarded the money I put on his cart and examined the small jar of face cream. He held it at arm's length away from his eyes to read. "Intensive moisturizer for face and throat. Thanks, Geri. I can really use this."

"Remember to put it on the back of your hands. They're the biggest indicator of age."

"Well, thank you kindly. I will keep that in mind." He started to search through the pile of boxes and sundry pieces of junk in the cart. I became scared that he would try to reciprocate by giving me a jar of beans or a broken iron. But instead he pulled out the old bell. "I lost the bowl somewhere in Union Square. I gave it to Charley for his dinner, but he never gave it back. But you give the bell another good rattle. You've earned it."

His chapped hand passed me the brass bell. Feeling confident and hopeful for the first time in what seemed like forever, I closed my eyes, took a deep breath and gave the bell a firm shake. My wish was simple. I wanted what Miss Ava had said to come true. That on this night, I would meet the man of my dreams. The sharp ping of the bell seemed to echo down the street. I opened my eyes and handed it back to Max, who was busy rubbing cream into his cheeks and hands.

"Did you wish that I would look twenty years younger?" he asked, smiling. "Because I think it just came true."

"Close," I said. "Very close. 'Bye, Max."

I left Max to his new beauty regime as I continued down the block. Smiling to myself, I wondered if Miss Lauder would be impressed by Max's prompt application of her precious beauty tip. After all, men are human just like us, according to Sally. I was almost at the front of my building when I heard Max cry out.

"You got it!"

My heart leapt into my throat. When I spun around, I saw that he hadn't moved from where I left him. He appeared crazed, with his arms open wide and his head tilted back over his shoulders. Although I assumed he was talking to me, he wasn't looking in my direction. His eyes stared wildly over the tops of buildings at the full moon. His one arm reached in the air, as if attempting to snatch it out of the sky. The other extended in my direction, pointing at me.

"You hear me, Miss Hepburn? You got it!"

18

A Date of Wreckoning

The final hour before my date with Nathan Ferry—
Photographer, I painstakingly applied my eyeliner while
overhearing Maria in the living room instructing Emmy on
breaking the bridge of an assailant's nose without the use
of one's right arm. Emmy and Maria had decided to make
a date night between themselves as I prepared for mine.

Looking at the list that I'd made that day, I checked off
each product I needed to apply. The copious notes I took
down on how to apply the four different shades of orange
eye shadow to my upper lid came in quite handy. It took
me fifteen minutes to finish one eye. Forty-five minutes to
control my cowlick. But by the time I finished applying the
eyeliner, lip liner, brow liner and a panty liner, I felt like a
lady worthy of a golden bra. The virgin bra lay at the bottom of my bag, still carefully wrapped in its pink tissue
paper. When I reached in and tore off one of the tags, I felt
a prick. A red bulb popped from the sliced skin of a paper
cut. I pushed the skin together to see how much blood
would ooze out of the wound. Only a drop managed to
peek out. I took in a deep breath and let it out. This isn't an
omen, I thought. This is a cut. And like everything else, it
will heal.

Emmy and Maria shouted from behind the door, chanting

for me to hurry up and come out so they could see the new me. I hollered that I would be a minute as I looked through the six rejection letters I'd received that week from various agents. At Emmy's request, I'd moved the letters off the fridge and onto a small bulletin board in my room with the proviso that she not enter the room, until I sold something or got an agent. Unfortunately this task was taking more time than I had originally thought, and the bulletin board kept falling under the weight of all letters. Instead of buying another board, I figured I would move them to the walls. In three weeks my room went from a neat cubicle with a flowered duvet and a *Doctor Zhivago* movie poster to the set of the *Synchronicity II* video. As I strained to tack a letter over the door, I heard a catcall come from behind me. I turned around and smiled at J. T., who sat on my bed looking over my pile of makeup.

"You don't need any of this crap, you know," he said as he sniffed a bottle of foundation. "And this smells like paint."

"Just trying to give inner beauty a night off," I whispered as I sat down next to him on the bed. "Not all guys can see through the motor oil."

"You should aim for one who does."

"I will. I'm just trying to put my best foot forward tonight, that's all."

"Still, I think this stuff's a waste," he said, shaking his head in mild disgust. "You look fine without it. How much did you spend on all of this, anyway? A hundred, a hundred and fifty bucks? And for who? Some guy named after a hot dog."

I moved my face so that J. T. had to meet my eyes. Looking in his soft expression, I let my gaze run along his jaw. "J. T., in real life, if we ever met, you wouldn't give me a second look." Suddenly a buzzer went off.

Emmy shouted from the other side of the door. "Geri! He's downstairs! Hurry it up!"

Getting up, I took another look in the mirror. Happy with the result, I grabbed my bra and put on my dress. As I reached for the door, he spoke.

"I see you just fine. It's you that can't seem to recognize me."

When I arrived in our lobby, Nathan was just putting out a cigarette. He jumped to attention and walked over.

"Hey, Geri. You look great," he said.

Forgetting whether I'd checked for any lipstick marks on my teeth, I mumbled, "Zank eww."

I figured I would keep quiet until I could check my teeth. This worked out perfectly as we walked down the sidewalk enjoying the red glow of sunset over the city. Although we didn't say much, he reached for my hand and pulled me closer to him. I peered at Nathan to check him out. His jeans looked like something off a movie set, so perfectly faded they made me want to put my hands in his pockets. He wasn't much taller than I, but his trendy dirty blond locks stood up at least an inch off his head, making him seem taller. The cigarette smoke mixed with his cologne, making him not only smell totally sexy, but also blocking out the smell of garbage that occasionally wafted up from the side of the buildings. And although his shirt seemed a bit tight and his nails manicured, I bet I could talk my dad into thinking he was cool.

As we walked down the sidewalk, in no real hurry to catch a cab to the gallery, I noticed all the flower boxes brimming with begonias and zinnias. He looked up at the boxes and smiled. The corners of his lips twirled up, giving him dimples like Todd's.

"I never thought I'd be on a date with a girl who lives up here."

"Is it such a bad place to be?"

He lifted my hand to his face and kissed it. "Nah, it's not a bad place to be."

I smiled back. Not a bad place to be, indeed.

We jumped into a cab and saw our lives flash before our eyes as we rocketed down FDR Drive. I was ready to throw up all over my new dress as we stopped abruptly at the Collective Unconscious Gallery on the Lower East Side. The line for the exhibit opening stretched down the block and around the corner. Nathan took my hand again and led me past the crowd and right up to the front door. Everyone stared at us as we sped past the line and into the gallery. As I waited for Nathan, who left to grab some drinks, I listened to a haunting tune played by a woman drawing a violin bow across a lumberjack saw. The warbling tone sounded as if she were playing the forestry tool underwater. I stood hypnotized until Nathan returned with two glasses of champagne. We walked into the main room of the gallery hand in hand. He kept his eyes fixed on my face as I looked up at his friend's massive sculptures.

Before us sat a ten-foot-high sculpture of a cockroach dressed in a velvet tuxedo, eating a man who appeared to be either Tony Blair or the guy who played Lenny in *Laverne & Shirley*. And there wasn't just one. Everywhere around the gallery sat enormous roaches in various states of rage. From the roach with the head of George Bush to the insect with televisions for eyes showing *A Clockwork Orange*, the theme of the exhibit appeared political, although the exact message wasn't quite clear.

"Let me guess, you're thinking of buying one," Nathan said.

A laugh burst from my mouth as I imagined Emmy's face when she saw the Bill Gates roach looming over her grandmother's china pitcher in the dry sink. "I don't think it would fit through the front door. They're just too fuc . . . fantastically big." Trying to curb my cursing was proving harder than I'd thought. But other than a loud "Shoes for brains" for the delivery truck driver who'd nearly hit our cab, I was holding my own. "Incidentally, how much would one of these cost?"

"Ten grand," he said matter-of-factly. "And that's for the small one."

As I looked up at a giant roach suspended from the ceiling wearing a pink homecoming queen sash, I smiled. "You know the artist. Maybe I can get a discount."

"I'll think up a few favors you can do for me. Then maybe I'll put in a good word."

I could feel a blush creeping up my face, so I turned away to hide my third-grade, I-got-a-crush-on-you smile. As I took a sip of my drink, I looked around the room at the other people milling about. The gallery was *Spy* revisited. Everyone was unsettlingly beautiful and oddly shiny. The wait staff looked like body doubles for the cast of *One Life to Live.* The female guests looked like they ate indifference for lunch and guys sported tattoos and strategically messy hair. "So who is this guy again?"

"Randy Cross. My roommate and the next big deal in modern sculpture. The whole setup works out great for me because we share clients, lab fees, studio time . . ."

Just as I began to take another sip of my complimentary champagne, a man screamed at me from behind.

"Breathe!"

My drink went down the front of my new dress as I whirled around to see who had just scared the crap out of me.

"Geri, this is Randy," Nathan explained.

In front of me stood a man shorter than myself wearing black leather pants and a tight black T-shirt that read FRESHLY FUCKED. I tilted my head and looked at him like a confused dog. Nothing about him made sense. His spiky jet black hair made his enormous head come to a point. If he were taller, he'd be frightening. And if art is only a reflection of the artist, then inside this five-foot-tall man was a fifteen-foot cockroach with the head of our forty-first president. He closed his eyes and yelled as if he were standing on the other side of the street and not five inches below me.

"I'M RANDY!"

I leaned in closer and yelled, "NICE TO MEET YOU!" thinking he might just be hard of hearing. Nathan looked jumpy as he made the introductions.

"Randy, this is Geri. I told you about her last night. She's the one from Spy."

"We met there," I added.

"Of course. That's where our little Nate picks up all his lovelies," he spat. I couldn't tell if Randy was high, insane or freshly fucked by Pol Pot. "So, Geri, who do you know?" he asked.

"In the tri-state area?"

"To get in to Spy. Who put you on the list?" Randy asked as he quickly pinched the skin under his nose. Sweat began to bead up between his shards of hair.

"A friend of a friend. We—my girlfriends and I—had never been there before. Didn't really fit in."

"Obviously," he answered as he looked me over. Like a mini-tornado fueled by ego and cocaine, Randy knocked me off my game. I wanted to reach for Nathan's hand just to feel as if I had a friend in the room, only Nathan seemed to have taken a step back.

"Nathan says you're a writer."

"Future writer." I felt myself begin to stammer. "During the day, I'm a manager at a children's book company, Junior Varsity. Maybe you've heard of us? We do Kibbles the Karate Cat and . . ."

"You're boring. Let's do coke." And with that, he grabbed Nathan and me by the arms and led us to a private side room. On one of the mirrored tables sat two piles of white powder that two vacant-looking stick figures were chopping up into rows with Sam's Club cards. As I stared at the scene, I wanted nothing more than for Maria to bust into the gallery with ten cops and slap the cocaine out of Randy's nose. I stood there motionless as Nathan leaned over to me and whispered.

"I thought you said you wrote?"

"I do. After work," I answered. Randy let out a mocking laugh as he pushed aside one of the women at the coke tables.

"So, Geri, you do?"

"Drugs? I've experimented."

"Pot and No-Doz don't count," he snapped.

"Well . . . then no."

Randy took one of the cards out of the woman's hands and continued to chop. "Are you just going to stand there and watch me, or are you going to join in the fun?"

Nathan and I stood there awkwardly as the three looked up at us.

"Come on, Nate! You bought half of this! Oh, fuck it," Randy said, giving up. He took out a dollar bill and rolled it into a fine tube. "So, tell me, Geri, what sort of stories do you write?"

"She writes movie scripts," Nathan blurted.

"Film noir? Avant-garde?" Randy asked as he and the two women geared up for a big snort.

"Young adult stuff. My script is about a group of pre-teen

carolers. Not quite like an after-school special because the older kids get drunk a lot, but . . ."

The three stopped in mid-snort and looked up at me. Randy broke the silence as he doubled over in laughter.

"What?" I said, confused. "It's not a total comedy. One of the kids has leukemia."

Randy gasped for air. "I bet my whole collection it ends happy."

"Yeah. Open-ended, but happy."

"Coming from someone who works for the company that brought us Katie the Karate Cat, it would have to."

"Kibbles the Karate Cat, and why can't it end happy? Shit . . . shoot, why would I put my time and energy into something that depresses me and anyone who might watch it?"

Randy shot up and cried out, "Because depression is reality!"

I wanted to finish my point, so I continued as if I wasn't having belittling discussion about art with a coke-addled psycho.

"Yes and no. Your life is pretty cool, agreed?" The two women looked at each other and nodded in agreement. "But for people who spend most of the day filing, faxing and dealing with customers, happy is kind of nice."

"Come with me!" Randy yelled as he marched over to one of his sculptures. Our whole vapid group followed Randy out of the room. Nathan ran up to him and grabbed his arm.

"Quit it, will you? You're high."

"I just want to have some fun with a fellow artist, Nate. Geri, come here."

I walked over to Randy, who stood at the base of a human-sized roach whose feelers were nailed to a cross. "I wanted to show you this. It's called Salvation. This—" he said, flinging his angry little arm in the air—"this is who your carolers sing about."

"They do?"

"Yes! They do! You see, Jesus was your God's only son, created in his own image. The only living being that could out live us all! Now, if the only form of life that can survive a nuclear holocaust is a cockroach, then wouldn't it be true to say that the roach is created in God's own image? That the roach is Jesus resurrected?" His passion caused him to start punching the air. "Isn't this God?"

The room grew even more silent as everyone waited for my reply.

"I'm not positive, but I really don't think Jesus is a New York City cockroach."

"Well, mine is." Two of his groupies broke out in applause. With that, Randy turned on his heel and began to storm away. As he passed me, he shot off another comment. "You can't even bend your mind to art."

Blood began to rush to my temples. All the advice given by my friends, that bitch Kelly Cox and the kind women at Bloomingdale's about being a graceful class act started to fade. I felt everyone's eyes on me as my mouth began to take on a life of its own.

"Are you kidding me? Just because I don't do coke or play the saw or think God is a bug doesn't mean I'm not an artist."

"Your *hobby* is writing. You are not a writer."

A vision of my room papered with rejection notices popped into my head. Then the dumbest comment popped out. "I have one hundred fifty rejection notices that say otherwise." I could hear people in the room begin to chuckle, but I kept going. "Okay, I might not be a successful one, but I am a writer. And let's get something straight. Just because I live on the Upper East Side, have a

401(K) and work for a company that publishes books teaching kids how to take a crap on the toilet that doesn't mean I can't create art. Anyone can do it. So on that note, thank you for your show. Good luck to you and good-bye."

I could overhear one of the stick figures ask the other, "What's 401(K)?"

She answered nonchalantly, "It's like Special K, but it messes you up longer."

Nathan walked up to me and began to steer me to the other end of the room. "Come on, Geri. Just let him go."

When I turned around, I saw the whole room staring at me in silence. I got halfway across the exhibit before I heard Randy shout out, "You don't need luck when you've got talent. If anyone's going to need luck, it's you."

At that moment all those fading voices whispering advice in my head shut off. Even the woman who played the saw stopped. The only sound I could hear was the sea. As I looked out at all the blank faces in the room, one stood out. In the far corner, among a room of black leather and denim, stood J. T., wearing khaki pants and a Tiffany blue shirt. He looked as if he'd just stepped off the side of the bus. His face appeared concerned as he looked at me. Then I felt a smile creep across my face. He knew I needed a welcoming face, and he showed up. Slowly I turned around and called after Randy.

"By the way, I never told you what I thought of your sculptures."

"Please don't keep me waiting," Randy said as he folded his arms across his chest.

I raised my voice so that even the people outside on line could hear me. "I think your sculptures suck as much cock as you do."

Crickets. That's what you would have heard had this

scene been in the country. But in that room, the only noise in the entire gallery was one man's laughter. When I whirled around, I noticed it came from J. T. He dabbed his eyes with his cocktail napkin as he slapped the back of the man next to him. As I marched up to the coat-check lady, I gesticulated wildly that I needed her to move out of my way. After insulting the artist on his opening night I figured a hasty exit was more than appropriate. When I pushed past a couple who were actually clutching each other in fright, I accidentally knocked over the coat-check lady's tip jar, sending money and change all over the floor. I could only whisper, "Sorry, I have to keep going."

When the gallery door shut behind me, I could hear the room buzzing with excitement. I waited a safe distance from the door for Nathan. As I stood there I couldn't understand how the whole night had gone so wrong. My mind kept shouting for Nathan to hurry up, but as the minutes passed, I realized Nathan wasn't coming. No one would be barging out that door to defend my honor or to see if I was all right. I was alone. And I would remain alone as long as I chose to stand there.

My heart sank as I walked into the street and hailed a cab. As soon as I got inside the taxi, tears began to spill down my face. The day I'd waited, prepared, plucked and planned for had ended in humiliation. Why did it go so wrong? While we were stopped at a red light, the cab driver kept leaning over, looking into the rearview mirror. I thought he was going to ask me why I was upset, but then I realized he was looking past me.

"My daughter's going to freak out when I tell her who I didn't pick up," he said as he shook his head and chuckled. The light turned green as he slowly turned the corner onto First Avenue.

"Huh?" I asked as I wiped my face.

"The guy who just shot out of that building. The one trying to wave me down. I think he's that stud hanging on her bedroom wall."

A rush of relief swept through me as the cab turned the corner on Seventy-eighth Street. I'd counted each block from Fourteenth Street up, knowing that with each light we passed, I was moving farther and farther away from that tornado of cocaine-induced nastiness. As the cab pulled up to the front of my building, I kept telling myself that it was going to be all right. After all, I was home. The place where people understood me and loved me for who I was. As I paid the cabby, the door was opened by someone on the street waiting to get in. When I looked up at the hand that held the door, I realized my nightmare hadn't quite wrapped itself up yet.

"Oh . . . Geri," Todd said as he stuck his head in the cab. The stench of burned oil flooded the car and I could see his Nissan smoldering in the background.

My first instinct was to yell "Gun it!" to the driver. Instead, I handed the money over to the cabby and reluctantly got out. Cassie stood behind Todd, talking on her cellphone. Todd and I faced each other in silence until the driver yelled out.

"Hey, is someone getting in?"

"She is," Todd answered without taking his eyes off me.

Cassie pulled her cellphone away from her chin as she corrected Todd. "We are, babe. You're coming back with my stereo, remember?" She continued her phone conversation as she walked between us into the cab. Feeling like a complete fool, I turned my back to him and headed into the building.

"Hey, you look really nice," he said. I turned around to look at him. His expression seemed tired and mirthless. If I could have seen my made-up face, I probably looked the same. Not even a thank you or a smile came from my lips. I felt spent and sufficiently rejected for one lifetime. All I wanted was to get into my bed and imagine J. T. rubbing my feet or doing a dance to make me laugh. I wanted to feel safe. I wanted to be someplace where I wasn't completely disappointed at every turn. Apparently the only place this could happen was in my head.

"Todd!" Cassie yelled. All I could do was turn my back to him and continue on my way and try, with all my heart, not to look back. After all, that was what Todd wanted. When I opened the second set of doors, I heard Cassie call out again.

"What are you waiting for? The meter's running!"

Maria had already left by the time I walked into the apartment. Emmy stood at the sink, cleaning up their dinner dishes. When she heard the door lock behind me, she came into the living room, wiping her hands on a dishcloth.

"You're home early. So? How'd it go?" I looked at her for two seconds before her hopeful expression faded. She put down the dishcloth and sighed, "Oh, Geri."

"What if Depeche Mode's right? What if God has a sick sense of humor?" I said as I plopped on to the sofa. Looking down at my feet, I noticed that my cute strappy sandals had dug blisters into the sides of each foot. Upon removing one shoe, I reopened my papercut. I looked at my finger as it bled. "Yes, when I die, I think I will find him laughing."

"Geri," Emmy said uncomfortably, "we need to talk."

I couldn't image what great discussion needed to take place this evening. "Can this wait until tomorrow? I don't feel like talking about bills or . . ."

"It's not about the bills," she said softly. "It's about you."

"Me?"

"I think you may need . . . help. Like counseling."

"For what? Bad choices in sandals?"

"No." She wrung the dishcloth nervously in her hands. "For depression."

I rolled my eyes. "What is this? A one-woman intervention? You have to stop watching those *Party of Five* marathons on Lifetime," I spat. This is nuts, I thought. I'm crazy but I've kept my craziness to myself for years. My friends couldn't figure me out without a team of specialists and a bottle of Boones Farm.

"Geri, I'm serious. I went into your room tonight. I saw your walls. I'm sorry. I know I shouldn't . . ."

"Em, I asked you not to go in there. Not until I sold something."

"Geri, you're scaring me!" she yelled. "And Maria too. You surround yourself with so much rejection and negativity that nothing good could ever possibly get to you. I really think, as a start, that you should take the letters down. They cover three of your walls already. And I can't stand thinking of you asleep in the middle of all that . . . bad chi."

"It's not doing any harm," I said, trying to calm her down.

"Yes, it is. And that's not the only thing." She took a deep breath. "Maria heard from the neighbors across the way that you nearly kill yourself doing pull-ups on the fire escape. Is that true?"

Just then I remembered Maria waving back at me from our naked neighbors' apartment. Shit, I thought. If anyone could catch my antics, it would be the watercolor-loving free lovebirds. New Yorkers may not look up, but they certainly look over.

I was busted. This would require some minor disaster management. "Sometimes, I slip when I water your plants. That's all."

"Well, that's not what the neighbors are saying. They thought it was so strange, they brought it up to Maria after that attempted burglary. Geri, I'm worried about you, damn it."

Emmy must have been really upset. She'd said a bad word. "I'm fine. Really, Emmy."

"Please, if you're not going to see a therapist, then at least take the letters down. Believe me, it's easier to face the day when you're not staring at rejection. If you let things go, it will all get better."

"Let things go?" I thought. What did I have to let go of? Anything I'd ever wanted had let go of me a long time ago. At that moment, a surge of anger rose inside me. "Easier? How so?"

"What do you mean?"

"I mean we all deal with rejection in our own way. Sorry if I put mine on the walls instead of letting it take me out for coffee three times a week."

Emmy went pale. I wanted to take my words back as soon as the comment left my mouth. But I couldn't. Tears began to well in her eyes.

"I'm sorry, Emmy," I whispered. "I shouldn't have said that."

Hurt and pissed, Emmy took a deep breath, stood up and composed herself. "Geri, all I'm saying is that you need to talk to someone. Other than yourself." With that, she walked back into her bedroom and shut the door. By the time I finished mentally kicking myself for being such a jerk to my best friend, her light was off. Standing in front of a shut door, I figured it was probably best that I wouldn't be able to say anything else. My mouth had made me into jackass enough for one evening. There was nothing left to do but turn off the rest of the lights, put the chain up and crawl into my room.

Sitting in the dark on the edge of my bed, I began to quietly whistle. My heart begged J. T. to show up. But he didn't. Some days are so bad, even your dreams don't want to be around you. When I lay down and closed my eyes, all I could think about was Miss Ava and Max. They'd been so sure I could pull off an amazing New York evening and all I'd managed to do was let them down. I had no grace, no dignity, no poise. Dignity doesn't call someone a cocksucker in a room full of art aficionados. Grace doesn't dash the fantasy of a best friend. Poise says "thank you" to a compliment given by a neighbor. All I had was a bad attitude, a case of depression according to Emmy's analysis and a hundred-and-fifty dollars' worth of Estée Lauder. So I lay there and waited. Looking out past the bars of my fire escape. Wishing someone would climb up to show me how to escape.

19

First Time, Second Nature

I didn't have to wait long. I was awake when I heard the knock. The clock read 2:18 A.M. as I lay frozen underneath my sheets. The knocking itself sounded soft and urgent. Not meant to alert everyone in the apartment; just the person closest to the front door. Too afraid to turn on the lights, I quietly maneuvered through the dark to the door. Peering through the spy hole, I saw Todd outside. His hands were stuffed in his pockets and his eyes stared back down the hall. I quickly unlocked the door and ushered him in, anxious to hear why he'd come up at this hour. I figured he must be up here to warn Emmy and me of a gas leak or that he'd found the rattler that lives with the freak in apartment #34 in his toilet.

"Is everything okay?" I whispered.

"Yes . . . and no," he said quietly. "Is Emmy awake?"

"No. She's been asleep for hours. Are you all right? You look kind of scared . . ."

He didn't let me finish my sentence. Todd grabbed my face and urgently pressed his lips to mine. The force of his kiss knocked us off balance and we fell back against the bathroom door and onto the wreath Emmy had made while watching a rerun of *Trading Spaces*. We continued our embrace unfazed as dried eucalyptus became entangled in my hair. For a half of the smallest increment of time known to humankind, I thought that this might not be the greatest idea. But my heart overrode all other organs as it threw my body into autopilot. I jumped into his arms. My legs wrapped around his waist and my ankles locked behind him. With one hand lifting me and another attempting to dig a nest out of my hair, he carried me to my bedroom.

We have to be quiet. We have to be really quiet, I thought as we landed on the futon with a thump. Rolling around on the hard mattress, we tried feverishly to take off our clothes without taking our lips off each other. His kisses tasted like butter pecan and basil; just like I remembered. He peeled himself off me to close the bedroom door as I tried to extricate a clump of baby's breath from my head. Hooking the small silver latch on my door, he chuckled.

"You need a better lock. Who is this supposed to keep out?"

"It's a latch, not a lock," I whispered.

"What's the difference?" he said as he looked down at me from the base of my bed.

"Latches just block things out. Locks keep people out."

"Is that right," he murmured as he began to remove the rest of his clothes. I sat up in bed to watch him. He grabbed the back of his shirt and pulled it over his head with one quick motion. "Who you trying to block out? Better not be me."

My gulp was audible. "No. Wouldn't think of it."

"Good," he said, and he unbuckled his pants. "It would take a lot more than that."

Todd's body looked both soft and strong. Every inch of him held just the right amount of muscle. His chest seemed so perfect, I wanted to reach out and run my hands over it to see if he was real. When he got down to his

UMASS SWIMMING 1999 boxers, he gave me a slight nod, signaling me to begin. I only got halfway down my nightshirt before Annette's face and her shivering hand clutching a bunch of rubbers popped into my head.

Before my date with Nathan Ferry—Photographer, Sally had given me a pack of three ultra-Sheik condoms. These were given with strict orders that they were not to be used for sex but rather to be placed in my top righthand drawer as a Feng Shui cure to bad dating. I didn't know if I possessed the guts to reach for the rubbers if Todd asked whether I had protection. The memory of him bolting and the vision of Tony Manero from *Saturday Night Fever* saying, "You wanna be a pig, Annette?" wouldn't let my arms move. My gaze left his and darted to the drawer. Todd, noticing where my eyes landed, put his hands on his hips.

In a soft voice he asked, "You haven't given them a new home, have you?"

I shook my head. He walked over to the drawer, opened it up and found the small black box of rubbers. Crawling back onto the bed, he rubbed his nose against mine and whispered, "Allow me."

Making love with someone for the first time can be tricky; however, making love with Todd that night felt like second nature. His smell, his taste, his breath felt familiar but exciting. Like I was having sex with an old boyfriend who'd just come back from a year abroad in Antarctica. It was sensual. Urgent. Needful. And had he been my actual boyfriend, the moans and cries would have been peppered with I love yous. But just as I'd stifled my swearing earlier in the night, I felt the same need to silence the voice of my heart.

After going through the full box of three (one being torn by my teeth as I tried to open the foil packet) we held each other under my patchwork flowered quilt. Although we didn't engage in any romantic post-coitus chat, he made no motion to get up and leave. Within a minute of him tossing a condom into my wastepaper basket, his breathing steadied and he fell asleep. Feeling completely awake, I sat up in bed. The streetlight filtered through the iron bars and lit up one side of his face. As I watched him sleep, I knew it would be only a matter of moments before the thousand why questions began to filter in. And just when I thought about waking him up to ask, "Why are you wearing underwear from 1999?" I stopped. Another feeling broke in. Instead of shaking him awake, I found myself reaching for his hand. It was strong and callus-free, and I ran my fingers over the lines time had etched in his palm. Suddenly I felt like a little girl in a room filled with dark velvet curtains. I brought his hand to my face and began to rub it with my cheek. Silently I'd repeated the fruitless mantra I'd repeated so many times before in my short life.

"Please, please, please be happy here."

She left us on a Tuesday. Her bags were placed neatly in the entryway when I went to bed. For years I pretended she did one of those tear-filled good-byes while I slept. Looked at me lovingly from the doorway and blew kisses as I slept under my Smurf blanket. But in reality, she probably skipped my room. I don't know. She didn't have the nerve to wake me up to tell me she was going. She was off to "find herself" and I guess March 2, 1988, was as good a day as any to start looking. I asked Dad why Mom had to "find herself" if we had a street address and not a P.O. Box. He said if she had to find herself, it meant she wasn't really here.

Mom never called when she landed in France. She never spoke to me or sent me heartfelt letters once she got there. Twice a year, I would get postcards with a quaint thatched house or cold stone chateau on the front. The messages would be brief, describing some "wondrous" place that I had no interest in ever seeing. Never did she mention that she thought of me or missed me. It was always, "Hugs until we meet again."

But we didn't meet again. Because she had found herself. In Limoges, France. She found a man to love named Jacques and married him as soon as the divorce from Dad became final. She found herself pregnant and had another child; a little girl named Juliette. After the baby was born, I knew she would never find her way back to us on Long Island. She had found her life. A life in a small town with lots of vineyards. Like Southold. A life identical to the one she had back here with Dad and me. Only this life had a new language, better food and worse television. Dad replaced by Jacques. Me replaced by Juliette. Grape vines replaced by older vines whose roots ran deeper and whose fruit tasted sweeter, only because of their location.

I was twelve and Juliette was two when Dad got a telegram that we were officially "next of kin." As Jacques zoomed down a French highway in his shitty foreign car, he plowed into a deer that found its way onto the road. Dad sat me down in the passenger seat of the Muntz and showed me on the speedometer how fast they were going. He said you can't walk away from an accident when you're going 130 kilometers per hour. Everyone died. Even little Juliette.

As I was forced to sit in Miss Flamholtz's guidance office for an hour between lunch and recess while she kept saying, "This too shall pass," I knew that therapy would never help. There would never be a day of reckoning. A day when I could walk up to her and yell, "Look what I made of myself!" Never a day when she would come back to beg for my forgiveness or plead to get back in my life. A BMW and a 10-point buck took that option away. I realized that she might not have ever said any of those things while she was alive, but at least I had hope. Hope that one day I would have closure or I would have a mother who loved me. But death took away those options.

Growing up, I had two fantasies about her. In one, she stands in front of me, fixing my wedding veil. I kiss her on the cheek and thank her for always being there for me. Thank her for giving me the love and confidence in myself so that I could grow up to be the perfect woman for the most perfect man I had ever met. I would thank her for the overflowing wisdom of womanhood she'd taught me so that I didn't have to resort to books on dating because I had no one to give me solid advice or the sense to take it. And she would be there with an embroidered handkerchief to wipe away every tear. And we'd hug each other, then laugh as we would fix each other's makeup. She would tell me I look perfect as Dad honks the Muntz's horn, yelling for us to hurry up or we'd be late for church. That was the first fantasy.

In the second fantasy I am the night nurse at L'Hopital Beaujon who had the honor of taking her off life support.

20

Aces Lose

Todd left early. After giving me three short kisses to wake me up, he made me walk him to the door.

"Get a better lock for your bedroom, will you? I don't want to worry about you."

"I'll get right on it. As soon as the sun comes up." I tried to stifle my yawn so as not to let out any morning breath.

"You'd better. I'm going to come up and try to break it down."

"Go for it."

He gave me a soft, tongue-free kiss and left. When I turned around to walk back to my room, I noticed a Post-it impaled on the nail where the wreath had hung. It read, *If you're mad at me, say something. Don't take it out on the decor.*

I picked up the remnants of Emmy's wreath, which she believed I'd demolished in a fit of depression-induced rage, and brought it to my room. As I attempted to fix it, I tried to think of how I could tell her I'd smashed it. How could I explain to her about my night of loving with Todd? I could barely wrap *my* head around it. The eucalyptus fit back together fine and with another foot of string that I took off my light's pull chain, all evidence of my sex romp with Todd would remain our little secret. Or so I thought.

When I looked under the futon for any stray pieces of eucalyptus, I noticed something shiny on the floor. NISSAN glimmered off a Knicks keychain. Todd had dropped his car keys. This would be my excuse to see him again, I thought. And soon. After tossing the wreath back onto the door, I washed my face and tried to put on a minimal amount of makeup using the "fresh face" picture I'd cut out of *Allure* magazine. Rain rattled the leaves on the plants that hung off the fire escape outside as I began to apply a layer of foundation. When I realized that the clean, get-out-of-bed look would take about forty-five minutes, I ran my hands through my hair, slapped on some lip balm and left the apartment. As I hopped down the stairs, I figured Todd would accept me as I was. After all, if he was happy to see me last night au natural, then he should be thrilled to see me after I brushed my teeth.

They say that your body knows what's going on long before your mind catches up. As soon as my knuckles rapped the door marked #18, I broke into a sweat. In my love-induced haze, I'd forgotten that he had a girlfriend. And if they had not yet broken up, and if she still needed her stereo, she could very well be inside. I became aware of all these facts within seconds of my hand hitting the door. The sound of light female footsteps approaching grew louder by the second. I figured it was too late to run back up the stairs, so I stood there frozen, squeezing his keys in my hand so tightly that I knew they would leave a mark.

Cassie's high voice chirped from the other side, "Who is it?"

"It's Geri from Twenty-two for Todd," I choked as all the locks unhooked. She stood in the open door, wearing his UMASS SWIMMING T-shirt. Suddenly I felt as if I had gotten off my barstool after drinking five tequila shots. The hallway began to spin and I thought I was going to throw up.

"Todd's not here. He walked over to the gym. Can I help you with something?" she asked.

I reached out my hand and opened it like a five-year-old handing over a piece of candy she shouldn't be eating. "I think these are Todd's. I found them by the mailbox," I lied as the keys slid off my wet, white palm. She studied them for a moment.

"Yep. You're right. How did you know?"

Because he left them on the floor of my bedroom next to an empty box of condoms. "I've fixed his car a few times. I know he drives an old Nissan." The bile worked its way up my esophagus and into the back of my throat. My eyes wouldn't move from her face. She looked nothing like me. Tall and thin with pin-straight, ink-black hair that looked as if someone was standing behind her with a bounce card and a spotlight. This was his type, I thought. Forcing myself to stop staring at her face, I looked lower. Which was worse.

"We're giving that piece of junk up for a new Jeep. Now that there're two incomes, we figure he can trade up."

And he would need two incomes after buying the teardrop diamond that seemed to laugh at me from her left hand. My vision went blurry as I imagined myself in the middle of Times Square, looking at an electronic newsreel that read, "HE DIDN'T CHEAT ON HIS GIRLFRIEND BECAUSE HE WAS CONFUSED. HE CHEATED ON HIS FIANCÉE BECAUSE HE WASN'T."

Cassie flipped the keys around on her finger. "I'll tell him you stopped by. And thanks again, Jeannie."

"It's Geri." *Geri, the Loser. Geri, the easily duped. Geri, the idiot.*

Then the self-mockery stopped. *I'm Geri with the ace in her hand.*

With one word I could blow Todd's pending marriage

out of the water. I had the ace. I could tell her right now what had happened last night. The dizziness stopped and the rage started. I became instantly clear. I could end this, I thought. I should end this right now. I put my hand up to stop the door from closing. The words started to form in my mouth, and then I heard him on the stairs.

Somewhere between the floors a man whistled, "Put on a Happy Face." Just as I was about to speak, I tore my eyes away from hers and looked up the stairwell. It was empty. Only the soft tread of a man's steps and the breezy sound of whistling bounced around the hallways.

"Do you hear that?" I asked.

"What?"

"That whistling?"

"No. But hold on—" She reached over and pulled a piece of statice out of my hair. "Here," she said, handing it back to me. I held the piece of love debris as the phone rang in the background. The machine picked up immediately, *"Cassie and Todd aren't here right now . . ."*

"Sorry, I'd better get that."

"I'd better go," I managed to say, trying not to let my voice crack. I turned on my heel and took the stairs by threes. It was a sign. And J. T. had sent it to me. The only whistle to be blown that rainy day was his happy tune.

My keys shook in my hand as I tried to open my door. By this time, the whistling had grown so loud I didn't even hear Cassie close the door behind her. When I got inside, I ran to my bed and threw myself under the covers. I could still smell him. I could still smell us. I tore the sheets off my bed and tossed them in a pile in front of the door. After pulling my pillow cases off, I noticed the whistling had stopped. I looked around for J. T., but he was nowhere. I called for him, but heard nothing. The only noise came from the rain bouncing like beads off my air conditioner and the shush of water from the street traffic outside. The crescendo of white noise rose and fell with each car passing, letting me know that even though I felt as though my life had ended, the world outside was going on.

21

You Are Not A Winner—Try Again

"Manhattan! The most exciting city on the planet! Where all your dreams can come true in a New York minute!" Hedda proclaimed to the darkened boardroom. The slide that lit up behind her hair showed two Chinese girls holding hot dogs and wearing Mets and Yankees caps. "The capitol of the world. The cities' city!"

I yawned. After my weekend, New York's ranking had dropped between Beirut and Baghdad as my favorite place to spend a day in the park.

But not Hedda. You could smell her excitement as she pitched her new idea for a series of children's books based on each major U.S. city. The sales and marketing departments scribbled her every word on company stationery with the eagerness of an astronomy class in fear of failing their midterms. As usual, I couldn't care. My extreme disappointment in the "cities' city" forbade me. On the handout Hedda had given us, we were supposed to write our first thoughts and/or anecdotes on the different aspects of the city she touched on. Since two Chinese kids with Kosher franks meant diversity, I thought my example would be that in the course of a normal Saturday night, I'd managed to have my pride, dreams and heart duly crapped on by three different men with completely different hairstyles.

Hedda went on clicking though various slides of Manhattan that she and her chauffeur had taken with her new camera phone over the weekend. "New York, where the air is always filled with electricity. The city where dreams come true."

Daisy Dickinson called out timidly, "Isn't that Chicago?"

"No. That's New York!" And with her hands raised in victory, she clicked onto her last slide. The image was familiar. Our great Statue of Liberty. Her tone dropped when she pointed out the one flaw in the picture. "Minus the homeless man."

"Max!" I heard myself yell out. I couldn't believe it. There he was. Lighting up the conference room wall. He appeared to have jumped into the frame right before she'd snapped the shot. His jolly smile stretched across his face as he waved into the camera. His skin looked remarkably dewy.

"You know him?" Hedda asked.

"Yeah, actually, I do," I said proudly.

The lights came on in the boardroom as everyone began to file out. Through the shuffling of papers and scraping chairs I heard Daisy ask, "Is he related to you?"

After being swept into the herd, I moved with the crowd onto the next available elevator. Hedda jumped in just as the doors were about to close. The vacuum-packed crowd politely made room for her as she inched herself over to me.

"Geri, sweetie. Are you all right?" she asked. She appeared sincerely concerned as she awkwardly faced me and the rest of the people jammed together in the elevator. All of whom were focused intensely on their floors and our conversation. My face began to burn as I, too, looked up at the numbers, desperately trying to avoid eye contact with her.

"I'm fine. Really."

"You don't look like your normal perky self."

I've been called many things in my life. Perky is not one of them. And everyone in that elevator knew it except for Hedda. "Is it still boy troubles?" she asked.

I couldn't lie to my boss. But I couldn't answer either. I prayed for the elevator to plummet us to our deaths as I nodded affirmatively.

"Same boy? Ahh, God. There are so many fish in the sea, Geri. A great-looking gal like you could have anybody." Just then I heard someone at the back of the elevator choke back a laugh. "Same problem as before? Was it like I said? You know—" She bent her finger to the left. Everyone's eyes now shifted to see what she was doing with her hands.

"No. No," I whispered. I pointed to her ring finger as if we were playing charades.

"He likes wearing jewelry?"

I shook my head and pointed again at her ring finger. She looked at me as if I wasn't giving her enough clues, so I pointed to Daisy Dickinson's hand, which sported a tiny diamond engagement ring.

"It's Ted? Daisy's fiancé?" she gasped.

"What!" Daisy yelled.

Unable to keep my cool, I cried out, "No! It's my neighbor! He was engaged! We slept together and I didn't know he was engaged!"

Everyone in the elevator let out a collective "Ohh!" Then Hedda turned around. Everyone's eyes, including Hedda's, returned to the floor numbers.

By the time I got back to my office, I didn't even care that Sally had made a lasso out of paperclips. She was in the middle of trying to wrangle a file when she caught sight of Hedda and me returning. She jumped from her seat and ran over to my office. As I plopped myself in my chair I noticed a Post-it with Maria's name and work phone number on it. Sally followed me in.

"She's been trying to get you all morning. She wants you to call her at work."

The heat returned to my face. Only this time it wasn't from embarrassment but fear. Something didn't feel right as my finger punched the numbers. The phone didn't even ring twice before a man answered.

"Nineteenth Precinct."

"Hi, this is Geri O'Brien. I'm returning a call from Officer Maria Pulchenic."

"You Geri?" asked the man in the thickest Brooklyn accent I'd ever heard. "Yeah, she's expecting you. Wait a minute. I'll get her." I heard him yell. "Pulchenic!"

Sally still stood in the doorway, looking worried. She mouthed, "Is everyone okay?"

I held up my hand to her as Maria's voice came through.

"Gere?"

"Yeah. What's going on?"

She let out a sigh. "Geri, it's Emmy. She's here. Could you come down? She's pretty messed . . ."

I don't remember hanging up the phone or knocking Sally over as I ran out of my office.

Patrick sat waiting for me by the front desk when I barreled through the doors of the 19th Precinct. He picked up his Nextel to page Maria and pointed me over to a long hallway.

"Is she okay?" I panted.

Patrick put a reassuring hand on my shoulder. "Define 'okay.'"

Maria appeared in the hallway and waved for me to come over.

"Thanks for coming so quick. I didn't know what to do."
We bustled down the long hallway and up a flight of stairs.

"What happened?"

"I don't know. She won't stop crying. I was finishing up
some paperwork when I heard some EDP bawling in the
waiting room. I turned around and there's Emmy in her
volunteer scrubs holding a bottle of soda in one hand
and the cap in the other, screaming 'I'm not a winner. I'm
a loser. You heard that, world. I'm a big fat loser.' " Maria
shook her head in exhaustion. "Friggin' girl's lost her
mind."

"You think it's Bryan?" I asked.

She stopped at the door marked WOMEN'S LOCKER and
looked at me as if I were the EDP.

"Oh, yeah," I mumbled.

The women's locker room was empty except for Emmy,
sitting on a bench, bawling into an old NYPD softball
T-shirt. Feeling strange and cruel for causing a fight with
her only thirty-six hours prior, I sat a safe distance away.
Emmy took her head out of the shirt and blew her nose.
She didn't look at me when she spoke.

"I know you told me so. I know that's what you're thinking. That's what I'm thinking."

Maria chimed in with a rare kindness I only saw her use
on crazy people. "No one here is thinking that, Em." Emmy
began to cry again until she noticed the maxipad machine
in the background.

"You need to tell them that no one uses belts anymore."

"I've been meaning to get to that," Maria answered as
she put her arm around Emmy. "Now tell us. What the fuck
happened?"

"Well," she said through her sniffles, "we were having
coffee at our usual place. He ordered his espresso and then

he bought me my double chocolate latte. He always buys them for me. He knows I like just a little whip cream and nobody ever took notice of that before and . . ."

"You guys got coffee and . . ." Maria motioned her to move along.

"Well, he said he really needed to talk to me. Said he's been doing a lot of thinking and well, he couldn't hold his feelings in anymore. He said he hadn't felt like this before about anyone. That he couldn't imagine being with someone who was so different from him, someone who loved and cared about kids so much . . ." Emmy began to break up as Maria shot me a glance.

"Go on, Em."

"Then he told me that there was nothing he couldn't do while I was sitting by his side. That I made him feel like he could conquer the world."

"That's great!" Maria said. "Isn't that great, Geri?"

"Yeah, Emmy. You should be happy."

"Happy? He said that he could never ask Ingrid out without me by his side for moral support!" She dissolved into sobs.

"Emmy, Emmy, Emmy. It's okay. Really . . ." Maria said.

"No, it's not. I was a fool. Again! You told me. Geri told me. Ten years of experience told me, but no, I couldn't take the hint."

She had a point. I couldn't think of anything to say. Maria stood up and ran her hand across her forehead in thought.

"If you think about it, Emmy, you and Bryan actually have a hell of a lot in common." Emmy and I both looked at Maria, wondering what station this train of thought was stopping at. Maria continued. "It's your faces. Neither of you could get past each other's faces to see the real deal.

He could never get past the fact you weren't some fucking super model to see the brilliant and caring girl Geri and I know. And you could never get past his Aryan good looks to see that he's a superficial asshole. Emmy, there're lot of available men out there. It's like your mom always said. While you're in here crying that there're no good men, there's probably some sweet guy out there bawling like a bitch at a hot-dog stand because he got his heart broken by the office skank."

"I don't think her mom said it quite that eloquently," I put in.

Emmy dried her eyes and began to fold the T-shirt. "It's just I get so lonely here. I feel like no one can see me. Like I'm no good."

"We feel like that, too, Emmy. Right, Geri?"

"You have no idea."

"It's going to be all right," Maria said. "You are too good a person for it not to be."

"You think?" Emmy asked with trepidation.

"I'm a cop. I don't think. I know."

Emmy's face melted in appreciation.

"I love you guys."

"Save that touchy-feely crap for your students. Just give me a hug, weirdo."

Emmy looked over Maria's shoulder and waved me in. I wrapped my arms around the two of them and soon the three of us were locked in the traditional girl group hug. But no matter how silly we looked, nothing that day could have felt better.

Until we heard men crying in the background. Maria got up and opened the locker room door to see Patrick and three other cops hugging each other and wailing out in agony.

"I love you, man!" Patrick cried out.

"Someone has to," another yelled.

"All guys suck!"

Maria closed the door on them and chuckled. "The great men in New York start *after* you leave this building."

22

Mustangs in Manhattan

Once a year, the stars would align, the comet would fly overhead and Dad and Poppy would make the two-hour trip from Southold into Manhattan for the annual Mechanics Classic Auto Show.

When I met up with Dad and Poppy at the Jacob Javits Center, Poppy was already in a heated discussion with his friend, Ned from Arkansas, over the merits of installing protective steel walls in the backseats of old Mustangs.

"But, Tony, they had drop-in fuel tanks! Would you let your granddaughter behind the wheel without a backing?" Ned argued, almost laughing at Poppy's blatant disregard for automotive safety. In the old Mustangs, the gas tanks were "dropped in" the trunk of the car and had a nasty habit of bursting into the backseat and torching the occupants during ten-mile-per-hour fender benders. Ned must have installed hundreds of steel walls behind the back seats of these old flame-throwers. But Poppy considered tinkering with the old Fords sacreligious. Ned was right but Poppy just folded his arms and grunted.

"If you can't stand the heat, you should stay out of the Mustang."

On this note, Dad turned to me.

"Want to take a walk, kiddo?" Dad asked. "Come on, let's share a soda."

Dad looked and smelled as if he were going to church. Clean shaven, buttoned-up shirt tucked into his good jeans and smelling of Stetson. His city finery. After buying a five-dollar Pepsi, we walked out of the conference area, past the old Fords and vintage box racers into the enormous open-air lobby.

We found a bench that overlooked the street. Dad took the soda and a long sip. After a moment of silence, he asked, "How's the writing going? Any takers on your screenplay?"

"Nope. No takers," I admitted shyly.

"Why not? It's better than 99% of the crapola I see on television now."

I shrugged.

He crossed his legs and put his arm behind me. "How's the boy downstairs?"

I felt my throat close up. I took the soda from Dad and gulped some down. "I can't talk about it."

"Technically you can, but you won't."

"Correct."

"You still like him?"

"Yes and no."

"Yes and no," he repeated as he looked at me in deep thought. "I think that's what we men like to call a mixed message."

I turned to Dad. "How did you know? About Mom. How did you know she was the one for you?"

The question seemed to catch him off guard. "Wow, how did I know?" he thought out loud. He puffed his cheeks and let out a big breath. "I guess it was like my first Mustang. You remember the pictures of that little green car?" He smiled to himself in thought. "I knew it was dangerous, but I also knew I had to have it. Nothing else would do. And if I didn't have it, I would spend my whole life wishing whatever I had would turn into it."

"But it was a death trap."

"I know. Maybe that's what made it more fun. I just loved everything about it. The way it looked. The way it felt. The way I felt calling it mine and taking it home. I guess it made me feel like a movie star," he said, smiling to himself.

"But it could've burned you alive."

"It didn't."

"But she did." I stared down at my drink.

Dad's hand stroked the back of my head. "You saying I should have settled for an Oldsmobile? Some big land yacht, because it was safe?"

"Maybe safe isn't so bad."

"You're right. Sometimes it's not so bad. Sometimes it's not so good either." I could feel him looking at me. He took my shoulders and turned me around to face the sea of cars inside the center. The shine of wax on their gleaming colors made the floor into a rainbow.

"Look in there. See all those cars? See that red Mustang over by Poppy? That was your mother. Beautiful, a bit dangerous and worth it. For me, at least."

"How, Dad? How can anyone be the right one if they leave you?"

"Because I knew she would," he said.

I looked at him in shock as he kept staring out over the convention floor. When Dad got lost in thought, it seemed he wound up in a better place. A happier place. A place with good memories that didn't sting or turn bitter. Like that photograph I kept in my underwear drawer, Dad would always at the barbeque, feeling the same happiness he'd known at the moment when the flash went off.

"Geri, I always knew there was something troubling her.

In those days we called it melancholy. I knew she had it, but I didn't care. I loved her anyway. And she loved me. Even when those gray days came in. I let her go because I knew she loved me. She could marry a million other men. I had her heart. Even if it was only for a few years. It would be better than never having it at all. I know it's different for you, being her daughter and all. But for me, if I had to do it all over again, I would. In a New York minute."

"Why? What did you get out of it?"

"A whole room full of shiny Mustangs could never equal one mint green Muntz given to me by the King himself. Geri, your mother was a Mustang. But you, sweetie? You're the Muntz. And that's the one I'm keeping for life. Whatever fire and hell I had to go through to get you, it was worth it." Dad put his giant arm around me as my head fell against his chest. Giant cockroaches, wimpy photographers and cheating fiancés left my head for that moment. Sometimes, a dad can make it all better.

"I love you, Dad," I said softly.

"I love you too, Geri Bean. Now, about this boy . . . You did get the tire iron Poppy and I sent you?"

23

Two for the Show

That night, after Poppy and Dad ate monster pastrami sandwiches and sped back to Long Island, Maria and I decided to have a poor girl's night-in. Being too broke to go out, we figured we would make do with the alcohol left over from last year's Christmas party. As Maria and I rounded up bottles of Zima and Chambord, Emmy prepared for her final date with Bryan.

Maria and I couldn't believe that Emmy had agreed to attend another of Bryan's company dinners, where she was to act as his lucky charm while he asked Ingrid out. Emmy explained that if she didn't agree, it would reinforce what he probably already surmised: that Emmy was as hopelessly devoted to him as an adult as she had been in elementary school, middle school, high school and every spring break throughout college. We'd tried to talk her out of it, but she figured if she did the opposite of what she felt, she might go out with a bit of dignity. Maria thought the odds of her not crying during the appetizers were slim to none. I was betting on dessert.

Maria and I were taking our first sips of the evening when the doorbell rang. Maria got up to answer it.

"Oh, hey, Bryan!"

Bryan stood outside the door looking handsome in a

gray suit and pink oxford shirt. "Hey, Maria! Long time no . . ."

Maria let the heavy steel door slam in his face. She called out to Emmy as she made her way back to the couch. "Emmy! Bryan's here!"

Emmy walked into the living room, putting the cap on her waterproof mascara.

"So where are you going?" I asked.

"Some Japanese place in Midtown. Japanos or Japos? Something like that."

"Keep your chin up," Maria said as we both looked at her with fake smiles.

"And if you feel like you're going to cry, eat some wasabi. It's a good cover."

"Thanks," Emmy said. She threw us a fake smile back and walked bravely out the door and into her nightmare. Our faces both relaxed as soon as the door shut.

"I hope she likes to sing," I said.

"Why?"

"Because it's a karaoke bar."

Maria laughed as she reached for her overnight bag. "She's having your kind of luck."

Wondering how she could have read my mind, I ordered, "Drink up."

"Wait," she said as she rummaged through her bag. After a moment of searching, she pulled out her gun. "Let me disassemble this first." She held the Glock proudly in front of her as she removed the magazine.

"Ahhh, God." I winced. "That freaks me out."

"What does?"

"You with a piece."

She looked at me as she cracked the weapon apart like a lobster. "Someone around here has to."

"Don't you ever get scared?"

"Of what?"

"Gingivitis," I said. "Getting shot?"

"What the hell's going to happen to me in this neighborhood? Other than that freak push-in burglar who, as we all know, doesn't strike during rush hour. The worst I'm going to get is a jaywalker with an attitude, a cellphone and a good lawyer." She laid each part lovingly on the coffee table next to her purple drink.

"I mean dying. Don't you ever think about it? That you could die in the line of duty?

"Well, if I do," she said as she leaned back on the sofa. "I'd like to go out doing something really heroic. You know, like saving kids from a burning church, or fighting off a perp holding hostages. Something that makes the papers and puts cops in a good light for a change. My mom would put that triangle-folded flag next to Grandpa's on the mantel. Something my Dad would be super proud of and my brothers could eat."

As I finished my own glass, the alcohol and the sheer patheticness of our night-in hit me. I jumped up and began to pace. "This is depressing. We should be out there," I said pointing to the window.

"On the fire escape?"

"No! Out there. In the scene. In the city. Not here drinking Chambord and Zima, talking about how we're going to die."

"Geri, it could be worse. You could be sitting at a karaoke bar waiting for the man of your dreams to ask out the woman of his."

Then it hit me. Where exactly we should be. "Let's get her!" I said as I threw my fist in the air. "Let's reclaim our friend. Let's reclaim our lives!"

"At a karaoke bar? Geri, dying of embarrassment isn't the way I want to go," Maria said as she poured herself another purple shot.

"Come on," I begged.

Maria held up her shot glass. "Geri, I'd rather eat glass."

I stuffed my hands in my pockets and felt some loose change. Then I remembered I was saving a California state quarter for Max. I pulled out the change and sifted through the coins to find it. I picked it up and presented it to Maria.

"Quarters. Whoever gets to five first. If I win, we go get Emmy. If not, we stay here until our teeth turn black."

Never backing down from a drinking challenge, Maria agreed. "You're on, crazy."

Holding the quarter between her thumb and index finger, she bounced the coin off the table, over the glass and into my lap. I picked the quarter up, rubbed it between my hands and made an affirmation out loud. "Our fate will be decided tonight and our lives changed forever."

"Whatever, just bounce it."

With a soft touch, I threw the quarter down on the table. The quarter appeared to travel in slow motion as it bounced off the table and landed on the rim of the shot glass. It spun on the rim as if by magic. Maria and I stared in amazement, wondering which direction it would fall when it finally came down.

24

Three to Get Ready

Lots of ideas sound great at the time. Marrying before the age of twenty-one, Vietnam, painting your walls purple, to name a few. But as Maria and I crouched on the kitchen floor of Japas Karaoke Bar-n-Grill, I wasn't quite sure what great idea had brought us here.

After showing Maria's badge to the kitchen staff, all of whom appeared to be taking turns smoking weed in the back alley, they allowed us to sneak through their kitchen to get to a view of the dining room. As Maria and I waited behind the swinging door, we understood why the cooking crew needed multiple bong hits. Each time the door opened, a burst of unapologetically bad singing barreled into the kitchen. All the staff who didn't have the luxury of a numbing drug just cringed as they angrily threw salads together. Figuring the diners' attention would be on the singer, we scurried into the dining room behind a waitress carrying a large tray of miso soup.

Once inside the dining room, we saw who was making all the noise. On the polished black stage illuminated by purple neon stood a plump, sweaty man attempting to find his way through Billy Joel's "We Didn't Start the Fire." I couldn't take my eyes off him as he burped and barked his way through the past fifty years of American history.

Maria couldn't be bothered as she searched for Emmy in the dark dining room.

"I can't see her," she whispered as she stood on her tiptoes, straining to get a better view of the back of the room. "Is this the right place?" When I was finally able to tear myself away from the man screaming about Cola wars I spotted her. Emmy and Bryan sat slurping soup no more than two feet in front of us, both with their backs to us. Immediately we crouched down, pretending to tie our laceless shoes. The fat man wrapped up his song to a flurry of applause at Emmy's table. He made his way back to the table of suits, slapping high-five to everyone in his path.

"Billy Joel's got nothing on me!" he cried as he used his napkin to wipe the sweat off the three rolls that made up his brow. He stuffed the tips of the napkin in his pants before plopping down. "And Christie Brinkley's got nothing on my Ronni!"

He reached over and grabbed the hand of the extremely thin, extremely large-breasted woman who sat beside him. She patted him lovingly on his bald spot as her brilliant diamond bracelet caught the streams of light beaming from her brilliant doorknob-sized diamond ring. In a thick, nasally voice she baby-talked to him.

"Me so love the miso soup," she said as she slurped the salty tofu.

"Me so love you," he cooed as he kissed her hand.

Maria's head dropped into her chest. "You gotta be fucking kidding me," she muttered.

"What can you say? Guys dig big boobs."

"Not our Bryan. He seems to have other things on his mind."

With all the men at the table trying in vain not to stare at the big guy's chick's breasts, Bryan's eyes never left Ingrid. Ingrid wasn't eating. She just sat with her elbows on the table, fingers laced together as she watched Bryan attempt to stick a spoon in his mouth. From behind, we could only see Emmy's head hang low. I imagined her using her napkin to periodically dry her eyes. Her head didn't even come up as Billy Joel Jr., stood up to make a toast.

"To a beautiful future with Far East Tech!" They all raised their cups of saki.

"To a beautiful future," Ingrid said, staring at Bryan.

"Beautiful," he answered under his breath.

"Beautiful," Emmy spat sarcastically.

I leaned in and whispered to Maria, "So how do you think we should get her out of here?" I asked. But there was no answer. Maria had vanished. I looked around until the lights dimmed. The Japanese MC took the stage.

"We now have a special dedication. To all the Southold High School alumni. Here is 'Settlers Strong and Free'!"

Bryan's attention finally left Ingrid. He jumped in his seat as he elbowed Emmy awake. "Hey, Emmy! Are you going to sing?"

"No," she muttered as she stared up at the stage.

"What is this song?" Ingrid asked as she turned around to face the stage.

"It's the song the soccer team used to sing," Emmy answered. "The only ones who know all the words are . . ."

Before Emmy could finish her sentence, she saw Maria standing in the center of the purple stage. Chest out, with fists proudly resting on her hips, Maria bellowed out the song she and her fellow teammates used to chant before every soccer game.

"For the glory of Old Southold High, our founders strong and free . . ."

Bryan, also being a big soccer star in his day, jumped up and began to sing from the table. Emmy just sat there with her mouth half-open.

"We fought and toiled for land that's loyal. For farmers all are we . . ."

Feeling I had to join in, I snaked my way through the tables and slowly climbed the three steps onto the neon-lit stage floor. I stood at least five feet behind Maria, mumbling nervously through the lyrics with my arms glued to my sides; looking like a third-grader trying to find her way through the word "indefatigable" in a spelling bee.

But not Maria. Her blue mouth proclaimed her unabashed love of her home team. Maria felt the words. And although there was no trumpet section to accompany her, she made the whole crowd feel them as well. With a hint of tears in her eyes, she walked to the back of the stage and slung her arm around my shoulders. She stuck the microphone under my lips as we sang the final verse in unison. Me squinting out over the restaurant under the hot lights and Maria with her eyes shut.

"The sun shines high, we do or die for Settlers land's for me."

The crowd cheered as Maria's eyes popped open. She grabbed the microphone away and screamed, "Tuckers take it in the face! YEAH!"

Although we couldn't see him, we could hear Bryan hoot in agreement. In a flurry of applause, Maria walked to the front of the stage and put the microphone back on its stand. After a quick bow to the fans, she turned around and walked up to me. Putting her hand on my shoulder she announced silently, "Your turn."

Bahh dum. Chit. Chit.

That was all it took. The strum of two chords followed by two brisk hits on a snare. I officially left my body. I found myself tipping Maria's hand off my shoulder as I swaggered up to the microphone. Releasing it from the stand, I stood proudly on the end of the stage and hollered out in perfect pitch "*Jailhouse Rock*," the song I'd sung at least a hundred times from the backseat of the Muntz.

I didn't recognize the voice. I didn't see the lyrics whizzing down the blue teleprompter. I didn't notice the shuffle of the crowd. I wasn't there. I was a kid singing into a Philips head screwdriver as she watched her dad rotate a tire and her mom tap her heels on the cement floor.

Midway through the second verse I thought I sucked so bad that the Japas patrons were getting up to leave. After my eyes adjusted to the light, I realized that the crowd had stood up to dance. Japanese waiters, businessmen, big-titted escorts, Swedish dream destroyers all stood at their respective tables and did some version of the twist. As I threw my hips around the stage, everyone seemed to feed off my energy. And how could they not? After all, I wasn't dancing. I wasn't singing. I wasn't even sober.

I was auditioning. And I got the part.

In the gaggle of dancing patrons, I noticed Maria lead Emmy through the crowd. Pulling her up onto the stage, I handed the microphone over to her so that she could sing the final verse. To my surprise, Emmy threw down her purse, grabbed the microphone and sang with complete abandon, unloading all her frustrations and disappointments onto one poor little Elvis tune. The crowd reached almost fever pitch when she dropped to her knees and shouted out the last line of the song.

The cheer from the patrons overtook the sound of the song fading. When the house lights slowly came up, we could see everyone cheering. Bryan shouted out Emmy's name over and over as he pounded his hands together in applause. But Emmy didn't notice. She was too busy looking at Maria and me with all the pride of an F student passing the Sequential II Regents exam. She grabbed our hands and raised them up in the air. We bent over and gave the crowd one of those exaggerated Broadway bows. Looking over at Emmy with her hair falling out of her bun and Maria with her blue teeth, I said to myself, "I will never forget this night." And if life ever causes the three of us to drift apart, we will always have this moment. This brilliant New York moment.

The blood rushed back into our heads as we stood up, and Maria and I stumbled backward.

Emmy picked up her bag and panted, "Come on, guys. Let's go home."

She dragged us off stage, into a nearby hallway, past the women's bathroom and out a back door marked EXIT. Once we got outside, Emmy walked into the street with her arm in the air to hail a cab. My head was still spinning as I gulped a mouthful of cool night air. I placed my hands on my knees to steady myself while Maria looked around the street in a daze.

"Didn't you forget your coat?" she asked Emmy as a cab stopped short in front of us.

Emmy held the door as Maria and I piled in. "I don't care," she answered as she slammed the door. Maria and I looked at each other and decided not to press the issue. We figured whatever she'd left in the restaurant wasn't worth going back to get.

Since the driver didn't want me to puke in his car, he let us off two blocks away from the apartment.

"Guess what happens in two hours?" Emmy asked.

"What?"

"Bryan notices I'm gone." Emmy and Maria doubled over in giggles. All I could do was hold my stomach. I tried to steady myself using a streetlight.

"Guys, stop. I'm going to get sick."

Emmy wiped her eyes and walked over to me. "Why

don't you go back to the apartment," Emmy said as she rubbed my back. "I have some money. I'll go and get milk and ginger ale for your tummy."

"Hey, just 'cause Geri's a lightweight doesn't mean we have to stop drinking," Maria said, pointing to Emmy. "Loan me a couple of bucks and I'll go to the liquor store on the corner. Geri, be a peach and buzz us in."

"Okay," I croaked as my mouth started to fill up with pre-puke saliva. Our huddle broke and the three of us hurried off in different directions. The street seemed unusually dark and quiet for a Saturday night, but still, I didn't want to be caught throwing up in front of my building. Todd had recently seen me in some compromising positions. I didn't want vomiting my brains out on our front stoop to be one of them.

My key was out and at the ready far before I got to the front door of the building. Jesus, Mary, Joseph and God don't let me run into anyone, I thought. If I don't, I swear I'll never touch Chambord again. This sounded like a promise I could keep as I didn't feel Chambord would be a very hard liquor to give up. It's considered a mixer, it took ten years to finish a bottle and, in a pinch, I could use Schnapps instead.

After pushing myself through the front door, I began to hustle up the first flight of stairs. As I reached the top of the flight, I could feel my feet begin to slow down. My stomach suddenly stopped hurting. All the senses that had been focused on my stomach began to refocus. The sweat kept pouring down my back as I stopped and listened. I was waiting for something. Waiting to figure out why I was suddenly sober and why suddenly everything felt so wrong.

25

Between Our Doors

Each of the thousand times I entered the front door to my
building, I would hear the double clicks of the lock closing
behind me. It took me until the second flight of stairs to realize what I hadn't heard tonight. And not hearing it
sounded like a siren. I stood still for a moment and listened for footsteps. Nothing. Hedda used to tell me that I
would know I was a true New Yorker when I had a hard
time falling asleep in the country. It would be too quiet.
Continuing up the stairs, I chuckled to myself. Maybe I was
a real New Yorker because the quiet is freaking me out.

Then I heard it. Strong, purposeful footsteps. Someone
had followed me in. I leaned over the banister to get a
look but could only see a sliver of the stairs below.

"Maria?" My voice just bounced around the tiled hallway. I stood there for a moment, waiting for her reply.
Nothing. Worse yet, the footsteps had stopped.

"Todd?" I called out as my voice cracked. I waited another moment to hear a reply, or the sound of a door opening. Still nothing.

Then the hallway echoed with the sound of my
shoes rapidly clicking up the stairs. As I got closer to my
apartment, I thought, *I'm paranoid. This is just me being
stupid, drunk and paranoid.* Once I get in the apartment

and hear the safe snaps of our deadbolt, I can exhale. When I got to my door, my hands shook with such force that I dropped my enormous key ring onto the doormat. When I stood back up I saw him.

A head wrapped in a nylon stocking peered at me from inside the shadow of a black hooded sweatshirt. A nervous cry hummed up my chest but stopped in my throat. When I saw him reach into the front of his hoodie and produce a small handgun, the cry dislodged itself from my throat and began to crawl out of my mouth. He leapt toward me and grabbed the back of my head. Smelling like stale cigarettes and garlic, he pressed his tightly wrapped mouth into my ear.

"It's worse if you yell. Much worse," he said. I pressed my lips together and nodded affirmatively. He relaxed his grip and continued, "Let's go, sweetheart. Inside. Fast."

My bulky key ring jingled with the sound of eleven keys bouncing off each other. When I looked down at all the metal teeth, I couldn't recognize which key opened which lock. Each one looked exactly the same. Each looked foreign. My hands shook so hard, I dropped the keys again. But as I felt him breathing in my right ear, I heard another voice in my left. Not my own. A female voice. A woman's voice. She sounded calm, firm and familiar.

"Don't let him in your apartment."

When I bent down to pick up the keys, another image came to mind. A gun. Maria's gun. She'd left her Glock in the apartment.

"Don't let him in your apartment," the voice repeated.

Then another object. A tire iron. I'd left it right by the front door like Poppy had suggested. A tire iron doesn't beat a gun.

"Geraldine, do not let him in your home," the voice insisted.

As I tried again to decipher which key opened the front door, he muttered impatiently for me to hurry up. But when I tried to stick the key that opened the door to Dad's shop in the lock, he had had enough. In an attempt to jog my memory, he grabbed a handful of my hair.

"I said fast!" he ordered through his teeth before smashing my head into our steel door. My eyebrow caught on the door's edge, causing a warm drip to run down my face. I stumbled backward in shock as he grabbed the key ring from me.

"Where's the fucking key? Which one?" he spat as he attempted to try to stick the twelfth-floor J. V. bathroom key in the front door. In his frustration he lifted up the stocking covering his face to get a better look. While he was madly fumbling through my key chain, his mistake began to dawn on me. He hadn't waited until I had actually opened the door before revealing himself. And when he heard another voice approaching, I could tell his mistake dawned on him as well.

"Geri! You puking in the hall?" Maria yelled from two flights below.

He looked at me, waiting to see if I would answer. Under the jaundice-yellow lights of the hallway I got a good look at his face. His eyes dug into mine, waiting to see how I would answer. As blood from the cut on my forehead made its way into my left eye, I calmly called out, "Is Patrick with you?"

His expression quickly changed from frustration to fear. The gun disappeared inside his hooded sweatshirt as he turned and hustled down the stairs. I rushed behind him to the top of the stairwell. Looking down, I saw Maria slowly plod up, each step carrying a brown bag with two bottles of red wine. The burglar kept his head down as he scurried past her.

"How drunk are you? Why would he . . ." she began to say as she lifted her head to look up at me. When she caught sight of the blood running down my face, she dropped the wine.

Her mind registered everything so fast that I couldn't stop her. The sound of the dropped wine crashing on the stairs made the burglar haul his ass down the next flight. Maria bounded after him, lifting her feet and taking the stairs three at a time. I ran after them with my heart banging in my ears. Mom, make her stop, I cried in my head. He has a gun. But I couldn't form the words. Instead, the only words that came out of my mouth were, "Don't, don't, don't."

Within moments, the sounds of feet banging down stairs were replaced by grunts. The chase had ended. I rounded the corner and ran straight into Todd's door. No light shone from underneath, but I pounded on it anyway, hoping he was just asleep.

"Todd! Todd!" I yelled, but no one answered. Just as I was about to scream out "Fire!" a shot rang out in the hallway. A shot that echoed loudly as the bullet ricocheted down the stairwell. My hands covered my ears as I threw myself onto the hallway floor.

"Don't, don't, don't . . ."

Crawling down the next flight of stairs, I saw Maria struggling with the burglar. She'd caught him on the first flight and was trying to wrestle the gun away from him. After a swift kick in the groin, the gun dropped from his hand. I winced, waiting for another shot. But none came; only the sound of metal smacking on marble. I scurried over to the weapon, picked it up and ran back up a flight, away from the struggle. The gun looked nothing like the one Maria had disassembled in the apartment. Maria's looked like a toy: clean with well-marked indentations and a clearly defined safety latch. This gun looked like it had been the property of many owners. The handle was worn smooth on the left side and shiny metallic scratches sliced up the barrel. The metal felt warm from being pressed against his body. I held the gun away from me like a piece of rancid meat or a smelly sock and placed it under apartment #11's welcome mat, which read, WIPE YOUR PAWS.

When I returned to the fight, the burglar was beginning to uncoil. Maria's elbow connected with his chin and knocked him back into the wall. His head bounced off the tile, causing a sharp chunk of ceramic to dislodge and fall. As he slid down the wall, he stared at Maria in total disbelief. I could only imagine that he was wondering how this short girl, the kind of girl he liked to target, could be the one to take him down? He reached out for Maria's arm in a feeble attempt to stand up. But as soon as he raised his hand, she grabbed his wrist and pulled his arm behind his back. She pushed him down onto his stomach as she grabbed the back of his head. Straddling him, she looked as if he were giving her a pony ride down the last flight of stairs. I stood a few feet behind them, frozen. She turned her head and looked back at me.

"The gun? Is it gone?" she asked, breathless.

I nodded.

"Good." Her attention turned to the man between her legs. Then with three hard thunks, she pounded his head on the marble stairs until his body relaxed. She'd either knocked him out or split his head open. When she let go of his wrists, his arms fell limp against his sides.

I put my hand on her shoulder as she looked down at the fallen fighter. Her expression seemed to be more surprised than angry. As if she'd just stumbled unexpectedly upon this horrific scene on her way home from a baby shower. Her voice rose two octaves into that of a little girl as she wiped her mouth with her hands.

"Oh, God, Geri. What have I done?"

Staring down at the man who lay motionless on the stairs I said, "It's okay."

"Geri, let's go. Let's go."

She grabbed my hand and we raced down the stairs. But we didn't get far. Just as we were about to step into the lobby, our feet froze. A puddle of milk was beginning to collect at the base of the stairs. Neither of us could breathe. It wasn't until we saw a ribbon of red swirl into it that our feet moved from the spot they'd frozen in.

Emmy.

Around the corner, under the mailboxes, sat Emmy in a pool of blood and milk. The shot that got away during the struggle had ricocheted off the walls and into Emmy's shoulder. She managed to prop herself up against the wall as a liter bottle of ginger ale rolled back and forth against her foot.

"Maria, what's happening?" she whispered.

Maria grabbed Emmy and pulled her forward, checking her back and head to see where the bullet had hit her.

"You're going to be fine, Emmy, you hear? You're going to be okay," she said calmly as she took off her belt to use as a tourniquet. I couldn't move. I just stood there in shock, watching Maria feverishly tend to Emmy.

"Geri. Geri!" Maria snapped. "Get help."

Smearing my way through the pink mess, I walked backward out of the front door and into the night air. I looked up at the other apartment buildings on the street. The darkened windows looked down on me, letting me know the block was filled with people who had no idea what had happened in our building. My mouth opened, but nothing seemed to come out. I could hear nothing.

But someone could. A light went on. A window opened. An older woman in a nightgown looked down at me with a phone in her hand. Then another light appeared in another building. Another window opened. Slowly the apartments facing the street began to wake up. Soon I saw flashing red and white lights at the end of the street. Only the siren didn't seem to blare. The men running toward me didn't seem to make a sound. The old woman who lived in apartment #17 with the ten cats stood on the stoop in her housecoat and curlers, directing the cops into the lobby. I saw Patrick jump out of one of the police cars in plain clothes. He ran up to me and flung his arms around me. I could feel his lips move next to my ear but could hear nothing.

Once I saw the three EMTs crouch around Emmy and Maria, my ears cleared and all the evening's noise popped into my head. The sirens, the cop chatter, the warbling voices, beeping radios and Patrick's voice trying to soothe me.

"We're here, Geri. It's going to be all right."

The police carried Emmy out of the lobby and onto the front stoop, away from the crowd of tenants that had started to form in the lobby. From baseball bats to frying pans to an angry beagle, almost everyone had brought down an article to defend themselves. But as I watched Maria hold Emmy's head while the paramedics cut the sleeve off her bloody blouse, everything went blurry. The tears mixed with the blood from my head wound made the entire scene appear as if it were happening underwater. Patrick held me with one arm as he pushed back the EMT who was trying to bandage the gash on my head.

"Geri, Geri, it's okay," Patrick pleaded. "You can stop screaming."

26

Visiting Ours

"May I see her?" I asked the Nurse Roshonda as she put the finishing touches on my bandage. Apparently, the doctor who'd worked on my head wasn't a fan of seeing blood. It took only six stitches to close the gash on my forehead but eight pounds of gauze and three reams of medical tape to cover it. Afterward Roshonda saw me looking like a fluffy pirate and was kind enough to spruce me up.

"I'd be surprised if you could," she said as she smeared a dollop of salve onto a small rectangular patch. "Doctors around here think gauze grows on trees and women don't have mirrors."

I chuckled until I felt a sharp streak sear through my temple. Roshonda shook her head as she poured a cup of water.

"That Percocet didn't kick in yet, huh?" She held up my chin as she placed the rose-colored plastic cup to my lips. "It will, honey. It will."

"I want to see my friend," I said. "Can I go up?"

"Visiting hours on the third floor are over. Besides, I think it's best if you just let her sleep."

"It was only in the shoulder, right?"

"Yes, it went right in and out. They patched her up real good. She's going to be fine. She just needs some rest. And so do you. It's the only way a concussion heals." She fluffed the pillow behind me and gently pushed me back onto the bed, lifting my ankles so that I would take the hint not to get up. "Now just lie here for a bit. I'll let you know when your family arrives." Roshonda gently patted my shoulder before turning around. Her long steely dreadlocks sat motionless on her back as she made her way to the door.

"Where's Maria? The other girl with me?" I asked as I propped myself up on my elbows.

Roshonda turned around in the doorway and rested her hand on the dimmer switch.

"The last time I saw her, she was talking to another police officer and two women outside. You need to tell the older one she wears too much perfume."

She dimmed the lights until they went off. I lay back down in the bed and listened to her sneakers squeak down the hall. When I felt certain she wasn't going to return, I rolled out of bed and crept to the door. Opening it a crack, I peered out into the empty hospital hallway. Other than a few stranded wheelchairs and abandoned IV stands, the coast seemed to be clear. Slipping off my shoes, I walked out into the hallway toward the swinging doors marked STAIRS.

The sign on the third floor had an arrow that pointed left to ICU, right to PRENATAL. The night nurse didn't notice me as I scurried past the nurses' station. I peered into each room through its sliver of a window until I saw the half-opened door at the end of the hall. When I stepped lightly into the darkened room, I saw her.

Propped up in bed, Emmy slept soundly with bandages covering her right shoulder and arm. The glow from the streetlights that filtered in through the vertical blinds allowed me to see the round stain of blood that peeked through her bandage. The only noise in the room came

from the soft ticking of the morphine dispenser that would
ensure her comfort during the night.

Shutting the door behind me, I slid across the floor in my
socks to the side of the bed. I dug her hand out from under
the covers and held it in mine. She felt cold and clammy as
I traced my finger over the rubber tube of her IV.

In the quiet of that room it finally dawned on me what a
fool I had been. So many times I had taken my own life in
my hands. Running in front of buses, licking power strips,
balancing on the fire escape four flights up, never caring if
I fell. Hoping I might. But, Emmy was the one who got
hurt. As I looked down at the hospital tag wrapped around
her wrist, a wave of guilt flooded over me. She was here
because I wasn't brave enough to get in his face and fight
him off. Because I wouldn't let him inside my apartment.
I indirectly put a bullet in her because when I had a
chance to really put myself in harm's way, I didn't take it.

"She saved you, you know," he said. Leaning against a radiator across the room stood J. T. His white suit was illuminated by the streetlight. "He would have killed you."

"No," I whispered. "I should have let him in. He would
have just robbed us and left. I have nothing worth stealing
anyway. Nothing that can't be replaced." As I tried to rub
some warmth into Emmy's hand, my head began to go
numb and a chill filled the room. I figured the painkiller
must have kicked in because I could no longer feel my
face.

"You're right. That's why he would have killed you," he
said as he walked over to the blue plastic chair tucked in
the far corner of the room. He sat down and perched his
elbows on the armrests as he folded his hands in front of
his face. His eyes studied mine. "There would be nothing
to take. Well, except for a pile of rejection notices and
cheap suits. The only thing in that apartment would have

been one girl. One girl who could describe his face perfectly to the police. And one weapon that didn't belong to
him."

The question escaped my lips as if I hadn't heard him.
"What are you saying?"

He moved to the edge of the chair and leaned forward.
"Geri, you would have been killed. And he would have
gotten away."

I shook my head in disbelief. I wanted him to stop, but
he continued unfazed. Like he was bringing me up to
speed on an afternoon soap opera.

"Maria would have found you first. Facedown on the
floor of your kitchen. You, admirably, would have been
holding a tire iron. But you were right. Gun beats tire iron."

"No." I felt myself begin to rock back and forth. "You're
making this up."

J. T. leaned back into the chair. He picked up a magazine that lay on an adjoining table and nonchalantly
flipped through the pages. "It's ironic. You, kitten, would
have been the one who got off easy. Maria would never get
over it. That image would have haunted her for the rest of
her life. And it would have killed your dad. Losing his wife
and his daughter! Who would blame him for running the
Muntz with the garage door closed? And Poppy! Forget
about that old man . . ."

"Stop it!" I barked. The room began to rotate slowly. I
steadied myself on the bed. None of this was real. None of
this could be happening. But as J. T. painted the grotesque
scenario, I could see the images fly through my head like
memories. They were as real as if they had happened.
Blood pooled around my chest as I lay on our kitchen
floor. The small hole the bullet made in my back seemed
so insignificant compared to the one it made going out my
chest. My arm extended to the tire iron, which lay only

inches away from my fingertips. My eyes were open and lifeless. They held the same shocked look as Maria's as she violently wrestled Emmy away from the kitchen so she wouldn't see. The same as my dad's as he drifted off to sleep in the front seat of his car with the sound of Elvis's "Teddy Bear" playing in the locked garage. But none of that had actually happened. I was alive. And Emmy lay before me. Sleeping, broken, medicated. J. T. walked up to the other side of the bed without taking his eyes off me. I turned my attention to Emmy as I tucked her bangs behind her ears.

"Was that supposed to happen?"

He shook his head. "She wouldn't allow it."

"You're saying Emmy chose to wind up like this?"

"No. I'm saying she wouldn't have it. Not on her watch."

He nodded to someone over my shoulder. Then I knew who *she* was. I could smell her. Windsong and cold cream. The skin on my back prickled to attention. It was as if I had walked into a dark room that I had not been in since I was a child, but could remember the location of every piece of furniture. My heart seemed to stop beating for a moment as I heard her voice behind me.

"You are supposed to live," she murmured into my left ear. That voice. That beautiful voice. I hadn't heard it in almost twenty years. This was the voice that had whispered in my ear by the apartment door. Her breath traveled into my ear and snaked its way into my brain. My heart begged my body to turn around to see her. To run my hands over her face. To trace her perfectly arched eyebrows. To feel her soft cheeks against mine. But my drug-inflamed head and abject fear kept my eyes and body motionless. Too scared to turn around to see if my mom was really standing behind me. Too frightened she'd disappear if I did. My mouth opened, but only empty air choked through. I wanted desperately to talk to her. I wanted desperately to say all the things that were bottled up in my heart. My throat hurt from holding them in but my mouth wouldn't let them come out.

Her voice crept closer to my face. "You are supposed to live."

Suddenly my back felt warm, as if I were being hugged. The chill left the room and was replaced by a rush of sweet-smelling air. I wrapped my arms around myself. In that instant, my courage rose and I tried to turn around to see her. But as I did, my eyelids sank shut. My head felt like a basketball losing its spin off a player's finger. My body sank down to Emmy's bed. My head rested by her feet. Then, for the second time that evening, I felt someone lift up my legs onto the bed. Tucking my feet under Emmy's pillow, I closed my eyes and let something larger than myself carry me off to sleep.

I don't remember what time it was when she shook my knee.

"Hey, girl," Emmy croaked. "Stop hogging the bed."

I opened my eyes and saw her staring down at me from the opposite end of the bed. Her chapped lips cracked out a smile. Still feeling heavy from the drugs, I could only lift up my head enough to prop it on the hump her feet made under the blanket.

"The bandages make it look worse than it is. Trust me," I whispered.

"Yeah," she said as she pressed her chin to her chest, straining to get a look down at her shoulder. "If my kids thought I was tough before . . ."

We both chuckled quietly, like the only two kids still up at a slumber party who are trying not to wake up the parents. As Emmy looked out the window at the lights of the city, tears began to drip down her face.

"Did Maria stop him?"

"Yeah, Em," I said, rubbing the white waffled blanket that covered her shin. "She got him."

She sniffled. "Good."

Then Mother Morphine and Papa Percocet ordered us to go back to sleep. We closed our eyes and drifted back from where we came.

"Geraldine Agnes O'Brien, you get your behind out of bed right now!"

Two enormous brown eyes hovered inches from my face.

"Aunt Bitsy?" I said in a daze.

"Wish I was. I'd kick your butt across the East River for sneaking out of that room," Roshonda said as she pushed me up to a sitting position. "Come on now, I told you I'd let you know when your family arrived."

"Who?" I couldn't seem to make out where I was.

"Your family. You know, the two bulldozers who call themselves your daddy and granddaddy," she said as she gently pushed me out of Emmy's room and into the hallway. "The old guy scared the guard into letting him keep his chain."

"Chain?"

Then I understood. Looking down the hallway, I saw Dad, Poppy and a nurse who was failing miserably to take away the metal chain Poppy had wrapped around his hand. Dad attempted to mediate until he caught sight of me.

"Geri!" His huge frame moved surprisingly fast as he jogged down the hall. Dad scooped me into his arms, lifting me at least a couple of feet in the air. He kept repeating my name over and over as his massive hands palmed my head. His chest heaved as he wept.

Poppy stood behind me and stroked my back. "What a

sissy your father is. He cried the whole way up here. Just the way you did when you were a little girl."

Dad put me down, then grabbed me by the ears. He gasped for breath between his sobs. "Nothing is allowed to happen to you, you hear me! You're my girl. You are my best girl." He threw me back into his chest with a thud and squeezed me so tight I thought I'd blow a stitch. "I'm not going to lose you."

Poppy leaned over and wiped a tear off my purple, asphyxiated cheek. "And if you leave me alone to deal with this pansy, I'll kill you until you're dead."

My arms reached out to Roshonda for help. After noticing my lack of oxygen, she gently asked my father to put me down. She then guided us down the hall toward the elevator. As the three of us walked slowly behind her, the other nurses stopped what they were doing and watched us pass. Being flanked by Dad and Poppy, I must have looked like a walk-up sandwiched between two skyscrapers.

"And from now on, I don't want you wandering off alone at all hours of the night," Dad said as he pointed his grimy finger at me.

Roshonda hummed loudly in agreement.

"Dad, in a couple of years I'm going to be thirty!"

"I don't care!"

Poppy reached out and tapped Roshonda on the shoulder. "Excuse me, ma'am? Could I have the room number of the man who did this? I just want to pay my respects."

Roshonda grabbed his chain and playfully yanked him into the elevator.

"You're not making more work for me, Grandpa. I've cleaned up enough messes already."

27

Fire Escaping

Maria and I left the hospital at 5:32 in the morning after I lied to a doctor that I had gotten one of the best night's of shut-eye in my life. They agreed to wait until seven o'clock to notify my father that I'd left. Whether my paranoia came from the Percocet or just the bad memory of Emmy sprawled out on the lobby floor, I didn't want to walk back to the building with anyone but Maria. I knew if I didn't, our building would seem less like home and more like a haunted house. So with two shopping bags filled with flowers that overflowed from Emmy's hospital room, Maria and I made the three-block trek back to the apartment. Neither of us said a word.

On our walk back to the apartment, a Bob White quail whistled at us. With as much breath as I could hold in my mouth, I answered it, just as J. T. had taught me that day in the apple tree on Poppy's farm a lifetime ago.

The first time Maria spoke was when I took my keys out to open the front door. "His name was Charlie Matteo."

My brain rapidly searched for a face to go with the name but none came to mind. "Who's that?"

"The guy who put that dent in your head. I went to visit him in the hospital during the night. He's in a coma."

The words fell out of my mouth as I stared at Maria in amazement. "Oh, God, why?"

"I don't know, Geri. I don't know. Maybe I needed to make sure that he wasn't going to hurt anyone again. Or maybe I needed to see what I could do to another human being. I don't know."

I leaned toward her and tried to peer into her eyes, which she hid from mine. "Maria, don't regret what you did. You saved our lives."

"I don't regret what happened. He was an evil prick. It's just—" She raised her head and looked at me. A lone tear made a track down her face. "Ever wish you could fix something that you broke on purpose?"

I shook my head.

"Geri, could you go in and let me know if they've cleaned it up?" She stared at the ground. Although Maria didn't move, one carnation from the top of an arrangement in the bag she held shook wildly back and forth.

I opened the door and walked up the stairway. I stood on the landing and inspected the surrounding area. There wasn't any blood. Only the ripped corners of bright yellow police tape stuck on the sill. A circle of white chalk surrounded a chip from the fourth marble step off the second-floor landing. The step where Maria had bashed Charlie Matteo's head in. I ripped every bit of tape off the window before I walked back down the stairs. I peeked my head around the corner and smiled at her, letting her know it was safe to enter.

We opened up the door to the apartment but didn't go in. The place looked frozen in time. Empty bottles of Zima littered the coffee table. Maria's duffel bag still rested in the corner and a quarter, heads up, stared at us from the bottom of a shot glass. A wave of medicated fatigue washed over me as I walked through the living room into

Emmy's bedroom. I dropped the bags and began to remove the flowers. Maria looked concerned as she stopped me from taking any out.

"Sit on your bed and I'll make some tea. You look like you're going to pass out."

I dragged my feet into my room, where the morning light had begun to creep in through the windows. I sat on the edge of my dented futon with its flowered sheets and lemon embroidered duvet. The sound of Maria shuffling around in the kitchen sounded as nice as the Bob White quail that I could still hear from outside. Within a few seconds I was asleep; I never heard the kettle go off, the bird finish its song or the knock on the door.

I awoke to realize the pain in my head was back. I overheard Maria's voice in the kitchen, talking to someone. By the way my heart raced, I knew who was on the other end of that conversation.

I sat motionless facing the window when I heard three slow raps on the inside of my bedroom door. The smell of him flooded the room, turning the marrow in my bones into something that felt like cold cement.

"Geri?" Todd asked gently. "Geri, how are you?"

I couldn't turn my body around to look at him. I couldn't answer him. The mattress sank slightly when he sat down.

"I wasn't home," he continued. "I was visiting my parents when I saw our building on the news. When they began to give . . ." His voice trailed off. After a few deliberate breaths he went on. "When they said a young woman was attacked. When they described you." Then he stopped.

"The thought of someone hurting you in this building tore me up inside."

A sarcastic chuckle burst from my mouth.

"Why?" I spat. "You wanted that honor for yourself?" And

with that, the bed straightened out. Todd stood up and began to pace.

I finally turned to face him. "Why didn't you tell me you were getting married?"

He looked shocked for a moment as his eyes found my bandage. He answered, "I couldn't. It just didn't seem right. It didn't feel right."

"And having sex with me while being engaged to someone else? That seemed right to you?"

He stuffed his hands in his pockets as his eyes searched the room for an answer. They finally landed on mine. "Yes, Geri. It did!"

My blood started to boil.

"How did it happen?" I demanded.

"What?"

"How did I go from a friend—from a neighbor who used to fix your car—to some kind of skank that you decided to use to get back at your cheating girlfriend?"

"Geri, wait . . ." he stammered as he walked toward me, his hand reaching out to touch my face. "You've got it all wrong."

I slapped it away. "Is it because I live right upstairs? Was I convenient? Maybe with your crappy car you couldn't afford to choose someone you had to drive to screw?"

"Geri, I didn't use you."

"Then what were you doing?"

He looked as if he was going to shake me. "I was falling for you!"

This comment made me want to rip his face off.

"You're a coward!" Todd tried to walk away from me, but I cut him off. "It's no wonder you can't stand up to Cassie to break up with her. Or to tell your father to fuck off. You can't even stand up for what you want."

But as I looked at him, all I could see was that green steel door marked #18. My fists pounding on it, praying he was inside. Praying he would come out to help me. But as he stood motionless, I realized there was no use. Even if someone was inside, he would never choose to open himself to me. No one would ever be home.

His voice cracked when he spoke. "This is what I want."

"Really? To marry someone you cheat on? Who cheats on you? That's what you want for your life?"

If Todd were a girl, tears of frustration would have welled in his eyes. Instead, his wide jaw flexed as he clenched his teeth. But I am a girl, and I could feel moisture begin to form in mine. Then I sat back on the bed and put my head in my hands.

I stopped talking to Todd. I finally found the words I wanted to say to my mother in the hospital. Barely audible, they squeaked out of my mouth.

"Why didn't you stay with me?"

This time, I let his hand touch my face. I let my cheek fall into the curve of his palm. His fingers stroked my cheek. My blood stopped burning. I didn't hate Todd. I didn't hate my mother. I didn't even hate that they'd left me. None of that seemed to matter now. What I hated was loving them but never being able to say it. They would never be open to hearing it. They would never say they loved me too. All the love I felt in my heart wouldn't change a thing. Both had left me long before I realized they were gone.

Then I lifted my head and looked at him for the last time. "Please don't come here again."

His nostrils flared and he forced down a wad of air. My eyes drifted back down into my lap. His steps got heavy as I heard him walk to the door, but he didn't walk out. I could feel his eyes boring into my head. I didn't want to look at him. I didn't want to read him. I wanted him to disappear, and twenty long seconds later he did.

After he left the room, I heard the apartment door lock behind him. Maria peeked her head in the doorway. "What happened? He looked like shit."

I flopped back down on the bed.

"Geri, what happened with you two?"

I rolled over and looked up at Maria, who was holding a steaming cup of tea and a plastic bottle of my prescription painkillers.

"Ever wish you could fix something you broke on purpose?"

28

Wash, Fold, Put Away

I opened my eyes. The only light in the room came from the sun outlining the shades that Maria had drawn over the windows. The last thing I remembered before lying back down was Maria giving me my painkillers. Now I hadn't a clue if the sun was coming up or going down. If I had slept the day away or just ten minutes.

My head dropped back down on the pillow as I stared up at the cracks in the plaster ceiling. When I rubbed my head, I realized that it no longer hurt. I sat up in bed and waited for the pain to rush up to my temples. Nothing. A breeze blew in and lifted the shade, bringing in more light and causing the letters on my walls to rustle. The dozens of rejection letters that I'd tacked around the room fluttered like October leaves that were too stubborn to fall off their branches. Walking over to the walls of shame, I began to do what Emmy had begged me to do for months: take each one down.

Frustration began to build in my heart. Each standard letter was crafted by some "assistant from the desk of " and stamped with the signature of the person who didn't have the time or inclination to reply to the likes of me. The statements in black and white foretold the future of my screenplay. *Unacceptable. Not at this time. Hope you find a home*

for this. Good but not for us. I began to read each one until
all the initials of all the agencies merged into an alphabet-
ical blur. CAA, IMG, ICM, NBC, CBS, PMA, GMC, all of the
fifty-two agencies and/or production companies I'd sent
my screenplay to had something in common with Todd
and my mom. None of them wanted anything to do with
me. I slammed the stack down into the garbage can as my
head fell into my hands.

"Of course GMC didn't want your screenplay, sweetie," I
heard J. T. say over my shoulder. "What's a car company
going to do with it anyway?"

I lifted my head and peered back into the garbage can.
The rejection letter sat at the top of the heap.

"Although your screenplay is very sweet, we here at General Motors cannot help you produce your film. However,
for all your future automobile needs, we hope you do turn
to your friendly local GM dealer . . ."

Go figure. I chuckled as I turned to J. T.

"I guess I should narrow . . . my . . . search. . . ." My voice
trailed off as I watched J. T. pick out a pair of white pants
from a pile of clothes on my bed. He folded them and
placed the pants neatly in a suitcase. "J. T.? What are you
doing?"

"What does it look like? I'll give you two guesses. And
I'm not making crème brûlée."

"I don't know," I said in a daze. "But whatever it is, please
stop."

He lifted up a pair of boxers and peeked at me through
the fly. "No, I'm not catching up on my tennis."

I walked over to the edge of the bed and stared down at
the suitcase. "Where did you get these clothes from?"

"It's for dramatic effect, kitten. You were a film major.
You should know what that means."

"Yes, but what effect are you trying to create?"

He dropped his drawers into the suitcase and closed the lid. After snapping the latches shut, he leaned over. "Geri, I'm leaving you."

I shook my head. "You can't do that."

"Yes, I can." He straightened up and picked up the suitcase. I followed at his heels as he walked around my bed.

"No, no, you can't."

"Yes, yes, I can."

"No, you won't."

"Watch me, Geri Ferry." Then he stopped and looked inquisitively into the air. "Geri Ferry. Ha! I loved that one. Glad it didn't work with that guy. He had no nuts." J. T. regained focus and kept walking. "Nuts are important. You'll realize that."

Panic and a sense of complete dread washed over me. I stomped in place, threw my hands on my hips and whistled.

J. T. stopped in midstep and slowly turned around. "Geri, don't make this harder than it already is."

"You're not allowed to go." Now my voice cracked. Tears poured down my cheeks. "I won't let you."

J. T. smiled and put down his bag. He walked back to me and placed his hands over my face, brushing away my tears with his thumbs. His spoke so softly that his lips barely moved.

"Geri, honey . . ."

"I don't care if you don't like me anymore. You have to stay."

"I didn't say that. I like you plenty."

"Then why are you going?" I begged.

"Because I think it's time."

"Time for what?"

"Time for you to know what this feels like."

For the first time ever, he leaned over and kissed me.

Only the kiss didn't touch my lips. It didn't make my knees buckle or make my hair stand up on end. Instead, it felt as if all my organs—liver, heart, brain, pancreas, intestines small and large—beamed white light into the rest of my body. My whole life felt like it had touched down at this very moment. And in that moment, everything made perfect sense. The rejections, the head wounds, the hangovers, the dent in the bed, all of it seemed perfect. It wasn't love. It wasn't passion. It wasn't acceptance, freedom or excitement. It was all of it tumbled in a white wash. It was my life. And for the first time, it made sense.

He pulled his lips off mine. I kept my eyes shut, trying to hold in that feeling as long as possible.

"And the great thing is, it doesn't go away when I leave," he said. "That's what I want you to have all the time. Every morning. But I can't give it to you here. Not like this."

I opened my eyes. The light stopped coming in through the shades. The room had turned dark. The sun wasn't rising as I'd originally thought. It was gone.

And so was J. T.

29

The Clock Strikes One

Out in the living room, Maria was watching television and eating a candy bar. When I finally emerged from my bedroom, an Asian man on the television was falling off a log and rolling into a pool of green slime. Maria let out a grunt and laughed once he made contact with the snot.

"He shouldn't have taken the dare. What a dope!" Maria said as she threw her hands in the air. "Now he's going to lose three hundred thousand yen and the car." She moved over so I could sit on the sofa.

"Where are Dad and Poppy?" I asked.

"They're fine. Hedda put them up at the Carlyle."

I pictured the two in the ultra-luxurious hotel suite. My father was probably sawing into his fifth porterhouse steak of the day while Poppy napped in front of free HBO with a bottle of Crown Royal balanced on his belly. It didn't surprise me that Hedda would put my family up in one of the swankiest hotels in town. I only hoped that the towels, bathrobes and ashtrays I knew Poppy would steal wouldn't run her bill too high. Thinking of steak, my stomach emitted a large growl.

"Do you want a Toblerone?" she asked, handing me one.

"I'll wait for dinner," I said sadly. I realized I hadn't eaten in twenty-four hours.

For the next half hour, I sat on the couch, holding a large Toblerone and watching *Super Showdown,* a show where Chinese couples nearly killed themselves by performing inane stunts in order to win a quickie divorce, possession of the larger assets and custody of their male children.

By the time Jing-Wei was ready to sink her teeth into a coffee can filled with beaver nuts, there was another knock on the door. I knew it wouldn't be Todd. My stomach growled as Maria answered it.

Patrick removed his cap as he walked into the room. His outfit looked more like the one he'd graduated from the academy in than his normal uniform.

"Who died?" Maria asked as she ate another section of her candy bar.

"We need you back at the station house."

"I put in for leave."

"I know, I know. They just need another statement."

Maria sat down in a huff. "Are you serious? Do I have to go? Really?"

"And Geri should come too," he said, pointing his cap at me. "They're going to need a statement from her as well."

"But the Changs are battling it out for their camper van," she objected.

"Look, I had orders to get you both. Now are you going to come quietly or am I going to have to shoot you?"

Maria grabbed her jumbo-sized wallet and stuffed it into her back pocket. "Guess I'd better go. With your astigmatism we don't want you to shoot the nudists across the street."

"Very funny, Pulchenic," Patrick said as he looked into a

mirror and fixed his hair. "Come on, Geri. We can all ride in the car together."

Inside the squad car, I realized I still had the candy bar clutched in my hand. I also noticed that there wasn't a hump in the backseat of a police car. There were no seatbelts either. The only thing it did have was a metal grate that separated the cops in the front from the perpetrators in the back. I thought it odd, as a metal grate would not make for a pleasant airbag, but Maria assured me that it was far less likely for an unruly stockbroker high on ecstasy to get hurt in a traffic accident than to rip out the seatbelt and choke himself with it.

The interior fittings of police cars weren't the only surprise of the evening. As soon as the three of us stepped through the front doors of the precinct, Patrick straightened up like a pin. Maria looked around at all her fellow officers. They were milling about in full dress uniform. Shiny caps, white gloves, squeaky black shoes.

Maria looked around. "Will someone tell me who fucking died?" she repeated jokingly.

Without warning, Patrick cried out, "Atten-tion!"

Suddenly every man stopped what he was doing. In unison they all turned and faced Maria. A wave of forearms lifted in the air as they stood at attention and saluted her.

No one said a word. We looked around in shock. Maria stood with her mouth half open and her eyes drifting from one corner of the room to another. Three older men walked past the front desk to Maria. One I recognized from the papers as being the Chief of Police, C. William Kelly. The man was always the first on the scene to explain to John and Jane Q. New Yorker the rationale behind every move a police officer made in the city. Whether a cop saved the lives of ten people from a gun-toting lunatic on a subway platform or was caught having sex with a minor on a mountain of methamphetamines, Kelly knew cops better than anyone because, "No one knows the breed like the steed."

Kelly extended his hand to Maria and gave her a handshake that shook her entire body. He pivoted himself to face a reporter who had been hiding behind a standing American flag just waiting to take their picture.

"Officer Pulchenic," he said in his hearty voice, "You have made the Nineteenth Precinct, the City of New York and every police officer in this state extremely proud. For putting yourself willingly and without hesitation in harm's way, I would like to award you this small token of our gratitude. Gratitude for catching an elusive and dangerous criminal." The man to his left handed Kelly a plaque, which he then gave to Maria. I couldn't catch what the plaque read, but I assumed it said something to the effect of #1 Cop or Employee of the Year. "We can all sleep better thanks to you."

Maria looked at the plaque, then back up at Kelly. Still speechless, all she was able to do was shake her head in disbelief. Camera flashes popped as Kelly maneuvered Maria over to a photographer. The reporter next to him raised his pen for a question.

"Officer Pulchenic! Hinkle from the *New York Post*. Could you tell me what went through your mind when you saw the East Side Burglar?"

Nothing but vowels came out of her mouth. Kelly, who never had problems finding the right consonants to match, jumped in.

"You don't have time to think. You just react. You see, Hinkle, you got to know the breed . . ."

Maria found her voice. "I didn't see him."

"Excuse me?" Hinkle said with a cocked head.

"I didn't see him. I saw her."

She pointed to me. All eyes shifted in my direction. I just gave a nervous smile as I held up my Toblerone.

"I saw her bleeding from the head and my first thought was that this prick hurt her. So I ran after him. It wasn't until I saw the gun that I realized who the sack of shit was."

Hinkle wrote feverishly, mumbling, "Sack . . . of . . ."

Maria turned to Chief Kelly. "I appreciate your stopping by and giving me this. It's great. This award and all. And I'm honored that all the guys took showers and got spruced up in their dress blues for me. But at the end of the day, I didn't put that man down because I was a cop. I put him down because he hurt my friend. And no fucking body has the right to do that."

I wanted to run over and hug her.

Hinkle was beside himself as he kept writing. "No . . . fucking . . . body . . ."

Kelly leaned in and said under his breath, "Clean up the quotes for the papers, will ya?"

After taking a dozen photos of Maria and Captain Kelly, the photographer asked if he could have a shot of just Maria and me. I walked over to her and we stood side by side in front of the American flag. Her right hand held up her plaque. My left hand held up my Toblerone. And with our other hands, we held each other.

30

Love and Other Lost Causes

A small crowd of teenagers had already gathered in the hospital room by the time I got up to visit Emmy at Lenox Hill. I slipped unnoticed into the room. Every available inch of space had a student occupying it. Each looked intently down into an opened textbook while one kid read aloud a series of letters and numbers that sounded like a locker combination. As I tried to find a place to sit, Emmy looked up from the book propped on her knees and gave me a wink. She seemed to improve remarkably with each visit. No longer hooked up to any machines, she'd regained the color in her face. It even looked as if she'd figured out how to wash and style her hair with only one good hand.

After finding a free patch of space on the radiator, I picked up a *Mathletes Monthly* newsletter which lay on the floor. The periodical, to which Emmy acted as supervising editor, was made up of all sorts of math-related fun. Fun by the standards of kids who considered chess a sport. I flipped to the section marked "Puzzles," and as I turned the magazine in circles, trying to figure out the difference between two seemingly identical boxes, I wondered why Emmy actually went to the trouble to look decent when she had a built-in excuse to look like crap. It wasn't until her doctor walked into the room that I understood the reason for her rapid recovery.

"Sorry, kids," said the powerfully cute doctor in the white lab coat. "Visiting hours are almost over and our patient needs her rest. Doctor's orders." To indicate his authority, he pointed proudly to the name tag pinned cockeyed on his lapel. It read, DR. BRADLEY PITT, M. D. I covered my mouth with the newsletter to hide my laugh.

Shoshanna popped her gum as she examined the good doctor up and down. "We're not visiting, Doctor Muffin. This is a study session."

"Really? What are you all studying for?"

"They have an AP Calc exam on Monday, Doctor Pitt," Emmy explained. "Everyone, this is the doctor who has been taking care of me. Doctor Pitt. And over there in the corner is my friend and roommate, Geri O'Brien."

One huge kid in the back piped up. "Was that you on the cover of the *New York Post* the other day?"

"Yes," I said. "Me and our other friend, Maria."

"You the one holding the Toblerone?" Shoshanna asked as she pointed at me with her long pink pen. "You know at my mom's shop we can do a wash and set for twenty bucks."

My face burned with embarrassment. "I was caught off guard."

Fortunately, Emmy diverted the group. "And Geri, Doctor Pitt, this is my AP calc class. I'll have you know that you are looking at the best of the best. Our future scientists, doctors . . ."

". . . Engineers that own a chain of beauty salons," Shoshanna interrupted.

"And entrepreneurs."

Dr. Pitt ran his hand through his shaggy golden brown hair. "Well, that sounds great. We need more of those."

Another kid wearing a Lady Liberty basketball T-shirt stood up in the back. "Tell us, Doc. Is Miss Kozak gonna make it? You can be honest. We can take it."

Dr. Pitt pulled a pair of Buddy Holly black-rimmed glasses out of his breast pocket. Then he took out Emmy's chart from the base of her bed. After a moment of close examination, he lowered his glasses on the bridge of his nose and looked down at Emmy. His green eyes seemed to twinkle when they met hers. "Should I tell them?"

"Sure, doctor. They can handle it."

"Well, I guess you all should hear it from me. After all, I am Emmy's, excuse me, Miss Kozak's physician." He pulled off his glasses and looked at the ground, shaking his golden locks sadly. "It doesn't look good. She only has a few more days left. Two or three tops."

"What!" Shoshanna yelped as she shot out of her chair.

"Here. At the hospital. She'll be out in a couple of days and back at school."

The students groaned in disappointment. The smile returned to Dr. Pitt's face. "Come on, now. Let your teacher get her rest."

The teens begrudgingly began to gather their things. As the long parade of good-byes began, Dr. Pitt walked over to me.

"They're going to be a minute. Let's look at that suture, shall we?" he said as he put back on his Coke-bottle specs. "Do you have any questions?"

"Yeah, what does the surface of Mars look like?" was what I wanted to ask him. His glistening emerald eyes were the size of golf balls behind those lens. Instead I answered honestly. "Nothing. Still get headaches, though."

"Good. That's real good," he said as he gently peeled off my bandage. Even though his hands were on me, his attention was clearly on Emmy.

"I tend to forget my name at times," I said.

Watching Emmy give kisses to some of the kids, he answered, "That'll happen."

"And some nights I sleep in strangers' apartments because I don't know where mine is."

"Try putting some ice on it," he said as he returned his attention to my head. "Looks good. In two days give the wound some air, but until then, keep the bandage over it." He reached into his pocket and produced a roll of medical tape. "I'll give you some fresh tape and you'll be good to go." He threw out his arm and yanked about three feet of tape off the roll. He went back for another pull, but I stopped him.

"It's okay, really. I can do this," I said as I ripped an inch off his ream. He tried unsuccessfully to roll the excess back onto the roll.

"You know, your friend must be a popular lady. I've never seen so many people at visiting hours here. The staff, family, her students, boyfriend . . ."

"No boyfriend," I said as I watched Dr. Pitt begin to tape up his own hand.

"Really!" he exclaimed. Dr. Pitt, like Emmy, had the worst poker face I'd ever seen. He tried to hide his smile, but his joy at this piece of information was palpable. I could only imagine how crappy he must be at telling patients they had two weeks to live or that a parents' conehead-shaped child was really beautiful. Taken aback by his own fervor, he instantly turned it down a few notches. "Really? That's odd. Smart, attractive and can take a bullet." He looked over at Emmy, then back at me. "Where has she been hiding?"

I answered matter-of-factly. "Seventy-eighth Street."

Just as the last few kids strolled out of the room, another visitor walked in. Emmy's face lit up as she saw Bryan's head pop through the door.

"You up for one more visitor?" he asked, holding a bouquet of pink flowers.

"Bryan!" Emmy said hopefully as she sat up in bed. Her cheerful demeanor changed abruptly once she saw that his other hand was connected to Ingrid's. They were officially a couple. Upon witnessing the international sign of dating, Emmy lay back on the bed and faked a smile as badly as Dr. Pitt repressed one. "Good of you to come."

Bryan gave me a quick nod hello and led Ingrid over to Emmy's bed. He gave Emmy a kiss on the cheek as he placed the flowers in her lap.

"Emmy, how are you?" he asked as he grabbed her one good hand.

Unable to take her eyes off the daisy chain of rejection in front of her, she called over to Dr. Pitt, "I don't know. How am I, doctor?"

Dr. Pitt, still fighting a losing battle with a roll of medical tape, pulled off his glasses and smiled. "She looks perfect from where I'm standing."

Ingrid, upon noticing the startling cuteness of Dr. Pitt, pushed out her breasts and threw him a gleaming Nordic smile. Her wicked powers of seduction, however, held no sway on the good doctor. He glanced at Ingrid for only a moment before impatiently looking up at the clock.

"Visiting hours are up in a minute, folks."

Let down by his blatant disregard for her beauty, Ingrid turned her attention to Emmy.

"We were so worried about you. You shouldn't have run off like that."

As Ingrid prattled on, Emmy's attempt to hide her disappointment began to unravel. Her lower lip began to quiver as she stared at her hand in Bryan's. This would probably be the closest she'd ever get to him. After all the pennies she'd thrown in fountains, after all the birthday candles she'd blown out, after countless prayers to any saint affiliated with love or lost causes and after memorizing a book on dating, all she would ever get from the man she'd loved for the better part of fifteen years would be a hand hold.

I felt rotten for her. Even if you are holding a bingo card with no matches, it still sucks when someone yells out that they've won. The whole scene reminded me of why I had an invisible friend to begin with. Inside I breathed a sigh of relief knowing J. T. was in my life. Then I remembered that he'd left, too. And I felt rotten for me.

To my surprise, Dr. Pitt seemed to size up the situation pretty quickly. He grabbed the flowers from Emmy's lap and made his way into the bathroom.

"Don't want these beauties to die," he said as he disappeared inside. Meanwhile, Ingrid wouldn't shut up. She explained that if it hadn't been for Emmy leaving, she and Bryan wouldn't have spent the rest of the night getting to know each other better.

Just as Ingrid was about to show Emmy the bracelet Bryan had bought her and I was about to throw up, a loud crash came from the bathroom.

"Everything's fine! Nothing to worry about!" Dr. Pitt cried from inside.

Bryan looked at Emmy strangely. "Is that guy really your doctor?" he asked.

Then Dr. Pitt walked out with the flowers. He'd stuffed Bryan's arrangement in a portable plastic urinal; the kind men with kidney stones pee into when their loved ones are driving them home from lithotripsy treatments. He put them on Emmy's bedside table with pride.

"There we go. I think this will do nicely."

The glow returned to Emmy's face. As the rest of us looked at the flora in horror, Emmy looked up at the doctor and laughed. Laughed as if rejection wasn't standing two feet in front of her.

A bell began to ring in the halls. Dr. Pitt slapped his hands together in happy anticipation of our departure.

"Visiting hours are over, everyone!" he said with more excitement than required. "It's time for me to give the patient a quick checkup."

I gave Emmy a kiss and told her I'd be back tomorrow. Ingrid gave Emmy kisses on both cheeks and Bryan went in for a full hug. After Dr. Pitt shooed us out of the room into the hallway, Bryan turned to me.

"That man's a surgeon?" he asked, perturbed.

I shrugged my shoulders. "He's one of the best bone and joint guys in town. So they say."

The three of us headed for the elevator. Ingrid slid her arm through Bryan's as I walked behind them down the hallway. She looked back at me from over Bryan's shoulder with a wry smile.

"That doctor's handsome, no?"

"The guy's a clown," Bryan interjected. "I doubt he got through medical school."

Just then I remembered the puzzle in *Mathletes Monthly*. I wanted to figure it out, if only to make myself feel smarter. Without notifying the two lovebirds, I turned on my heel and headed back to Emmy's room.

But when I reached the door, I stopped. Inside I could hear them laughing. Instead of entering, I quietly opened the door and peeked inside. Dr. Pitt sat in a chair pulled right up next to the bed. The clipboard and glasses lay idle at the foot of the bed, while he explained something to her using swooping hand gestures. Emmy looked up at him, completely enthralled. And although I couldn't hear him, I knew he wasn't fixing any bones or showing her what activities she should refrain from when she got out. Whether he knew it or not, he was healing a more delicate organ.

The door closed without making a sound. I jogged back down the hall and resumed my place behind Bryan and Ingrid. Bryan kept talking. Neither of them had noticed I'd been gone.

"So Geri, you think that guy's for real?" Bryan demanded.

I looked back in the direction of Emmy's room. Thinking of that look on her face, that look once reserved only for lattes with Bryan and the biography of Andrew Wiles, I crossed my fingers that Emmy was well enough to let the good doctor fall into the enormous crack Bryan had made in her heart.

"Yeah," I said smiling. "I think he just might be the real deal."

31

Finding Lightning

After I said good-bye to Bryan and Ingrid and watched them glide away in a taxi together, I decided to go for a walk. The late summer night air felt good, and it seemed like a lifetime since I'd last strolled down Second Avenue or seen Max.

But as I walked past the Irish bars and the people eating outside with their dogs, a sinking feeling pulled at my gut. So much had happened in the past week, yet nothing had really changed for me. I still walked the same streets, past the same restaurants, past the same customers, past the same small dogs. Meanwhile, Maria had found recognition and Emmy had found what I hoped to be a fresh crush on a new man. The only thing I found was myself walking to the Soupberg Diner in hope of seeing a homeless man whose only income came from suckers like me who thought fate and karma responded to spare change and brass bells. And if I found Max and if I rang that bell, I would still be terrified that I'd run into Todd or his fiancée in the hallway. And if I did run into Todd, J. T. wouldn't be around to lean on. Neither would Emmy. All I had waiting for me at home was a mailbox soon to be filled with more rejection letters. And tomorrow all I had waiting for me was a day of work at a place that made cannibalism marketable.

With each passing block I came to realize that the more things changed, the more I stayed the same.

This fact became even more evident once I walked up to the corner of Seventy-second and Second. During the past week, without my knowing it, the Soupberg Diner had changed hands. In place of our weekly hangout, where the wait staff freely handed out insults, now stood Sid's Snack Bar & Internet Café. The pale pink and blue tile tables had been replaced by bright green and orange counters lined with flat screen monitors and keyboards. The low burgundy stools that always had stuffing coming out of the split down the center had been replaced by stools that I'd need a rappeling harness to climb into. And where a shelf filled with day-old pies had sat, there was now chalkboard that listed fifty different fruit smoothies. All of which required breaking a twenty.

The one thing that remained the same was the shopping cart filled with Max's possessions and the RING A BELL sign that sat in front of the door. But Max was nowhere to be found. I walked up to the cart and found a sign placed on top of a bag of clothes.

Back in ten minutes.

Figuring he would be a homeless man of his word, I walked inside Sid's café and sat at one of the counters facing the street. The Polish waiter who'd told me to eat him had been replaced by a Hunter College student who was more than happy to tell me the top-ten fruit combination shakes and the health benefits of each one. I ordered a kiwi fig on her recommendation and swiveled in my seat until its arrival.

As I sat suspended in midair, I looked out the window at Max's pile of possessions. It was Tuesday night in Manhattan. Max had somewhere to be and I didn't. Max seemed happy and content and I wasn't. And Max wore a Hefty bag. My eyes kept shifting from the cart of crap to the computer screen glowing in front of me. My hand seemed to instinctively drag the mouse around its pad. Words suddenly popped up on the screen.

Thirty-two minutes left on card.

I hadn't paid to access the Internet, so when the waitress stopped back, I asked if it would be all right if I used it.

"Sure. The person left a few minutes ago. They paid for the time, so you might as well take advantage of it."

I thanked her for the smoothie, which not only looked like the inside of a colon but tasted like it as well, and began to access my work e-mail. Ninety-seven e-mails had come in during the time I had been out of the office. My eyes glazed over at the long list of messages I needed to answer until I saw that I had one item marked as a draft. Not being able to think what I could have typed and never sent, I called it up .

It was my ill-fated resignation letter. The month and day had been updated to today's.

Before I left Sid's, I ordered an organic peanut butter and challah sandwich (which I made them cut into small squares) and the closest soup I could get to corn chowder. Although Max hadn't returned, I searched gingerly through his stuff for something flat to place his food on. Underneath his sign I found an old newspaper. It was the *New York Post* with Maria and me on the front page. My picture was circled and a small star drawn in the right corner.

"Perfect," I said as I laid the paper on a bunch of empty soda cans and placed the food on top of my face. For a moment I thought about leaving him my fig smoothie too, but figured Max didn't need that kind of drama.

The walk back up Second Avenue seemed scarier than the walk down. The garlic wafting out of the restaurants smelled the same. The dogs yelping sounded the same. But now, finally, everything looked different.

My shoe stayed on the elevator as I struggled to break through the pack. Once I was in the reception area and able to breathe, someone threw out my Hush Puppy, hitting me in the shoulder. "Don't you read the *New York Post?*" I thought, but then none of the sixteenth-floor blue bloods would probably be caught dead with that paper. They were more likely to read *Mathletes Monthly* than anything with color photos or a horoscope page.

I hopped on one foot as I tried to put my shoe on. As always, Berta didn't look up from her new cowboy romance to greet me.

"Good morning, Geri. How's the writing going?"

"It's not, Berta, but thanks for asking," I said as I walked toward the door and into Howard.

"Hey there, Geri. Always on time, like the sun," he said, holding the door open.

"If only I were as hot." I rolled past him and into Sally and Daisy. They flew past me in a whirl of paper. Sally held a stack of color-coded folders while Daisy struggled with about twenty pounds' worth of handouts. Both wore green foam Statue of Liberty crowns. Daisy called out for someone to hold the elevator as Sally yelled over her shoulder.

"Geri, I printed your e-mail out from last night. It's really great."

"Who helped you write it?" Daisy asked. Her teeth were so bleached, it looked as if you could see through them. "Or did you go to one of those paid . . ."

Sally pushed her onto the elevator. "The managers are going to flip over it, Geri. Really. Hedda said she's running late, so we're going up early. I'll meet you upstairs in about five . . ."

Not moving from the doorway, I called back, "I'm not going to the meeting."

Sally stopped. "What? Geri, you have to present the copy. It's your copy."

"Nope. I'm giving it to you."

Sally cocked her head and looked at me as if I'd lost my mind. And she might have been right. All I could do was smile. "You'll do a great job, Sally."

"But, Geri . . ." she pleaded as the elevator doors kept slamming against her leg. Daisy yanked Sally inside. Before Sally pulled her head and those giant green foam spokes in, I gave her a wave. She had nothing to worry about. The managers would love the copy. They would love her.

I could smell Hedda in my office before I walked inside. She sat in the guest chair. A small stack of papers rested on her lap as she read a printed version of the e-mail I'd sent her last night. My hands started to sweat as I walked behind my desk and turned on my computer. She held the paper far enough away from her face to read the small type.

" 'In the city, Timmy found one thing true. You don't have an experience with Manhattan, she has one with you.' " She put the e-mail down and looked up at me. "This is a great tagline."

"Thank you," I answered as I pulled a shoe box filled with sundry office supplies from my desk. Dumping out the stapler, sixteen yellow Post-it notes, and three un-usable vials of White-out, I began to fill it with my business cards and stationery.

This act seemed to bother Hedda. "Geri, you have real talent. You left television . . ."

" 'To find a new place here in publishing,' " I said, finishing her sentence. "I'm sorry, Hedda. My heart's not here. It never really was."

"I wasn't talking about publishing. I was talking about writing. You have a real gift, you know."

If she could see the stack of rejection letters I'd just thrown out, she would know that every major literary agency and production company in New York and Los Angeles begged to differ. As well as three car dealerships in the greater Denver area. I ignored the compliment and began to take the picture of Elvis off my bulletin board.

"All of my files are under the c-drive. I listed everything first by the author's last name, then by ISBN. It's pretty easy to figure out."

Then Hedda lifted a copy of my screenplay as if it were Exhibit A. The air flew out of my lungs.

"One of your scripts was sent back," she said as she opened the text. I waited to see if she was going pitch a fit for using the company copy machine or throw the screenplay at me for using the company mailroom to send it out. Instead, she calmly thumbed through the pages. "You put the wrong zip code on it and used a company label with our return address. It came back to me. I read it last night. It's pretty good. I like the whole idea of friends coming together to help each other find the meaning of Christmas. Just the right amount of sweetness without being sappy."

Normally, I would be happy to hear such a nice review. But it didn't seem to matter much now. I walked over to the bookshelf and grabbed Kelly Cox's dating book and a stray *New York Post* that Sally had left in my office. Sally had stuck a note over my face reading, "No one gets laid with hair like that." I crumpled the note and tossed it in the trash before Hedda could see.

"If you don't mind, I'd like to send this to a friend of mine at Universal. You never know, right?"

"Thank you. But you don't have to."

"Geri, stop," she ordered. I sat down, and for the first time looked her in the face. After studying her eyes for a moment, I realized Sally was right: her eyebrows had to be tattooed on. "I know you've been through a lot in the past week. And I know your dream isn't here. But have you thought this through? What are you going to do once you leave these doors?"

"I don't know, Hedda," I said. I absentmindedly grabbed the courage rock and rubbed it vigorously. "I don't know. But what I do know is that lightning is hitting everyone but me. And I got to thinking that maybe I'm standing in the wrong place."

"Maybe you are." She looked back down at my screenplay. "Or maybe you've been doing a damn good job of dodging it."

I tossed the rock into the box. "I wish that was the case."

Hedda stood up and held my screenplay to her chest. Her wide smile seemed sad but sincere. I think it's about as sad as Hedda would ever choose to be. "Well, if you'll excuse me, I have a presentation to get to. There's some great stuff that's going to be read during that meeting that I don't want to miss." Hedda held out my screenplay. "I can keep this, right?"

"Merry Christmas."

As Hedda was about to leave, she turned to me, looking slightly confused. "By the way, the only problem I have with your story is the mom. It seems as if you've got the two reversed."

"I don't understand."

"The mother and daughter are separated, but the daughter is haunted by the mom. It should be the other way around."

"No," I said as I shut off my computer. "The mom left the

daughter on page five. Remember the scene with the Christmas tree fire?"

"That might be the case, but a mother can't really erase thoughts of her child," she said as she walked up to the edge of my desk. Her perfume overcame me as she leaned in to explain. "Your main character is ten years old. Now Geri, in fifth grade, how many times a day did your dad run through your head?"

Looking up at the ceiling in thought, I answered, "I don't know. Twice, maybe? If it was his turn to pick me and Emmy up from CCD, then three."

"Let's make it even and say four. Geri, I have two kids that I get to see every other month when their father doesn't have them, and a job where I'm in meetings over half the day. Even if I'm in the middle of sweet-talking a bunch of crazed IT guys, there aren't ten minutes that go by without one of my little monsters and their fifteen food allergies running through my head."

"So you're saying I should make my main character allergic to peanuts?"

"No. What I'm saying is that no matter where you go, no matter where you hide, you can't run away from your child. It's impossible. And it's not Christmas or their birthdays or seeing other kids their age that remind you of them. It's your heart that does."

I wanted to believe her so much, but I thought I knew better. "Some mothers feel different. Maybe that's just you."

She smiled knowingly as she turned to walk toward the door. "You should know by now, I'm always right. You come visit me when you're a mother. We'll have a gin and tonic and a talk."

As I watched her leave, I wondered if her kids would turn

out like Hedda. Smart, dynamic and olfactory-challenged. If they were lucky, they would.

"Hedda," I called out before she could walk out of the office. "I don't think I ever told you this, but you're a great boss. Thank you."

"No, sweetie. Thank *you*." The smile stayed on her lips as she gave me a wink and disappeared behind the door.

I sat back in my chair and looked up at my bulletin board. Only one photo remained. It was one Patrick had taken of the four of us at Madison Square Garden during their police induction ceremony. Maria made Patrick stand on a chair to get us all in the frame. In the photo, Maria, Sally, Emmy and I look petrified as we lunge forward to help Patrick, who is in the middle of falling off the chair. The photo always made me laugh. But I knew if I took it home, it would make me miss Sally more. I decided to leave it on the board for the next occupant.

Then I leapt out of my chair and out of my office in hope of catching Hedda. I'd forgotten to tell her what I couldn't write down in my resignation letter. Thank God, she hadn't gotten very far. One of the CEO's assistants had accosted her in the reception area.

"Hedda," I called out. "I know someone really great who would just love . . ."

"I know," she said as she initialed a folder and handed it back to the assistant. "She'll start on Monday."

32

Washed Ashore

"Keep up the writing," Berta said with her nose still buried in her book. I gave a slight wave that she didn't see and stepped onto the elevator. To my surprise, it was completely empty. Instead of being squashed in a crowd with my back jammed up against someone's groin, I stood in the center, alone. Holding my shoe box in one hand and the old *New York Post* tucked under my armpit, I waited to see if anyone would join me for my descent. But this day, it seemed I was the only person in the company going down.

As the floor numbers got lower, I could feel my years at Junior Varsity Publishing rewinding and vanishing. The lit numbers seemed to count down the seconds to my new life. Within moments, I would be on the ground floor. The doors would open and I would be in awe of the new world that lay in front of me. But when the elevator finally landed, all I saw was the lobby: the shiny brass ceiling, the marble floor and one lone security guard counting the minutes to lunch. By this time, all the employees of J. V. Publishing were already in the building, starting their day in the exciting world of children's books. My day was over. Listening to my shoes click out of the building, I wondered whether I'd just committed the bravest act of my life or whether I should be committed to an institution.

Once outside, everything my eyes fell on was seared into my memory. The silver breakfast cart where the Pakistani man sold coffee and bagels in the morning, Howard, even my last look at Berta the receptionist. Their lives rewound and became new. They would now be the everyday characters in somebody else's story. Berta would ask about me through Sally once a week, then once every so often, then never. Daisy would use me as a scapegoat for every file that went missing in the department. Howard would notice the lack of packages I'd mail to California and my greeting at 8:55 A.M. Only then would he inquire about my whereabouts.

And what would Sally tell them? Would I have left Manhattan for Los Angeles or would I move back home to Southold? Would I have a job in film or would I rotate tires at Dad's shop? Would I move into an apartment of my own because I was loaded or would I not be able to afford my half of the rent? On that clear and sunny day, the fog surrounding my future wouldn't lift from my head. Was Hedda right? Should I have taken more time to think this through? After nearly getting hit by a bike messenger and two U-haul vans, I realized I needed a sign. Something that would point me in the right direction. But as I focused on the bustle of Manhattanites around me, I only saw people rushing to places they needed to be or swinging bags from stores that I could no longer afford to shop in, like the Burlington Coat Factory. The bells that chimed at noon from the Episcopal church didn't give me a sign. They were too busy letting people know it was noon and letting me know that I not only needed to find a job, I needed to find a purpose.

That question looped in my mind as I zigzagged though the cars that were stuck in the middle of the crosswalk. The police were setting up blockades on all of the side streets. After making it safely to the other side, I walked up to the policeman who stood on the corner drinking a cup of coffee and watching the road rage unfold.

"What's going on?" I asked.

"Queen's in town."

"You mean the borough?"

"No, I mean the broad from England. We had to clear a path from the East Side to Midtown. She's going to be at the United Nations and then wants to go to a taping of Maury," he said, taking a sip of coffee.

"This gridlock's for a talk show?"

"Hey, lady, we just do what we're told," he said, pointing his coffee cup at a honking car. "Not my fault she's got a thing for paternity tests."

While he walked over to the car to write a summons for noise, I walked down into the Thirty-second Street subway station. I, too, would probably come to love Maury since I would be home at eleven every day to watch him.

Even with all the traffic outside, the platform held only a few frustrated commuters, most of whom were people who couldn't take their cabs or town cars to the gym and seemed generally pissed off that the Queen had forced them to go down underground with the likes of me and people who worked in shifts. When the train finally came, I'd barely stepped inside the doors before a woman with a real Birkin and fake cheekbones barreled into me, sending my box of worldly office possessions all over the floor of the train. She didn't offer an apology as I crouched down, trying to gather up my business cards while fighting back my frustration. This wasn't a good way to start the rest of my life.

After picking up my mess and probably a case of typhoid, I sat in an empty row of seats. I was looking through the box to make sure I had everything when a hand appeared under my nose with my courage rock. And above that hand came a familiar voice.

"Excuse me, but I think this belongs to you."

There he stood. Like he'd never left.

J. T. stood above me, holding my rock and looking magnificent in a white T-shirt and a pair of jeans. In his presence, my heart managed to heave a sigh of relief and skip a beat all at the same time. He abandoned his normal cheery hello for only a hint of a smile. But I didn't care.

"Hello, you." I grinned as I took the rock from his hand. "I knew you'd show up sooner or later," I said as the train began to move. He looked at me, perplexed, as he took the seat next to me.

"You did?"

"Sure." I put the rock back in the box and laid the newspaper over the top. "Especially today."

As I studied J. T., his eyes kept moving from my picture on the paper to my face. I figured that extreme stress had fogged my imagination, because his demeanor and face appeared just slightly different from the way I last remembered it. His voice sounded deeper, more resonant, with almost a hint of a Midwestern accent. His hair was more brown than blond. His face more puzzled than happy.

"Why? What happened today?" he asked.

"I quit my job."

He crossed his legs and looked back at me with interest. "Is that a good thing?"

"I don't know."

"Well, why did you quit?"

"I just couldn't get promoted again."

J. T. looked up at a woman who was busy reading the same cowboy romance novel as Berta. "You hit the ceiling at your job?"

"No, I thought if I stayed there long enough, Hedda would make me a vice president."

"Oh," he said, scratching his head. "That would be horrible."

"Tell me about it," I said in agreement.

The bell chimed as the train pulled into the next station. The doors opened for new passengers. An elderly couple shuffled in. The two slowly made their way to a seat at the far end of the car. The older woman, gnarled with osteoporosis, tried to steady herself as she leaned back into the seat. The husband stood by her and held her arm with one hand until she made it down safely. In the other, he held her stately white purse. After she was situated, he sat down next to her and placed her purse back in her lap. The two said nothing to each other. But even though they said nothing, the man held her hand. Gently stroking her liver-spotted skin as if he were petting a bird, applying just enough pressure to convey warmth and love but not enough to break the delicate bones. I looked up at J. T., who also seemed intrigued by the couple.

"I just want it to all mean something," I said.

J. T.'s head swiveled back in my direction. "Being vice president would mean something."

"But not to me. It's not about the position. It's not about selling a screenplay or being famous or . . ." I shook the newspaper in frustration. "Or being a friggin' hero. At the end of the day, it doesn't mean anything. It's about that," I said, pointing to the couple.

J. T. gave them a second look. "It's about getting enough calcium in your forties?"

"No, J. T. It's about finding your place. And maybe having someone along to help you settle in when you do."

I relaxed into the seat and rested my head on his shoulder. Taking in a deep breath, I could smell the soap he'd used that morning in the shower. I turned my mouth toward his arm and spoke into his triceps.

"Why can't you be real?"

He pulled back with a startled look on his face. "I'm sitting next to you. How real do you want me?"

For the second time, the box fell onto the floor. I leaned over, grabbed a handful of hair at the back of his head and kissed him as hard as I could. His mouth stiffened as he began to pull away. But it only took a moment before his mouth succumbed. Everything about him tasted and felt so real. His tongue, his lips, his mouth felt alive in mine. And just like before, everything that seemed to be wrong in my world suddenly felt like it made perfect sense.

And then it didn't.

All the lights on the train went out. For two seconds, the entire car was in complete darkness. But in those two seconds, I realized my lips were firmly planted on someone on the subway. The stress of quitting my job had made me lose my mind. When the lights flickered on, I slowly pulled my head away from the man I'd so innocently sexually assaulted. My eyes widened in horror as I stared into the face that I normally saw moving at thirty miles an hour on buses and taxis all over Manhattan.

This was not J. T., imaginary friend. This was Joshua Tenor, molested khakis model.

My hand covered my mouth as he jumped to his feet. His face was contorted in shock.

"Who are you?"

"Oh . . . my. . . . God . . ." I stammered as I slowly got up from my seat.

Joshua wiped his lips with his hand and studied his fingertips as if he were searching for clues. His voice rose an

octave in excitement. "I've seen you before. At Spy. And
that horrible art show . . ."

The train began to spin. The woman across from us sat
with her mouth open and her romance novel folded in her
lap, her thumb still holding her page. I staggered backward
as I held my palms up toward him, the way someone does
when caught in a room with a hungry Doberman pincher.
The bell that chimed from the doors signaled that escape
was only a few feet behind me.

"I'm sorry. I'm so sorry."

Everyone on the subway seemed paralyzed except for
the new passengers. They walked on and wove around us
as if nothing had happened. With our gazes still locked on
each other, I stepped backward through the doors and
onto the subway platform. After the final bell rang, the
doors closed. He still stood motionless in the car. His expression didn't change until the train began to move. Then
he yelled out one word. I couldn't hear it, but I could read
it on his lips.

He appeared to have shouted the word, "Wait."

Raw energy surged into my legs. I ran down the platform
toward the exit. Something in me needed to get out from
underground and into the open air. As I pushed past the
other passengers on the platform and spun through
the turnstile, my heart thumped in my ears. Had that happened? Had that really happened? Did I just make out with
Joshua Tenor on the 6 Train? My head wanted me to run, to
distance myself from my mortification. But as I charged up
the stairs into the light of Fifty-ninth Street, I found my horror
abruptly fading. I could still taste Joshua on my lips. And as
I looked around at all the New Yorkers trying to get into
Bloomingdale's, I realized that incredible feeling remained.
Everything felt right. Everything looked clear. Everything
still made perfect sense.

Even Max in a tuxedo.

On the block past Bloomingdale's stood Max. Not wearing a garbage bag or pushing a baby carriage filled with junk, but rather in a black-vested tuxedo. Max had just walked out of Zeller's as a sales clerk from the store searched the street to find a cab. Max brushed down a long coat that he had slung over his forearm. A cab driver who had been sitting idle in traffic yelled out for him to jump in. The clerk ran over to the cab, held the door open and ushered Max inside. I watched the whole scene in amazement until I found myself running toward the cab.

"Max!" I cried out as I ran into traffic. "Max!"

Max rolled down the window and stuck out his head. "Geri! Wish me luck. I'm off to Atlantic City!" he cried out.

The cars were packed so thick I couldn't squeeze through. "Max, it works! It really works!" I shouted over the horns.

"What?"

The traffic started to move and Max's cab began to pick up speed. I ran back onto the sidewalk and jumped up on a newspaper dispenser. I cupped my hands around my mouth as I shouted, "The bell! It works!"

He laughed as he shouted back, "I told you it would, Ms. Hepburn!" Max gave a wave before pulling his head back inside the taxi.

"Thank you!"

Standing on top of the newsstand, I waved until the cab finally disappeared up Third Avenue. I looked up at the gigantic buildings that lined the canyon. Holding my hands out toward the city, I cried out in joy for everyone to hear. Near and far. Past and present.

"THANK YOU!"

33

Four Months Later . . .

A sea of single women threw their arms in the air and reached for the bouquet that came soaring across the dance floor toward my head. Maria and I ducked with our hands firmly planted over our Zima and Chambords. The cluster of pale pink roses and baby's breath landed at my feet with a soft thud. Instead of looking at the bouquet as a sign from the fates that our true loves would appear this year, Maria and I stared down at it as if someone had hurled a chicken wing by our dyable shoes.

Sally scooped up her eight-foot-long bridal train and turned around. Upon seeing whom the fateful flowers had landed in front of, she rolled her eyes in frustration.

"Will one of you pick it up?" she called out.

I lifted up my red silk sari, reached out with my open-toe shoe and nudged the bouquet in front of Maria. Maria lowered her drink to her side.

"Mia Hamm is going to win another gold for the U.S."

Just as Maria took a step back in preparation for punting the bouquet back across the dance floor, Dr. Pitt bent over and picked up the fallen flowers. Amid a chorus of "Oohs" and "Ahhs," he walked over to Emmy and handed them to her. Everyone gave the two a round of applause as they kissed. I let out a sigh as I turned to Maria.

"Emmy's got quite the guy."

Maria leaned her head back and downed the rest of her drink. "He's going to seem quite the guy in about ten minutes when another dude tries to ram a garter up his thigh." She let out a deep belch and handed me her glass. "Be a dear, will ya?"

Maria made her way back to our table, where Emmy and Dr. Pitt sat canoodling. I shuffled across the dance floor to the bar, praying I wouldn't trip over the red silk sari Sally had made me wear. Although Sally wouldn't give up her dream of wearing a Vera Wang dress to her wedding, she could gladly give up the idea of having her bridesmaids wear one. Habibe's sisters had been instructed to help me show up looking like a woman going to the wedding of an Indian king and not like I was going to a toga party. But after four trips to Jackson Heights, I had enough silk wrapped around my torso to cover a football field and enough gold jewelry to cover the professional football team that played on it.

I never attended Celine Dion's wedding, but I couldn't imagine Sally's being any smaller. The wedding coordinator almost crapped his Calvin's when he found out that Sally was the only daughter of a wealthy Long Island Jewish doctor and Habibe, the eldest son of a wealthy New Jersey Indian doctor. Apparently, in the wedding planning world, this combo is called the "Triple Diamond" and guarantees a 300-person, $300/plate minimum. The only way to beat this bride/groom combination is if either set of parents is going through a divorce.

The wedding was to be a mix of Jewish and Indian traditions. The matzo ball soup preceded the dal, guests danced the "Hava Nagila" around a flaming pit of fire, the DJ played "Greased Lightning" before Bhangra techno. But at the Puck building on this cold New York night, in the middle of the carnival atmosphere, the wedding appeared picture perfect for a couple who loved their families as much as they loved each other, and who also believed a virgin couldn't get pregnant the first time she had intercourse.

After the bartender handed me my order of two Zima and Chambords, I turned around and bumped into a small cluster of Habibe's aunts, all of whom were hunched in a circle around Hedda. Hedda gave me a wink as she proudly held out her hand. She shouted over the music at the huddled women, who were gazing in awe at her six-karat yellow diamond.

"Husband number three," she yelled as she shifted her ring to catch the light. "You know what they say: 'Three's the charm.'"

"That's quite the charm," one of the aunts said in a thick Hindi accent.

"He had quite the bank account in the Cayman Islands. And I had quite the lawyer." This comment caused the gaggle of aunts to erupt in giggles. Hedda smiled as she took a sip of her bubbly and waved me over. I nodded hello as I squeezed my way through the group to Hedda. Hedda flung her diamond-studded hand around me and pressed me proudly to her side. I smiled as I watched my drinks slosh onto my sari.

"What do you think, ladies? Doesn't she look . . . just so . . ." She paused as she looked me over. I couldn't tell if the tears forming in her eyes were from pride or impending hysterics. "Festive?"

All the aunts nodded with smiles of approval. Hedda couldn't stop herself. "You all know who this young woman is, right?"

One of the woman yelled out, "She the matchmaker. She introduced Habibe to Sally by . . ." The woman grabbed her throat and did her best impersonation of throwing up. "On Habibe's restaurant window."

This bit of news, which appeared well known throughout the family, elicited a second wave of laughter from the women. I raised my voice over the laughter to refute.

"Excuse me, but you have it backward. You see, Sally . . ."

"Sally!" Hedda interrupted, "Sally is the one who replaced Geri at work because Geri here left to be a famous screenwriter!" The joking laughter stopped and changed to a collective gasp. "She sold a screenplay about Christmas to a big movie studio in Hollywood. Isn't that exciting?" Hedda said, her eyes gleaming brighter than the rock on her hand. She couldn't have been more proud of me if I were her own daughter. And if I wasn't holding two dripping purple drinks that were guaranteed to stain her pink Chanel suit, I would have hugged her back.

When Hedda had told me that she knew someone in film, she hadn't told me that her old college boyfriend worked as the head of development at Universal. An old college boyfriend who, incidentally, was still madly in love with her. If I'd written my name sixty times on a napkin, he would have made it into something starring Vin Diesel. He sent me a contract before he even finished reading my script. His assistant said he loved Christmas stories, especially ones featuring dogs. There wasn't an animal in the script. I didn't care.

"With a lot of Hedda's help," I interjected. I did my best to show my affection by putting my head on her shoulder. We exchanged a knowing look until one Punjabi woman spoke up.

Looking confused, she asked, "Don't they make movies where things go boom!"

Hedda yelled out, "Yes, they do! Boom! Right to the top of the box office it will go." She held her champagne glass in the air to toast. "And boom, so will the young adult tie-in book Junior Varsity will publish. Boom! Right to the top of the bestseller lists."

All the women held up their respective glasses filled with rum and Coke and shouted, "Boom!" I took a sip from what was left of my drink and excused myself.

"I'd better get back to Maria. She's probably wondering where her drink is."

As I walked away, I tried with my free fingers to wave to the happy group of women smiling back at me. Only Hedda's face continued to smile. The rest of the women pretended to throw up. None of it was done maliciously. They just wanted me to join in the laughter and to let me know that they recognized me. I could only imagine the hours of entertainment Sally's lie must have provided. But I didn't let it faze me. After all, Universal wanted to start shooting *The Carolers* for next Christmas. And if I was going to be a famous screenwriter, I would have to learn how to take the heat. Sally's aunts would just be the start.

By the time I made it back to the table, Emmy was smelling her soup and Maria was eating a potato pancake with her hands. I placed the drink in front of her. Maria held up the half-filled glass to the light.

"I'm not driving, you know."

"Look, I'm wearing the other half of that," I said as I plopped down next to Emmy.

Emmy looked around the room in awe. "I think they did a great job with this place."

"It's not bad for a quickie wedding. Considering Martha Stewart doesn't have an issue devoted to Jewish-Hindu shotgun weddings," I said.

"Jesus," Maria said with a mouthful of potato pancake. "Who still thinks you can't get pregnant the first time?"

Emmy and I turned to Maria and answered in unison, "Sally."

Suddenly, Emmy's face began to beam as she caught sight of Dr. Pitt walking across the dance floor with her glass of Merlot. With medical tape wrapped around the hinge of his eyeglasses and a red stain down the front of his dress shirt, he looked like the Poindexter version of a young Paul Newman. His expression lit up as he walked up behind Emmy. With his face pressed to her ear, he put down her drink.

"Here you go, sweetie. Sorry it's only half full. Had a bit of a slip by the Chuppah of fire," he said as he kissed her cheek.

"No shit?" Maria said as she looked at his shirt.

"It's okay, honey. Do you want to sit down?"

"I can't now. I promised Sally I'd talk to her cousins about volunteering for Habitat for Humanity. They seem really interested, and the program could use all that great energy."

I looked over at Maria, who was leaning over her plate, spitting out her food. A wheeze of laughter burst from her lungs. Thinking Maria was choking, Dr. Pitt sprang into action.

"Maria! Are you okay? Are you choking? Do the international sign for choking if you are." He stood in front of her, his legs in fighting stance, with his hands crossed over his throat.

Red-faced, Maria just looked at him and held up her middle finger. Dr. Pitt slapped her playfully on the back. "Very funny." She continued laughing as he gave Emmy a final kiss on the head. "I'll be back soon. Save a few dances for me."

"Take your time, hon," Emmy said as we watched him walk away. "And next time let her choke!"

Maria took a napkin and dabbed the corners of her eyes. With Emmy's eyes still fixed on Dr. Pitt, Maria leaned back and mouthed to me behind Emmy's back, "Watch this."

"Hey, Emmy, I went back home and visited the family last weekend. I saw Bryan on the bus. He asked about you."

"Bryan Starr?" Emmy said as she searched the crowd for one last glimpse of her man. "I thought he lived in Cincinnati."

Maria and I looked at each other and smiled as we took another gulp of our drinks. Although Maria loved nothing more than to tease Dr. Bradley Pitt, we both were indebted to the good doctor for his sheer persistence. After all, it only took two follow-up visits, six dinner dates, five dozen roses delivered to the school and four makeout sessions at the Seventy-seventh Street and Lexington subway entrance for Dr. Pitt to cure our best friend of the worst crush in the history of Southold High School.

"Speaking of visiting, when are you coming to my class?" Maria asked me as she wiped her lips with the back of her wrist. "You can never be too sure around those Hollywood types. Never know when you're going to have to throw down," she said as she spiked a piece of broccoli on her plate.

"She has a point, finally," Emmy said. "I took a few of Maria's classes and felt totally empowered. You should go."

Hunter College had approached Maria about teaching a self-defense night class. She'd agreed, figuring it might be good for a few bucks and a couple of laughs. But after a stellar write-up in *Time Out New York* and an appearance by Sarah Jessica Parker in the "Nail His Nuts and Bolt" class, Maria's self-defense course had a three-year waiting list. Now, on any given Saturday night, you could walk by the Lenox Hill Emergency Room and see at least four men nursing bloody broken noses all because they tried to sneak up behind their girlfriends to give them a hug.

"Guys, the average age of the kids acting in my picture is eight. I can take an eight-year-old."

Maria grabbed a fresh potato pancake and pointed it at me. "I'm just saying things might get ugly. And if you need to take one of those little perps down, you'll need the skills. You know who to call."

"Yeah, their moms."

The bell and base-filled Bhangra music began to fade as a slow, familiar love song took its place. Everyone cooed as Sally grabbed Habibe's hand and led him to the middle of the dance floor. This was a song that I'd requested. It was my parents' wedding song.

The Bengali DJ grabbed the microphone and called, "This goes out to Habibe and Sally from a thankful friend. Come on, everyone, get out and join the happy couple." Then the words to Elvis's, "Can't help falling in love with you," drew all the older couples out on the dance floor. Their elegant gliding, perfected by years of slow dancing made all the younger couples look downright arthritic.

"This calls for a toast," Emmy said as she held up her glass. "To Sally."

"To Sally," I repeated.

Maria proudly raised her glass as well. "To the woman who made dry humping an art form."

We all called out, "Hear, hear," and took a sip of our drinks.

Emmy smacked her lips with satisfaction. "Well, ladies, one down, three to go."

"Two to go," I corrected. "You're done."

Emmy seemed confused. "What do you mean?"

"She means that next year we'll be here in god-awful dresses drinking to you and Dr. Dufus over there."

Emmy shook her head in disbelief. "I don't know. Maybe one of you will be next."

The Zima almost flew out of my mouth. "Right, when the planets line up and a comet flies overhead . . ."

"And the earth collides with the sun," Maria continued.

"Come on, guys. Stranger things have happened. And remember what my mom always says—don't say there're no good men out there, because as you're saying it, there are probably nice men saying that there are no good girls."

"And they're right," Maria said.

"Yeah, it's just me and Maria left. Slim pickin's," I said as I hastily took a sip of my drink. But I lied. I wasn't left. I'd found someone. But I wasn't going to tell a soul about him. Not until I knew for sure. He was someone I'd known for a long time. Someone who felt like home. Someone who'd finally seen me.

Emmy just looked at the two of us and smiled. She raised her glass yet again. "To kismet."

I smiled as I raised mine as well. "To my New York minute."

"Ding fucking dong."

We clanked our glasses and put them to our lips. Just as we were about to take a sip, our eyes drifted over to the other end of the long rectangular table where Dr. Pitt sat with two of Sally's very handsome cousins. It appeared as if they, too, had just finished drinking a toast. The two cousins both threw Maria shy sweet smiles. Maria grabbed the champagne bottle off the table and stood up.

"Two for me. None for you. Sorry, Geri."

"That's quite alright." And it was. I had one for me. I always did. I just never knew it.

Maria got up, walked to the middle of the table and waved the men over. The heavy base kicked in again as Elvis's "Blue Suede Shoes" began to play. Emmy and I just shook our heads and laughed. Then we all got up and met each other halfway.

INT.   DINER   NIGHT

Geri sits alone in the diner writing in a notebook. A waiter with a thick Polish accent approaches.

                              WAITER
    Are you finished with that?

Geri looks over at a half-eaten burger sitting beside a copy of the *Village Voice* newspaper.

                              GERI
    Yeah, I am. Wasn't that hungry.

                              WAITER
    I meant with your story. Are you almost finished with it?

                              GERI
    (looks at notebook) I think I'm done.

                              WAITER
    What's it about?

                              GERI
    It's about three friends.

                              WAITER
    Well, I hope it works out well for you.

                              GERI
    It already has.

Geri smiles at him, gathers her things, puts down a ten-dollar bill. She leaves the *Village Voice* lying face down on the table. In the bottom corner of the classified section a personal ad reads, "To the woman who kissed me on the subway. Can't stop thinking of you. 'Til we meet again. J. T."

Fade to black.   THE END

Epilogue

"Well? What did you think?"

I couldn't breathe. For the past hour on our flight to Los Angeles all I could do was study his face in the reflection of my vodka and orange juice. I'd looked forward to this trip for weeks. I couldn't tell which was more exciting, pitching my new screenplay to a real live movie star who wanted to option the rights or spending a week watching him wear nothing more than his cute, blue-flowered bathing trunks. My nerves and my deathly fear of flying made me get up to pee six times an hour.

Normally in a plane, my hearing becomes as keen as a bat's. I notice every decibel change. Every clank of the drinks cart, every change in pitch of the air conditioning. But on this flight, instead of thinking what I would look like embedded in the seat of the person in front of me, I wondered what was running through his head as he read my screenplay. Would this scare him? Would he think I was totally screwy for writing about doing pull-ups on a fire escape? Would he think I was incapable of having a healthy relationship? Would he be repulsed by the fact that I like Zima?

He poured over the lines the way Emmy read her students' homework, with a slight scowl of concentration.

When he came across something he knew or thought was funny, his face eased into a smile. He never laughed, never commented, never looked up from the page. But every so often he would wipe the grin off his face when he felt me looking at him. Finally, he closed his eyes and put down the screenplay.

"You made me look like kind of an asshole," he said as he opened a folder marked *No Good Girls* and placed the screenplay gently inside.

"I didn't mean to. But did it, well—" I looked at him without finishing my sentence.

"Did it what?"

"Scare you?" I said.

"Was this supposed to be a horror film? If so, I think you need to do some revising, kitten," he said as he took a sip of his seven and seven. He looked calmly up the short aisle of first class as he considered his drink and his thoughts. It seemed like even a plane crash wouldn't manage to ruffle his feathers. The opposite of cool and poised, I repeatedly tried to wipe the sweat on my hands off on my jeans. Not getting the answer I needed, I pressed on.

"I mean, did it freak you out? Like, I'm not suicidal or anything, but . . . say if I were, would it freak you out?"

"Geri, I dated a model once who used to put cocaine in her eye so that it wouldn't ruin her nose. Nothing you will ever do will freak me out."

A sigh of relief left my lungs. But still I needed to know.

"But did you like it?"

And then a look crept across his face that I couldn't quite place. He turned his whole body toward me and cupped my face in his hands. As his eyes concentrated on mine, I couldn't tell if he was looking at me like I was a lunatic or loved. My eyes pleaded for an answer. And then he gave me his response. It was a very, very big smile.

It was on that flight that I stopped trying to figure out life. When I stopped waiting for some magical minute to strike. Because I didn't want to miss any of the moments that were happening in between. The present seemed so good, I stopped caring about the future. Or trying to predict it. Because if I could, I wouldn't want to know that my green suitcase would get lost when we landed at LAX, that a woman in first-class would stop me on the way to the bathroom and ask if I was the personal assistant of the stunningly handsome man I sat next to or that there was a man sitting in coach who broke up with his fiancée because he realized when his car broke down on the way to his bachelor party that he really loved another girl. I didn't care. I didn't want to know any of it. Because even though we were thirty thousand feet in the air, my life finally felt like it had touched down.

~My Yearbook~

Like Geri, this writer has seen her fair share of rejection and redemption. These are the people who brought me into the second camp.

The Coaches—

First, I must thank my agent, Susan Raihofer. Her enthusiasm for the girls and my ability means the world to me. Thanks doesn't begin to cover it.

My editor, Alicia Condon, Alissa Davis, Erin Galloway, Brooke Borneman and the team at Dorchester for giving my book a spine and a life.

The Teachers—

Thank you, Mom and Dad. Your love and influence from heaven and earth never fails to find me. You are the best teachers I could have ever asked for in life. I feel so lucky to have you as parents just as I know you feel so lucky to have me as a daughter because Beth and Rich are such brats.

To my high school English teachers Ms. Teresa Taylor and Mr. Larry Presby. Your lessons still point me in the right direction. Thank you.

The Upper and Lower Classmen—

Beth and Rich. Thanks for the pillow fights when you used the pillow with the big brass zipper, for using me as a jump rope, a curling iron tester, for giving me your chocolate side of an ice cream cake and teaching me how to handle everything from a broken heart to a job interview. Your little sister loves you the most.

Thanks to Grandma and Grandpa Grigonis, Grandma and Grandpa Pierson, Aunt Carol and Uncle Bill, Eric and Shelby, Ethan, Ava and Evan, Doreen, Cliff, Tara, Renee, Aunt Boots and the Rowe families, the Carrig, Smith and Normann families, Mr. and Mrs. Allen, Parker Wickham, John Ross and my students at Hunter College.

My Classmates—

Thanks to Stephanie Blumenfeld and Becca Cancro for always being there and for listening to it. To the lovely ladies of contracts: Jennifer, Robin, Melissa, Katie, Lisa, Jessica and Caroline. To John, Zareen, Joel and Phaedra for their encouragement and expertise. To the women of Sigma Phi Pi, especially Erin, Melinda and Stephanie. To Sanford, Bob and Mark, who are the good guys waiting at the other end of the table.

My 9th Period English Class—

Finally, and most importantly, thanks to the XR Bar writing group: Claire Marie Israel, Chris Kelly, Jennifer Campaniolo, Damian Sadeghi and Mike Shohl. These were the people who were able to hear me yell this story out ten pages at a time over the music at a bar on Houston Street. This is the only page you didn't get to read and it's because of you I get to write it. Our little corner of New York will live on in my heart.

~Book Club Questions~

In the very first scene, Geri, Maria and Emmy discuss what situations they would want their characters to be in if Geri wrote them into a movie. Maria wants to kick butt, Emmy wants to fall in love and Geri wants to write an edgy New York story where there are no models. How many times did the events they talked about actually occur during the course of the book?

The author bookends the novel with the beginning and the end of a screenplay. Looking at what happens in both scenes, do you think the novel is one large act of kismet or do you think the novel is just another one of Geri's stories? Did the story really happen at all?

After all, how often do you run into a homeless man who looks like Santa Claus wearing a garbage bag? Geri mentions that Emmy and Maria never noticed Max. How many other characters interact with Max? Do you think Max is Geri's guardian angel, a regular homeless man who likes to spend his money at casinos, or a scam artist? Is there any other proof in the book that Max exists?

Geri found herself in a position where she could have blown the whistle on Todd's cheating. Do you think she did the right thing? Would you have told his fiancée and blown the whistle on Todd, or walked away?

Which character is most like you? Geri, Maria, Emmy or Sally? Hedda? *Ingrid?*

The author not does give a man's name in the epilogue. Do you think Geri wound up with Joshua, Todd or someone completely different?

Geri's emotions toward her deceased mother range from idolism to hatred. At times she wishes that her mom was around to teach her how to be a real woman. Other times she wants to be nothing like her. How do you think the chapter in the hospital room affects Geri? Would you have turned around? In what ways does Hedda act like a surrogate mom to Geri?

During the attack, Maria did not have any time to think. She just reacted to seeing her friend get hurt. Have you ever had to make a snap decision with regard to the safety of another person? What ran through your mind?

How long have you known your oldest friend?

If your friend wrote you into a movie, who would you like to play your character? What story from your past would you want (or not want) told? What type of movie would you like to be in? Comedy? Romance? Thriller? Horror? Science Fiction?

MARIANNE MANCUSI

NEWS BLUES

All 27-year-old Maddy Madison wants is a cute guy, a designer handbag and to work at Newsline. What she has is a dead-end job at News 9 San Diego, a psycho boss and a counterfeit Kate Spade. One with a badly glued-on label.

Oh, and no guy.

Just when Maddy's sure her days of producing sensationalistic puff pieces will never end she's offered a promotion. She's now an investigative producer—and partnered with the station's newest photographer: sexy, motorcycle-riding bad boy Jamie Hayes. But every silver cloud has a stormy lining. Her new job is with News 9's narcissistic anchor, Terrance Toller; Jamie's getting married (not to her); and reporting the truth is about as easy as watching your divorced parents get remarried (not to each other).

So, how does Maddy get to produce real news, bag her boss and win her man?

Stay tuned. It's the story of a lifetime.

AVAILABLE MARCH 2008

ISBN 13: 978-0-505-52749-3
